Red in Tooth and Claw

Book Four of Underdogs

Geonn Cannon

Supposed Crimes LLC • Matthews, North Carolina

Published in the United States.

ISBN: 978-1-952150-91-3

www.supposedcrimes.com

This book is typeset in Goudy Old Style.

The wolf in you speaks
To the wolf in me
It's the language of beasts
We speak it fluently

There are no words
For what we need
The hunger bites and burns
The wolf heart beats

It's not like this
For everyone
Our wolves run wild
They might just eat us up

Wolf tugs at the leash
Leads me astray
Leads you to me
Are we a pack
Or running free
How big our eyes
How sharp our teeth
- "Wolf Song," Charming Disaster

CHAPTER ONE

ARIADNE WILLOW didn't have the luxury of going to a regular doctor for her check-ups. She didn't get the fancy hospital waiting room where she would wait on a padded table in a sterile room while nurses made announcements over the PA system. Instead she went to a quaint suburban house with a garden next to the porch and a neatly-trimmed backyard. The garage doubled as an emergency room, but patients who were only getting a checkup stayed in the dining room.

For the most part Ariadne was completely normal, with nothing to throw up a red flag. She could visit a doctor to get a flu shot. It was anything more invasive than a cursory examination that caused problems. Most of the bones in her body had minute, perfectly healed fractures that nonetheless showed up on X-rays. Those would be hard to explain without claiming she was a daredevil trapeze artist who wasn't very good at her job.

In truth she was a *canidae*, a werewolf in pop culture parlance, and every transformation required her skeleton to break and shift into a new position. Her spine became bowed, with a tail extending from the base of her spine. Her hands and feet snapped and folded to enable her four-legged stance, while the phalanges of her fingers became paws. The most telling evidence was her skull. Any doctor in Seattle would be alarmed at the roadmap of faded fractures across the front of her face. The human head didn't easily reshape into a wolf's snout, but Ari made it happen at least four times a month.

So she, like every other *canidae* she knew, had a *canidae* doctor. Aaron Frost was also a wolf, and a former veterinarian. Even before he retired he'd kept a side business at his home for others like him who needed help. Ari had once compared it to being a mob doctor, patching up the aches and pains and bullet wounds that couldn't be taken to a regular emergency room. He had considered the similarities for a moment before agreeing that she had a point.

Ari sat on Dr. Frost's couch after her most recent examination, staring at her hand as she flexed the fingers and then curled them into a fist. Her fingernails dug into her palm with a dull ache before she relaxed. Directly in front of her was a window seat with the curtains pushed open to let the sun in. The doctor's neighbor had a cherry-red bicycle lying in their driveway. Next door to them was a basketball goal flanked by garbage cans. It was so ordinary, so mundane, that she felt as if it was another world entirely. She wondered what those ordinary people would say if they knew the kindly old doctor was running an off-the-books health center for werewolves.

She looked down at her hands and the marks her fingernails had left in the palm. In the past few months, since the craziness of wolf manoth and the hunters, she had been experiencing moments of paralysis. Post-transformation pain had always been more acute for her than it was with most *canidae*, but lately the pain was different. Now it lingered in a way that alarmed her. And if she was alarmed, she could only imagine how Dale felt.

Dr. Frost came in from the kitchen where he had been running a few tests, and he smiled as he joined her in the living room. She was amazed at how different he looked from the first time they'd met. His white hair was tamed and a razor had been employed to remove the silver fuzz from his jawline. A jaw which, it had to be noted, was sharper and more defined than she remembered. His clothes were crisp and freshly-laundered. Marriage was doing him worlds of good.

"How's everything look?"

"Good, good," he said. "You're in perfect health for a young woman. Slightly better, in fact. You get more exercise than the average girl your age."

She smiled warily. "Perfect health for a young woman. What about for a young *canidae?*"

He rubbed his hands over the knees of his pants. "Yes. Well, the good news is that I don't see any indication that your condition is getting worse. You've stopped the half-way transformations, which helped. You're putting more time between your transformations which gives your joints the opportunity to heal and relax."

"In January you told Dale that I might be paralyzed by the time I'm forty."

He nodded somberly. "That is a possibility."

"Doc, that's less than ten years from now."

He nodded again.

Ari put her elbows on her knees and covered her face with both hands. Most *canidae* didn't have to deal with issues like this, but hers was a special case. Her birth was the result of an attack, her mother raped by a group of hunters. When she was born she lacked the ability to transform naturally due to her mixed blood. Her mother found a disreputable version of Dr. Frost and asked him to perform a wholly unethical procedure: he removed the blood from the newborn Ariadne and replaced it with a pure-born *canidae*. It worked and, when Ari reached puberty, she was able to transform like anyone else. When she complained that it hurt, her mother would say it hurt for everyone. She claimed it would eventually get easier and the pain would get less noticeable, so Ari just assumed she needed to toughen up.

Her mother finally revealed the truth a few years later. Ari's pain wasn't normal and was, as feared, worse than what everyone else experienced. Because of the artificial way she had been "created," and exacerbated by the fact her father was a hunter, her body was more reluctant on both sides of the transformation. She had been coping with the pain for years thanks to Dale, but now the pain was getting worse. She didn't even want to think about the terrifying moments when her hand would be frozen and stiff. If that was an omen she would one day be unable to move at all...

Frost patted her arm. "Have you been... medicating... as we suggested?"

Ari pushed her hands through her hair. "You can't smell that shit on me?"

He smiled. "It is rather pungent. But you can cook it into food, there are pills and fluid extract..."

"But I don't like pills or pot cookies, and smoking is more convenient all around." She sighed. "The stink, though. I smell like someone shit a skunk."

Frost laughed. "Have you tried heating vanilla extract on the stove?"

"Yeah. It just makes me want cookies."

"So make some pot cookies."

She smiled. "Thanks, Doc."

He folded his arms in front of him and leaned back. "I won't lie, Ariadne. This is a serious situation, and a unique one. I've never had a patient like you. That's why I like you so much." She smiled. "It could become life-threatening in a few years. But we're catching it early enough that I'm confident we can do more than just manage symptoms. You're health-conscious and determined to take care of yourself, so I think we have a fighting chance. You also have a very good partner looking out for you."

"I'm not the only one."

Frost chuckled and self-consciously reached up to touch his hair. "Yes, Caroline... hm. Yes." He shrugged and then patted her arm. "One way or another, we'll find a way to work this out. Okay?"

"Sounds good."

He patted his pockets, looked around, and spotted his prescription pad on the coffee table. He picked it up and flipped it open.

"I'm writing you a prescription for Rimadyl. It will help any symptoms that might be manifesting when you're in wolf form. Have Dale give it to you when you're transformed. If you try to take it as a human, there will be issues."

"It's an animal medication? Does that mean I can't change back until it's out of my system?"

Frost shook his head. "No, no. I've done this sort of thing before. The transformation doesn't affect the medication. Don't ask me how the body knows." He continued writing on his pad. "I'm also going to prescribe medical marijuana. Get whatever form of it works best for you."

"A lot of vets write scrip for pot?"

He winked. "No one will give you any guff for it. They know me down at the pharmacy. Besides, it's a legal drug now, Ariadne. They're even giving the stuff to elderly dogs to alleviate pain. Besides, it does help, right?" She reluctantly nodded. "The smell, eh, yes. That can be an issue for us. But there are a myriad of solutions on the internet for dispersing the aroma. If there's one thing that humanity has banded together on, it's tactics to conceal the fact they've been consuming mind-altering drugs."

"Okay." She took the prescription from him. "Doctor's orders."

"Indeed. Now, how is Miss Frye?"

"Dale? She's doing really well."

Frost nodded, obviously waiting for her to continue.

"Business is, uh, doing well, too."

"She's giving you massages still?"

Ari said, "Yeah. They help. They help a lot."

"How is she sleeping?"

"Fine. I guess." Ari furrowed her brow. "No offense, but why the interest. Dale isn't *canidae...*"

He chuckled. "I'm well aware. But she's dating a *canidae* with a complicated health issue. Since she became your employee, Miss Frye has come to your aid. She puts together stashes of clothing and supplies and hides them throughout the city, she wakes up whenever you call to come pick you up, she gives massages, and now she monitors your condition post-transformation to make sure it hasn't gotten worse. Caregivers have a nasty habit of not showing how much it weighs on them. You should be sure you aren't making the mistake of taking her for granted."

Ari nodded slowly. "Yeah. Yes. I understand. Thanks."

Frost stood up and rubbed his hands together. "All right. That should do for now. I'll see you again in a few weeks?"

"Yeah, sounds good."

"Unless something comes up. You don't have to worry about making an appointment in case there's a... a..." He gestured vaguely at the garage. "I'm saying if any of your foreign friends come back and cause a ruckus, you can always come here."

"Thanks, Dr. Frost. I don't anticipate anything like that happening again, but it's nice to know we have options if it does."

\#

Even though Ari had offered several times, Dale simply wasn't interested in becoming a licensed private investigator. She knew that it would make them equals in the business, but it would also change the dynamic of their work relationship. She liked sitting in the office and working on the computer while Ari was on stakeout or tracking people. Dale liked digging through computer trails while Ari seemed to have a good time following the real thing. She did appreciate the offer of promotion and what it indicated about Ari's perception of her, but she was perfectly happy where she was.

At the moment that was recovering cell phone records for a client who believed her wife was cheating on her. Dale hated cases like this, but they made up a majority of their workload. Everyone was jealous, and everyone was suspicious that their perfect world might not be so perfect after all. In this particular instance it seemed as if their client had reason to be suspicious. That was another reason Dale preferred staying on this side of the business; Ari would be the one who took the client into the office, sat her down, and found a way to reveal that her wife was indeed being unfaithful. She could keep that.

She had just printed off the pertinent records when Ariadne came in. "Hey. I have cell phone records for the Bertram case."

"Good news?"

Dale wrinkled her nose. "Mm."

"Damn." Ari picked up the printout and scanned it. "Damn it. Okay. I'll have her come in and break the news. Is that the last thing we have on the books?"

Dale tapped her keyboard and opened the calendar. "I think so. We're still waiting on final payment from Mr. Harris. Other than that we have a few days free. Why?"

Ari came around the desk and turned Dale's chair to face her. She got on both knees in front of her and took Dale's hands.

"Dr. Frost said something today that kind of freaked me out."

"Are you okay?" Dale immediately began stroking Ari's knuckles, subtly seeking for signs that they were seizing or in pain.

"I'm fine." Ari patted Dale's hands away. "It didn't have anything to do with my health. But as far as that goes, I'm healthy. He told me I needed to smoke more pot..."

Dale chuckled and Ari could hear the relief in her voice. "Okay, so what did he say?"

"You've been taking care of me for years. Even before we were together, you were always putting me first. I know I've thanked you for that. I know you know how much I appreciate everything you do for me. Nothing is being taken for granted here. But lately you've been so on top of my health that I feel like it deserves a special reward. So I'm going to take the week off and take you somewhere special. Just the two of us. No wolf. No transformations, no middle of the night calls, no stashes to maintain, just you, hanging out with your partner."

"Whoa." Dale leaned back against the seat. "That sounds awesome, Ari."

"And of course, my presence is negotiable..."

Dale leaned in and kissed Ari's lips. "No, it's really not. That's a really sweet idea, Ari. Thank you. But just so you know, I wasn't feeling neglected in any way, shape, or form."

"I hardly ever say thank you."

"You do. Every day."

Ari brought Dale's hands to her lips. "It's sweet of you to say that, but... really? I mean, what do I do for you? I need a calculator to add up everything you do for me, but in return you get... what?"

"I get you."

"Oh. Oh, you got boned."

Dale laughed and kissed both of Ari's cheeks. "We've been through this before."

"And yet I haven't gotten any better."

"You just need to learn that a relationship isn't about doing things for each other or keeping balance. It's not tit-for-tat. It's a cumulative thing. You don't know what you give me? Look at yourself, Ariadne Willow. You're the strongest woman I know and you're on your knees in front of me. You're the most impressive, most amazing woman I've ever met, and you're stressing about how to show me how much you love me. That blows me away, Ariadne. All you have to do is keep wanting me."

"But that's easy."

"Just like taking care of you is easy for me." Dale grinned wider and kissed the tip of Ari's nose. "You need me. You want me. That's enough."

Ari sighed. "Okay. Fine. If you want to let me off easy."

"I do."

"Fine." She stood up and pecked Dale's lips.

Dale gripped two of Ari's fingers to keep her from retreating. "Hey. Just so we're absolutely clear. You gave me a life. You gave me a job I love. You gave me the means to stay in a city I adore. I probably would've had to go back home with my tail between my legs if I'd never met you. That's what you give me. And if you're not aware of that, then maybe I'm the one who has been negligent. I should say it more often."

"We'll both try to be better, then."

"Agreed." She bent down and kissed the middle knuckle of Ari's index finger before letting her go. "I'll start thinking of places we can go. Nothing too far away, I'm guessing."

Ari said, "Nah. We'll save Paris for one of the big anniversaries."

Dale smiled. "Okay. I'm on it. Ari?"

She stopped at the door of her office. "Mm?"

"I love you."

Ari laughed. "I love you, too. Now get back to work."

"Yes, Miss Willow." Dale smirked and glanced at Ari out of the corner of her eye before she went back to her duties.

Dale suggested they stop for groceries on the way home, but Ari pointed out they would most likely be away from home for most of the week and anything they bought ran the risk of being wasted. So instead they splurged on some fast-food and took it back to their new apartment. Ari's home had been one of the casualties of wolf manoth, burned down by hunters after they realized she was a wolf. The material damage hadn't worried her too much, although she did feel guilty about her neighbors, but she was actually grateful for the loss because it forced her to take the step of officially cohabitating with Dale.

After a few months of searching they finally found a great place. It was a basement apartment in a Central neighborhood. Their landlady was younger than they were, a Duwamish woman in her twenties named Neka Teller who was studying to build boats. They were still trying to work out their relationship with her - were they friends who occasionally handed over a check? Was it simply a neighbor situation? - but everything seemed copacetic so far.

They had an exterior entrance that led to the backyard, and Ari was able to use it to get in and out for the wolf's nocturnal excursions. Dale had apologized in advance to Neka if their late-night comings and goings ever bothered her, but she said it was just part of living above a private investigator. She assumed investigations required a lot of unusual hours for stakeouts and whatnot. The cover was good enough that Ari let her believe it.

The apartment was just the right amount of cozy without feeling too small. They could be in completely different rooms without ignoring one another, but it also prevented them from getting in each other's way. Ari had never considered living in a basement apartment before, but so far it had been ideal. The place felt like a den, and she was lucky to share it with someone like Dale.

After dinner, Dale went to lay on the couch and stare at the TV while Ari set up her laptop on the dining room table. Dale liked her to fill out the final report to firmly entrench the details of a case in her mind if it was ever taken to court. Ari knew it was a good routine, and it had been necessary on more than one occasion, but that didn't make it feel less like homework. And in situations like this, when she was detailing the timeline of someone's infidelity, she found it more distasteful than usual.

The show Dale had turned on ended and some reality monstrosity began. When Dale didn't change the channel Ari looked over and saw she had fallen asleep. She smiled, saved her work, and went to crouch next to her. The remote control was on Dale's stomach, held in place with one hand while the other was hanging down to brush the carpet. Ari slipped the remote away from her and turned the set off. Dale took a deep breath and brought her hand up to rub her eyes.

"I wasn't sleeping," Dale murmured.

Ari said, "I know you weren't. But maybe you should go to bed anyway."

"Mm. Fine." She sat up and stretched. "Are you coming with me?"

Ari gestured at the laptop. "I'm still working on the report. I'll be there soon."

Dale nodded. "Going for a run tonight?"

"Not tonight."

"Good." She kissed Ari again. "I'm going to take a shower."

"Okay."

Dale went into the bedroom and Ari returned to her laptop. She rested her hands on either side of the keyboard and stared at the screen, which currently detailed a loving relationship as it turned sour.

Megan Bertram met Lisa Sneed in college. They met in Chem class, formed a study group, and eventually discovered they had feelings for each other. They moved in together after graduating and began a grown-up life with real jobs, mortgage, bills, and all the stress that came with those things. They'd been together eight years when same-sex marriage became legal in Washington, so they went down to City Hall and made it official. Now, barely two years later, Megan had hired Ari to find out if Lisa was cheating on her.

That alone was enough to be a sad story. Even if it turned out Lisa was completely faithful, the fact Megan had sought outside confirmation of her faithfulness made Ari depressed. How could someone spend eight years with another person, then take vows to love each other forever unconditionally, and then throw it all away?

In Lisa Bertram's case, her ten year relationship was destroyed by a young copyeditor who worked at her firm. From the records Dale dug up, they'd been seeing each other for almost fifteen months. Ari did the math and was disheartened to find out it started less than a year after their wedding.

"You didn't even make it to the first anniversary," Ari muttered. She pressed two fingers between her eyebrows and massaged. It wasn't her place to judge. She was an impartial, reporting the cold hard facts as she witnessed them. She was only a hired gun. Still, it made her angry. And sad. And it really made her want to hug Dale. In her heart she knew there was no reason to worry. She and Dale had a strong foundation. Their relationship was strong enough to weather temptation and the seven-year itch. But Megan and Lisa probably thought the same thing when they got married. And then six months later, Lisa was texting a younger woman about all the things she wanted to do to her.

Ari shut down the computer. The file would still be there in the morning, and she'd already spent enough of the day dealing with infidelity. She went through the apartment to make sure everything was turned off or locked. Their living space was separated from Neka's by a short staircase with a door at either end and a laundry room at the top. Ari made sure that door was locked as well, even though she still felt odd about doing it. On one hand, they deserved privacy. On the other hand it felt as if they were specifically barring Neka from entering part of her own home. Still, she knew it was necessary. And she knew Neka didn't object to the fact the door was locked. So she put aside the anxiety and went to bed.

Dale was still in the bathroom brushing her teeth, but she opened the door when she heard Ari moving around. Ari slipped in behind her, kissed Dale's neck, and turned the shower back on so the water could warm up while she was undressing. The bathroom was cramped, with a shower stall, a toilet, and a meager countertop. It was barely more than they might expect from a nice hotel, but they were able to make it work. When they moved in, Neka told them they had permission to use the larger bathroom upstairs if there was ever a need, but so far it hadn't come up.

Dale was already in her pajamas, a pair of shorts and a thin-strapped top. Her hair was pinned on top of her head, which gave her a passing resemblance to Pebbles Flintstone. She had removed her makeup and was rubbing cream onto her cheeks. She looked at Ari's reflection in the mirror rather than turning her head to make eye contact with her.

"So I was thinking about where we could go on our vacation."

Ari pushed back the curtain and stepped under the spray. "Yeah? What did you come up with?"

"I thought we could go to Grandpa Willi's cabin."

Ari smoothed her hands over her hair as she considered the suggestion. The cabin was where they fled during the Gavin case two years ago almost to the day, their hideaway when the police were on the lookout for Ari as a person of interest in a murder. More importantly than that, it was the place where she and Dale finally took the step from coworkers and friends to lovers.

"I think that would be the perfect place," Ari said finally.

"Yeah?"

"Absolutely. We didn't get a chance to enjoy it last time. I mean... other than..."

Dale laughed. "I know what you mean. The whole island is beautiful. There's a cute little town that is basically the blueprint for every Hallmark movie ever made. A real-life Smalltown USA. You'll love it. I used to love going up there when I was a kid." Dale finished her ablutions and went into the bedroom. A few minutes later Ari finished her shower and joined her. Dale paused what she was doing and tracked Ari's progress through the room with her eyes.

"What?"

"Nothing. Just... you, walkin' around all naked and stuff."

Ari grinned as she pushed back the covers. "You like that, huh?"

"Yeah. Something about it makes me smile."

"'Something'?" Ari crawled across the bed to take Dale in her arms, and Dale twisted to look at her. "Care to be more specific?"

"Hm. Not sure I can put my finger on it."

Ari pulled Dale down and began kissing her neck. "Well, maybe you should try harder."

They fell asleep together after making love, but years of waking up in the middle of the night to go rescue Ari meant that Dale was a light sleeper. She woke to the sound of movement in the house above them and quickly determined Neka had come home. Their landlady-slash-potential new friend had come home from studying. She was obviously trying to be as quiet as possible as she made a midnight snack. Dale distinctly heard the silverware drawer and the muffled clatter of plates. A brief silence and then the soft thuds of footsteps moving eastwardly across the house.

In the silence that followed, Dale put her cheek against Ari's breast again in the hopes she could fall back to sleep. She focused on the soft inhale and exhale of her lover's breath and the beating of her heart, but she quickly discovered it was a lost cause. She looked up in the hopes Ari was available for a second round of sex, but she looked far too peaceful to disturb. She was a beautiful sleeper, Dale noted. She reached up to brush the lightweight strands of hair away from Ari's lips and eyes. She knew that if she stayed in bed she would only toss and turn until she ended up waking Ari, and Ari lost enough nights of sleep to let the wolf run wild. She carefully extricated herself and padded out of the bedroom on the balls of her feet.

The moon was shining through the living room windows enough that she could see without turning on a light. She had planned to grab a light snack, maybe drink some milk, but the moonlight drew her to the door. They'd searched long and hard for a home that would give Ari the opportunity to slip away in the middle of the night without attracting attention. Just beyond their tiny porch was a short series of steps that led up to a wide backyard. It was enclosed on three sides, and Ari's wolf would be perfectly capable of watching for the coast to be clear before she ventured out for a run.

As Dale looked out, an idea occurred to her. She pushed down her underwear, peeled off her top, and then unlocked the door to slip outside.

Even though the backyard was mostly out of sight from the street, she remained close to the house. The cold was almost immediately an issue, and she pulled her arms in tight as the first shudder ran through her. She waited to make sure the night was totally still before she climbed the steps onto the grass. The blades were wet with dew, and her toes sank into the soft dirt. She shuddered again, her breath rising up in a cloud around her face.

She forced herself to stand in the frigid air, not even freezing but cold enough to be uncomfortable, and shifted her weight from one foot to the other. She told herself that she wasn't at home; she didn't know where she was or how far away home was. She didn't know where she would find clothes or money to make a call to come save her. She didn't know what she had done or where she had been that night. She didn't know how she would get home.

Moments like this were reality for Ariadne several times a month. Confused, sore from the transformation, and with the added bonus of being exhausted from whatever the wolf had made her do. The wolf could run for miles and strand Ari at the far reaches of the city if it wanted. Dale knew how unsettling and scary it was, but she'd thankfully never experienced it for herself. Now that she had approximated it, she knew it would lead to a new appreciation of everything Ari went through after a transformation.

After a few minutes she went back inside. She made sure her feet weren't muddy before she stepped on the carpet, then put her clothes back on. When she got back to the bedroom Ari had rolled onto her back but wasn't yet awake. Dale crawled under the blankets and her leg brushed against Ari's.

"Shhee!" Ari hissed through her teeth. "Babe, you're freezing..."

"Sorry, puppy."

Before she could retreat, Ari had found her hands. She closed her own hands around them and, eyes still closed, brought them to her mouth and blew on the cold fingers.

"Where were you? Were you outside? Why were you outside?"

Dale smiled. She didn't know if Ari was aware she wasn't waiting for answers. "I just wanted to see something real quick."

"Oh. Come here. Roll over." Dale rolled onto her other side and Ari spooned her from behind. Dale smiled and closed her eyes as Ari rubbed her arms. "Next time put on a jacket or something..."

"I will," Dale promised.

Ari kept hold of Dale's hands, and Dale brought them up against her chest as she settled in. By the time she drifted off again, this time for the rest of the night, she was already feeling much warmer.

CHAPTER TWO

THEY DECIDED to leave on the second ferry Monday morning. The way Dale figured it, that trip would be mostly empty of commuters, but still early enough that the tourists wouldn't be out. They woke up and headed out as the sun was just beginning to paint the city golden. Ari dozed in the passenger seat until Dale turned on the radio, and they sang together on "Just Like a Pill." They had spent the weekend packing and, true to her word to the doctor, Ari hadn't transformed at all. She didn't have to change every day, but keeping the leash on meant she could feel the wolf pacing in her mind. Even though she promised Dale the vacation would be completely wolf-free, Dale insisted on letting the wolf run around in the practically untouched wilderness at least once or twice.

"The poor thing has to make do with city parks and asphalt paths the rest of the year. She deserves a vacation, too."

The ferry lanes were half-full when they arrived. The sun had followed them from Seattle to Anacortes and danced off every hood and windshield like an array of solar panels. Dale added her car to their number and scanned the radio station for someone playing music. Ari found a baseball cap in the glove compartment and used it to shield her eyes, slumped in the seat, and tried to get some more sleep. Dale found Radiation Canary on a station in the high hundreds and sang along under her breath. When the ferry arrived, it trailed sunlight across its windows like something out of a fairytale. It looked like a sun-ship come to take them to a magical otherworld.

She reached over and gently rocked Ari's shoulder. "Hey. Our ride's here."

Ari breathed in deeply through her nose as she pushed the cap firmly onto her head, blinking in the sudden brightness. "Ugh. Too much sun."

"At least it makes the ferry look beautiful. Ethereal."

Ari grunted.

Dale laughed. "What's wrong? I know you're not grumpy from sleep-deprivation, because you actually got seven hours last night." She brushed Ari's hair behind her ear.

"I'm not grumpy. It is beautiful." She looked out the passenger-side window. "It's the water. Most *canidae* don't really like water. We avoid it if we can."

"I thought that was cats who didn't like water."

"I can't say about cats. And oddly enough, wolves... like, authentic wolves? They love the stuff. But *canidae* are different."

Dale said, "But I've seen you in water."

"Shallow water. This is going out on water, going out on deep water with an entire ecosystem underneath us. *Canidae* are connected to the earth, the ground under our feet. Dirt, mud, grass. You put us out on the water without land in sight, we get... antsy."

"I never knew that. I'm sorry. Why didn't it come up last time?"

"Last time I was running from the police. I thought I was going to jail for the rest of my life. I had bigger problems than being on the water."

She stroked Ari's hair. "We could go back, get tickets for a flight on one of those little island-hopper planes... it might have the same problems but at least it'll be shorter."

"No. Thank you, but flying would be a lateral move. Besides, we've already come this far. If I thought it was going to be an insurmountable problem I would've said something earlier. Maybe just... hold my hand when we're out there?"

"Well, that's a given." Dale picked up Ari's hand, kissed the knuckles, and smiled at her. "I don't think I've ever heard you mention a phobia like this. It's kind of nice."

"You like knowing I'm terrified?"

Dale shrugged. "Sort of. It makes you more human."

"Gee, thanks."

Dale stretched between the seats and kissed the top of Ari's head. "I'll take care of you. Promise."

"Good." She smiled. "I think I can take it now."

"Let me know if you need any special attention once we're aboard."

They drove aboard and left the car to go up to the passenger section. Dale took Ari's hand, nodding toward the stern.

"Want a window seat? You can look at all the little islands we pass so it won't feel like we're adrift in the middle of nowhere."

Ari chuckled. "I appreciate the offer, but I think I'll pass."

Dale nodded her understanding and led Ari to the center-most seats she could find. Once they were finally underway, Ari looked out the windows. Even from where they were sitting she could see the little islands clustered just off the coast.

"It is pretty, though. I can admit that."

"It's very pretty," Dale said.

Ari looked down at their joined hands. "Is it weird I'm really excited about this week? We're not doing anything special. I'm just going to be hanging out with you."

"Gee, thanks."

"You know what I mean. We work together, we live together. The only difference will be that we're not working. Well, and that obnoxious wolf won't be getting in the way very much."

Dale said, "I like the wolf."

"Good. But I am. I'm excited about it. Just you and me and the great outdoors."

Dale nodded. "I'm excited, too. I used to come out here with my parents."

She remembered how huge everything had seemed when she was a little girl, how those weekends had shrunk the entire world down to a single cabin surrounded by trees. Grandpa Willi would lead her out the back door, down a winding trail that had been tamped down by countless trips, and she would hurry to keep up with him. Then they would sit on rocks slickened by the tide and green slimy things, and he would cast his line out into the water. He always threw back what he caught. "We just wanna say hi to 'em, that's all," he said as he would gently return the creature to its own atmosphere.

"Your father brought your mother here, you know," he said more than once. "When they were first dating."

At that time Dale couldn't imagine a world where her parents were young, when they were just dating. She had just nodded and tried to keep up with his long-legged gait. He had reached back and put his hand on her shoulder to hurry her along.

"One day you'll come back here with some special man, and it'll be a special place for you, too."

Dale looked at Ari, who was distracted by her hydrophobia. Her chin was lifted and Dale could see the silver clasp of the leather collar she wore. It had only been two years since they became lovers, but so much had changed that she wasn't surprised it seemed like a lot longer. Of course it could feel like more because she and Ari had been friends for so long before they started sleeping together. They might have occasionally kissed or held hands, but it never went further than that. They were convinced that their working relationship was so important and so fragile that they couldn't risk adding a physical component.

Of course, when the whole world turned against them and they only had each other, they finally surrendered to the inevitable. Afterward there was no going back, not that either of them wanted to. Dale's only regret was that they hadn't taken the step sooner, and she knew Ari felt the same. And she knew that by waiting, they proved their feelings for each other were more than just a passing infatuation.

Ari finally realized she was being stared at and looked over. "It's okay. I'm fine."

"I know. I'm not worried." She smiled. "Thank you."

Ari said, "You're welcome. What for?"

"I'm not sure."

Ari said, "Well... you're still welcome."

Dale kissed the tip of Ari's chin and put her head on Ari's shoulder. "Wake me up when we get there."

"Hey. You're supposed to be protecting me."

"Hey, you got to nap on the drive up."

"Hey." She bumped Dale's head with her shoulder.

Dale nudged Ari. "Hey."

"Hey!"

They nudged each other with increasing violence until Ari put an arm around Dale to pull her down across her lap. Dale laughed and reached up to touch Ari's face, and Ari sighed in defeat.

"Fine. Nap. But if the boat tips over, I'm using you as a floatation device."

"Deal."

Ari took off her baseball cap and plunked it down on Dale's face. Dale moved the hat to her chest and closed her eyes. She never succeeded in completely falling asleep, but she drifted off enough that the sway of the ship and the feel of Ari touching her arm, her hair, her shoulder felt like a dream.

The island was shaped like a horseshoe, its two outstretched arms curling back in protectively around an almost-enclosed harbor. The eastern side had a resort tucked neatly away in the elbow, while the western wilderness concealed a community of private homes that could only be glimpsed briefly through the trees. Some houses were only evident because of long piers leading up to clearings with no actual residence in sight.

"Good place to hide away," Ari said, kissing Dale's temple.

The ferry docked at the apex of the horseshoe which had developed into a small tourist-driven town of antique shops and kitschy boutiques. It was as if the little souvenir sellers had been washed ashore by the tide, clustered around the ferry lanes like a clowder of cats who heard the can opener. Just beyond them were the necessities of everyday life: a post office, a grocery store, a library, a bank. Dale drove them to the grocery store where they stocked up on everything they would need for a week in the wilderness. Neither of them believed they would go the entire week without making a supply run, but the less they had to go fetch the better. Dale bought Ari a lollipop for "being a very brave girl" on the ferry, and Ari threatened to stick it to the back of Dale's head when she wasn't looking.

When they checked out, the clerk glanced at Dale and seemed to file through a mental list of people she knew as she put their items in a bag. She was almost finished when she closed one eye and pointed a finger at Dale and smiled triumphantly.

"Willi Frye."

Dale didn't even try to hide her surprise. "Wow, that's right. He was my grandpa. I'm Dale Frye, and this is Ariadne."

"I knew it. That red hair, you can see it a mile off. I'm Noreen, but most people call me Nora. Feel free to call me whichever. I knew your granddad when... boy, I was about your age, I guess? He was certainly a character."

"He was. Yeah."

"Back for a visit?"

"Yeah, we're going to spend a week up at the old cabin."

"I heard your whole litter moved out to, uh... where was it?"

Dale said, "Pennsylvania. But I came back for college and stayed in Seattle."

Noreen nodded. "Ah, I gotcha. Welcome back. You need anything you can find it here."

"Good to know. Thanks."

They paid and took their groceries out. Dale put the groceries in the backseat and smiled at Ari as she got behind the wheel.

"One thing I remember about this town? Odds are good that by tonight everyone will know that Willi Frye's granddaughter is staying up at the cabin this week."

"I guess it's good that people know where to find us. They... won't just drop in, will they?"

Dale laughed and patted Ari's knee. "If they drop by and see you running around naked, that'll be their fault. You have nothing to be ashamed of, puppy. You got it, flaunt it."

The cabin was a mile outside of town, beyond the point where the pavement turned into a dirt road, and at the end of a well-hidden access road that Ari still didn't see until Dale turned onto it. Branches brushed over the top of the car as if they were passing through a veil to another world. The sun was momentarily blacked out by the thick canopy before exploding back to life when Dale pulled into the clearing. There was a single tree in the middle of the space, like the spindle on a sundial, and it still held the bicycle Dale's grandfather had left leaning against a stump seventy years earlier. The tree had grown around the bike and eventually lifted it to its current eye-level position.

Dale parked in the shade of the bike tree. Ari got the luggage from the trunk while Dale unloaded the groceries. She had arranged to have the power turned on, but she still braced herself for failure when she switched on the lights. Fortunately the electrician had come through. The switch on the wall controlled four lamps through the living room but, as it was still bright enough to see without them, she turned the light back off and carried the food into the kitchen.

"I'm just going to leave the bags here for now," Ari said from the door.

"Okay." Dale loaded the fridge and freezer with their drinks and dinners. Their canned goods were lined up on the counter next to the microwave. When that was done she wandered back to the living room. The main space of the cabin was one large room with counters and strategic furniture locations to delineate the different areas. One of the two bedroom doors was open and Dale crossed to it.

"Puppy? You handling everything okay?"

Ari appeared in the doorway. "Yeah. Just putting blankets and pillows on the bed."

"Okay. Why~"

She was cut off by Ari's kiss, her hands going up in surrender as she was embraced and pulled close. The force of Ari's embrace knocked Dale back a step, but she corrected herself and put her hands on the back of Ari's head. Ari flattened one hand in the small of Dale's back and gripped her belt with the other. She lifted and leaned back, and Dale found her feet lifted off the floor. She gasped in surprise and felt Ari's tongue against her teeth as she tightened her legs around Ari's hips so she wouldn't fall. Ari turned and carried her into the bedroom, grunting when she reached the bed.

Dale yelped as she was dumped onto the blankets. Ari took a second to yank the shoes off Dale's feet and toss them aside before stretching out on top of her.

"The same bed where this happened for the first time."

Dale smiled and nodded. She put her hand on Ari's cheek, and Ari turned her head to kiss the palm. She moved her head to take Dale's forefinger into her mouth and she circled it with her tongue, then looked down and smiled.

"Undress me, puppy."

Ari's smile widened and undid Dale's belt. She pushed Dale's jeans down and let her kick them off herself so she could focus on the buttons of her blouse. Dale tried to help but Ari pushed her hands aside. "You told me to undress you," Ari said as she kissed the exposed skin between Dale's breasts. "So let me do my job."

Dale chuckled and stroked Ari's hair, only moving her arms to get her shirt and bra off. She scooted back and put her feet on the edge of the mattress. Ari kissed her stomach and Dale closed her eyes, lips parted and trembling slightly with anticipation. She gathered Ari's hair in her left hand and dropped her right hand to grip the blanket. Ari teased her with quick, glancing kisses to her thighs before she finally settled in, using her tongue to tease the sensitive flesh between Dale's legs.

"Ariadne, please," Dale whispered, flexing her right hand but careful not to pull Ari's hair too much. Ari didn't make her beg twice. Dale's jaw dropped and she arched her back, giving up on control and pulling Ari's hair.

"Sorry..."

"S'okay," Ari mumbled. "Look at me..."

Dale forced her eyes open and, after a moment of staring blindly at the ceiling, she looked down at her girlfriend. Ari winked and Dale smiled, struggling as long as she could to keep her eyes open until Ari's lips and tongue went back to work. Her eyes rolled back in her head and she sank back down with a grunt of extreme pleasure, curling her lip as she lifted her feet and rested them on Ari's back.

"You're still dressed," she murmured dreamily.

"But I'm still touching myself."

Dale groaned. "You're horrible..."

"Mmm." With one hand apparently busy, Ari brought up the other and wet it with her tongue. She pressed it against Dale's clit and curled her tongue to push it inside, and Dale finally surrendered to her orgasm. She flattened her hand against Ari's head, curled the other into a fist in the blanket, and came with a quiet cry. She moved her hand down to Ari's neck and curled her fingers around the collar, biting her lip as she gently tugged on it. Ari kissed Dale's stomach and breasts before settling her weight between Dale's legs.

"You're... still... dressed," Dale said between kisses.

"I am. Wanna do something about that, Miss Frye?"

She kissed Ari's chin. "I suppose I could."

Ari braced her hands on either side of Dale's head and lifted herself up as Dale pushed her jeans down. Ari straddled Dale's thigh and sank down on it, sitting up to shed her shirt and bra. Dale put her hands on Ari's stomach, stroking down and then along the curve of her hips. Ari was lean and muscular from all her nights as the wolf, miles and miles run on all fours had left her with a flat stomach and powerful arms and legs even when she was in human form. She started to lean down for another kiss, but Dale spread her fingers on Ari's chest to keep her sitting up.

"Wait. I'm not done looking at you."

Ari smiled and stroked Dale's arm. As Dale ogled her, she began to rock her hips, riding Dale's thigh in a slow and steady manner. Dale slid her hand over Ari's navel, down between her legs, and watched Ari's face as she found her clit. Ari's eyes narrowed but didn't close, and she tightened her legs around Dale's thigh. As Dale rubbed her, Ari moved faster, her lips parting as she reached down to rest her hands on Dale's shoulders. Her hair hung over her left shoulder, veiling one breast, and Dale sat up to kiss the other one, stroking the nipple with her tongue before gently biting down.

Ari cradled Dale's head and closed her eyes, still thrusting as Dale kissed her way up to her neck. As soon as she kissed the spot between Ari's ear and her jaw, Ari tightened her fingers on Dale's shoulder and slid down onto her back.

"Dale," she said. "Don't stop." She nuzzled Dale's neck and wrinkled her nose as she came, clenching her arms and legs around Dale as they collapsed onto the mattress together. She exhaled slowly through her lips, then moved to kiss her way along Dale's jaw until she found her mouth. Dale teased Ari's lips with her tongue before Ari let it in, and they settled into a more comfortable position for their post-coital kissing. Dale lifted her head to kiss Ari's eyebrows.

"Huh. Wow. Okay. So, the vacation is already off to a fantastic start."

Ari chuckled and kissed Dale's forehead before she rolled off of her. They lay side by side on the bed and found each other's hands without looking.

"Seven days of this," Ari said.

"Yep. Think you can handle it?"

Ari rolled onto her side and kissed Dale. "I think I'll find a way to deal."

They napped together until hunger forced them to address a need for lunch. As they dressed, Dale offered to make something fancy so they could inaugurate the kitchen and dining room. "We knocked the cobwebs out of the bedroom already, so we might as well clean out the kitchen, too."

Ari agreed. "While you're cooking, I think I'll take a quick run. Not far. Just to see the lay of the land. Any suggestions for my route?"

"It's been so long since I was here." She paused and rubbed the divot above her upper lip as she thought. "The road south keeps going, and it mostly hugs the coastline of the island. Such as it is. You'd probably be fine going that way unless it's become overgrown or something."

Ari nodded. She dressed in shorts and a pullover, made sure her sneakers were snugly tied, then kissed Dale as she headed out. She started to cut through the trees, but there was so much debris and undergrowth between each trunk that she decided to stick to the well-worn paths. It wasn't going to be a real run, just an exploratory jaunt, but there was no reason she couldn't get in a little exercise. She felt fine but an ounce of prevention and all that. Plus she felt it was necessary to see what the island looked like when she was in her normal, human form. The wolf was good with new places, but she liked to give it some sort of idea where it was before going out at night.

She jogged back to the main road and turned south as Dale suggested. The path was mostly straight with the occasional zig or zag to avoid natural obstacles. Occasionally she was close enough to the shore that she saw water through the trees to her left, while other times the forest seemed to close in on her completely.

Ari stopped at one of the thin spots and stepped through the trees to look at the water. There was no beach, just a rocky border where the land dropped away and gave way to the harbor. She crouched down and ran her fingers through the waves. She didn't mind it when she could see the bottom, when falling in meant she would get a little wet and a little embarrassed. She looked out over the deceptively calm waves. It got very deep very fast, and that was when the tremor of unease found its seat.

Movement further on down the shore caught her eye. A few hundred yards further south was a pier with a small boat anchored to it. Ari could see the back of a cabin at the top of a rise, its harbor-facing wall seeming to be almost all tinted glass. A woman was standing on the pier, her arms crossed over her chest, head down and hip cocked as if she was waiting for someone. Before Ari could retreat from the intimate moment, the woman looked up and spotted her. They seemed to make eye contact across the water, but the woman's expression didn't change.

Ari lifted her hand in greeting but the woman didn't return the gesture. Ari flicked the water from her fingers and stood up. Dale said people on the island were gossips, but they could gossip while still appreciating their privacy. The fact that every cabin along the shore was hidden behind a wall of greenery supported that theory. The woman probably didn't appreciate someone peeking into her backyard. Ari decided to leave her to whatever she was doing.

When she got back to the path she looked back. The pier was empty now, although she didn't know how the woman could have gotten back to the house so quickly. Odds were good that the woman was a long-time resident and knew all sorts of little paths and hidey-holes to duck into until the prying stranger had left.

Still, Ari couldn't help but feel a little unsettled at how quickly the woman disappeared. There one minute and gone the next, as if she had been swallowed by the forest.

CHAPTER THREE

THE FIRST day was spent, as promised, in various acts of a carnal nature. After lunch they played a game called "Shut Up and Kiss Me" in which they were allowed to say whatever they wanted to each other but they couldn't actually do it. They had to face each other and explain exactly what they wanted to do or what they wanted done to them, and the first one to give in and touch their opponent was the loser.

Ari won by suggesting something that had always proven to be Dale's weakness in the past. Dale pulled Ari down onto the couch with her.

"I didn't know you would play dirty," Dale said.

"I thought dirty was the whole point." She began nuzzling Dale's neck. "So what do I win?"

"You get to do everything you threatened me with during the game. And I get to do you."

"Best prize ever," Ari said.

In between rounds they simply enjoyed each other's company. Ari had brought a couple of books, and Dale had a Kindle that would provide enough reading material for the week. There was no television in the cabin, and when Dale tried to connect to the internet on her laptop she was unable to find a signal. The idea of being that far away from civilization was a bit unsettling at first, but Dale reassured her that the town had an internet cafe if either of them had a desperate need to check their email.

They had a light dinner, read for a while, and then Ari went to fill the bathtub. When it was ready Dale joined her, with Ari tucked into the corner of the tub with Dale sitting on her lap facing her. They splashed around a bit, managed to get a little actual bathing in, and eventually Dale retreated to the opposite side of the tub. She put her feet up in the middle of Ari's chest, and Ari took the opportunity to clip her toenails for her.

"I wish we had a tub like this back home," Ari said as she blew away a clipping.

"We could rip out this one and try to sneak it past Neka. She'd never know."

Ari smiled. "Or we could just break our lease and come live out here."

Dale pursed her lips. "Hm. Not much call for a private investigator out in the middle of nowhere. Besides, I'm a city girl. One week without wifi, that's fine. But if you want me to give it up permanently, we'll have a problem." She moaned and closed her eyes as Ari pressed against the arch of her foot with her thumb. "But yeah. I admit. It's really nice." She splashed the water with her other foot. "Uh-oh. You're in the water. Do you need me to save you?"

"Don't tease me about that."

Dale became serious. "I'm sorry. It's just that I never realized it was an issue for you. So baths are okay?"

Ari nodded. "Baths and swimming pools. Big bodies of water are the problem."

Dale considered that information. "Okay. I'll keep that in mind. I won't book us on any cruises."

"Good." Ari pushed Dale's legs apart and leaned forward,

kissing her lips. "I'm going to go lie down. Join me?"

"In a few minutes?"

"Okay." She kissed Dale again and smiled. "This vacation was a really good idea."

Dale frowned. "It was your idea."

"I know. I'm complimenting myself."

Dale laughed and swatted Ari's shoulder. "Get out of this bath and let me soak in peace." She admired the shape of Ari's body as she stood up, resting her elbow on the side of the tub with her hand in her hair as she watched her towel off. Ari stopped in the doorway and let the towel droop just enough to show one cheek of her ass.

"I'll be waiting, Miss Frye."

Dale blew her a kiss and sank lower in the water, closing her eyes as she spread out into the space Ari had just vacated. They hadn't done much with the first day of their vacation, but they'd done enough. Sex, jogging, food, sex, reading, sex... She knew they wouldn't spend the entire time jumping each other but she was looking forward to the peaceful, quiet moments that came between just as much as the bedroom antics.

When she was a girl and her parents would tease her about coming to the cabin with her husband, she would scoff. Not at the idea of a husband - she didn't know that about herself yet - but at the idea of spending her entire life with someone. She didn't really have long-term friends; they drifted apart during the summer and she met new people when school started again. She never kept in touch with college roommates or former coworkers. Even as a little girl she'd known that she wasn't the sort to settle down with someone for keeps.

But now she knew. Now she knew what she would do for the right person, and she knew what it was like to crave another person more than... anything else, really. Ari was her partner, her girlfriend, her employer, and the most important person in her life. All her life she had just been searching for her person. Now that she'd found that person, she would move heaven and earth to keep her.

Something startled Ari awake in the middle of the night, jarring her from a sound sleep to full alertness in seconds. She was initially confused; she had just started getting used to waking up in their new home and now she was in an entirely new environment. Dale was with her, which helped soothe the initial fright, and she quickly remembered where they were. She'd gone to sleep with Dale's head on her shoulder, but during the night Dale had rolled onto her back. The room was cold, but that wasn't why she'd woken up.

There were animals in the woods. Deer, foxes, owls, otters... the beasts came out at night. She slipped out from under the covers and went to the window. They were out there and her wolf could sense them. Prey and fellow predators alike out in the darkness. Her heart raced at the thought of joining them, but she had made a promise to Dale. It was a romantic weekend for two, and if the wolf did eventually have to make an appearance, she wasn't going to cave in on the first night.

She let the curtain fall back into place and walked on the balls of her feet back to bed. It wasn't until she had gotten back under the covers that she realized Dale was awake and watching her.

"You can go," Dale whispered.

"No. I won't. But thank you." She kissed Dale's eyebrows. "Go back to sleep."

Dale cuddled up close and Ari pulled the blanket up over her shoulder. She was still acutely aware of everything happening outside, but it didn't hold a candle to having Dale in her arms. She spent too many nights giving in to the wolf's urges. For one week she was going to focus on what she needed and what she wanted. And that included spending the entire night holding the woman she loved.

Ari surprised herself by waking up with the sun. Dale slept for another forty-five minutes and Ari spent the whole time watching her. When Dale finally woke up she stared at Ari for a beat before lifting her head off the pillow and looking around.

"You've been up for a while."

"Not long."

Dale grumbled and raked her fingers through her hair. She looked for the glass of water she'd forgotten to leave by the bed, kissed Ari good morning, and then went to the bathroom. Ari went after she was finished, then dressed in shorts and a pullover in anticipation of going for a run. Dale offered to make breakfast for them both while she was gone.

"You're getting kind of domestic out here. Cooking your lady meals while she's out in the wild woods." She stepped up behind Dale and put her arms around Dale's waist. "I kind of like it."

"You like it now. You're the one who has to wash the dishes."

"Uh-oh."

"That's right, uh-oh. You already have yesterday's dishes waiting for you. Better get cracking when you get back from your run."

Ari kissed her neck and put in her earbuds before heading out. She went south again on the theory that the path sort-of traveled was better than running back toward town. It was strange to run without sidewalks underfoot or pedestrians in her way. No traffic to contend with, no fumes or fog or distracting bakeries or coffee shops to test her will meant that she could let her mind wander. The terrain was steeper than she expected. The island had a distinct incline the further away from shore she moved, and she made a mental note to explore further inland to see if there were any-

She skidded to a stop and pulled the earbuds out to let them dangle in front of her. Dash Warren had been singing over the sounds of nature but now she could hear all the chirping and cooing birds all around her. The wind rustled the leaves of every branch and made it sound like people were moving in the woods around her. She turned toward shore and sniffed, then slowly panned her head back from left to right until she could pinpoint the source of the smell.

Blood.

The smell was sharp and unmistakable, like sucking on a coin. The air seemed to be thick with it but she knew that was only due to her wolf senses being piqued. The smell was coming from her right, inland, so Ari left the overgrown trail she had been following and moved west between the trees. Every few steps she would pause to triangulate the smell's origin before she started moving again. She corrected her course a few times, worried that she would end up lost in the woods, but now she could almost taste the blood. It was stronger from the left, so she rounded a tree and stopped with her foot on the trunk of a tree that had fallen long ago.

The woman was lying face down a few yards away, one arm extended over her head in a protective hook shape. Her thick blonde hair had fallen across her face. She wore a black-and-blue windbreaker and a pair of jeans that were shoved down to her knees, although her underwear was still in place. Ari crossed the distance without thinking about doing so, gently touching the woman's shoulder. There was no life in her, no hope that she would feel a pulse when she felt the woman's neck. Even as she had the thought she could see the jagged tear just above the woman's collar where someone had tried to slit her throat. Blood covered her front, with a pool of it underneath her in the leaves and mud.

Ari fought through the initial burst of nausea and panic to take out her cell phone. She expected the sight of no signal but it still frustrated her almost to the point of tears to see that the damn thing was useless. She looked around for signs of who had left the woman there. The blood was fresh, incredibly fresh, and all of her wolf senses were jangling for attention. There were no killers lurking in the bushes and no threat waiting to leap out at her.

She forced herself to move down to the woman's nearly-removed jeans and patted down the pockets. No wallet, no phone. She checked her phone again, as if some miraculous satellite had moved into position over the island in the past few seconds, but it was still useless. She put the phone back in her pocket and put her hand on the woman's shoulder.

"I'm coming back for you. I'm not going to leave you out here."

She stood up and fished her keys out of her pockets. As she went back toward the trail she made marks in the trees she passed. She knew she would be able to follow her nose back to the scene, but the cops she planned to bring would need plausible evidence of how she was navigating. She cut gouges into the bark without slowing down, grateful that she found the trail without getting turned around. Once she was on it she ran, pumping her arms and lifting her knees, drawing off every store of energy she had. She didn't know exactly how far she'd gotten from their cabin before the blood pulled her off the trail, but she kept track of the distance in her head.

Nearly two miles, she estimated as she ran back onto the porch. That meant the woman was lying three miles away from town. The crime scene was almost on the farthest end of the island. She burst through the door at such a speed that she scared Dale, who nearly fell out of her seat.

"Ari!"

"Get the keys. Someone was murdered."

Dale's eyes widened as she ran to the kitchen counter. She snatched up the keys and ushered Ari back out. "What the hell are you talking about?"

"Running. Smelled blood." Ari gasped for breath. "Off the trail, in the woods. Body. Woman's body. Throat..." She dragged a finger across her own neck.

"Jesus. Okay. Come on."

She put her hand on Ari's arm. "Breathe, Ariadne. You had a shock, you had to have run full-speed to get back here. Just take a second to breathe or you'll pass out." She went to the kitchen and came back with a bottle of water. "Take this. Drink it on the way into town."

Ari nodded her thanks and let Dale lead her outside. "Have you already called the police?"

"No signal."

Dale checked her phone as well. "Okay. We'll find them in town. There has to be a police station somewhere in town."

Ari drained the water bottle as Dale drove. Now that the adrenaline had worn off, she was exhausted and shaky from what she'd seen. She had caught her breath but her hands were still shaking. It wasn't her first dead body, but she still wasn't used to it. She hoped she never was. They had just reached the borders of town when Ari realized something.

"You got the keys."

"What?"

"I ran in and yelled that someone had been murdered, and you went for the keys."

"You told me to."

Ari said, "Yeah, but there wasn't a moment of doubt. You just... did it."

"I trust you. I didn't need to know the details."

Ari put her hand on Dale's leg and squeezed. Dale patted the hand with her own and then pulled to the curb. It was after nine in the morning, so the streets were flooded with the cars of tourists from the mainland. Ari guessed that the population of the town had doubled since she and Dale arrived, but she knew all those extra people would flow back out with the tide. She wondered if one of those tourists was hiding a murder weapon under their seats.

Dale checked her phone and saw that she had a weak wifi signal, so she searched for the police station. It was three blocks away near the center of town, and Dale navigated by finding the high school and driving east. An entire block was made up of government buildings, one on each corner: city hall, fire department, post office, and in a squat gray building facing away from the harbor, the sheriff's office. Dale parked as close as she could to the front entrance and motioned for Ari to go ahead of her.

Ari ran across the manicured lawn and up the stone steps. Inside she found herself in a small public area with alternating benches and potted plants along the walls. The main room of the building was blocked off by a tall desk where a uniformed officer was tapping at the screen of an iPod. Her entrance was less dramatic than the one she'd made at the cabin, but he still put his phone down and furrowed his brow at the sight of her.

"Can I help you, miss?"

"I need to report a murder."

The shock was evident on his face. His posture improved as he turned in his seat, moving his body toward the back of the building without taking his eyes off Ari.

"Sheriff? Need you up front."

Ari said, "The victim is still out there. It happened... it had to have happened within the past hour. The blood was still fresh."

"Who is talking about blood?" The sheriff was a beetle-browed black man with a shaved scalp. His eyes fixed on Ari immediately, the laser-point of a law enforcement officer locking on to the only unknown entity in the room. Under the weight of his stare, she felt as if he'd pulled a weapon on her. His uniform was tan, the brass polished, and the tie neatly knotted against his throat. Dale arrived as he finished sizing her up, so he shifted his attention to her.

"I'm Ariadne Willow. I'm a private investigator, I work in Seattle. I was out jogging this morning and I... heard a noise. I thought maybe it was a wild animal but something made me check. So I tracked it down and I found a woman's body lying in the woods. Her throat had been slit and her jeans were around her knees."

"Oh, God," Dale said, and Ari realized she'd neglected to share that piece of information.

The sheriff moved a finger between them. "You two are together?"

"This is my girlfriend, Dale."

"Dale Frye," Dale said.

"I'm Sheriff Drexler." He looked at the desk sergeant. "Donny's not out fishing this week, right? Give her a call, tell her to sit tight near a phone. We might have a job for her. I'm going to take Vaughn out with these ladies to see what's going on. Miss... Willow?" Ari nodded. "You'll ride with me. I want the whole story before we get out there."

Ari explained who she was and what they were doing on the island as Sheriff Drexler followed her directions through the woods. When she spotted the trail she'd taken, he stopped the car and left the light bar on the roof flashing as he followed her into the underbrush. Behind them was Dale and another police car, driven by Deputy Vaughn, a young man who looked as if he had just joined the police department instead of going to college. Drexler and Vaughn followed Ari into the wilderness, and she pointed out the marks she'd made in the trees as she followed her nose. The scent was drastically less noticeable now even to her senses, occasionally obscured by the wind, and she was grateful that she could use the markings as a cheat sheet.

She was relieved when she saw the fallen tree where she'd first spotted the woman's body, and she hurried up to it now. She stepped onto the rotted trunk and stared with growing dread at the empty clearing in front of her.

"Oh, no..."

Drexler arrived first and followed her gaze, then looked in both directions as if trying to find something that even resembled a dead body.

"Miss Willow...?"

"It was here. It was right here." She went into the clearing, no longer worried about destroying evidence. There was obviously no body, but also no sign of spilled blood. She crouched down and saw that the mud had been churned up and patted back down before it was covered with leaves. "Here. Someone was digging up the mud here. They were trying to cover up the blood."

"Or some animal was burying food. Squirrels, maybe." He sighed and turned in a slow circle to scan the surrounding area. "Look, it's easy for people who have lived on this island all their lives to get turned around out here. Maybe..."

"I left the marks on the trees." Ari looked inland, hands on her hips. Someone had come through after she found the body, moved it, and covered up all the evidence of their crime. "It was here."

"Maybe you were confused, disoriented."

"Her panties were light blue," she said, "and they had a little ribbon on the side. Her windbreaker had a patch on the sleeve. Why would I hallucinate something down to the smallest detail like that?"

Drexler didn't answer that. He kept his hands on his hips and scanned the clearing again. Deputy Vaughn was standing by the fallen tree looking like a cub scout who had wandered onto the scene.

"Your phone," Drexler said. "Did you take a picture?"

Ari cursed inwardly. "No. It never even occurred to me."

"Managed not to get any blood on you, too."

"Sorry about that. Next time I find a body, I'll be sure to take a selfie with the corpse and then roll around in the evidence." He started to respond but she shook her head. "No. I really am sorry now. That was uncalled for."

"You have to put yourself in my shoes, Miss Willow. If someone ran into your office back home and said they found a body on the sidewalk, and then you found... this..."

Ari said, "I'd probably think they were a lunatic."

"We won't go quite that far. I'll have Donny come up here and check things out just to be sure there's nothing to be found. If someone did move a body they couldn't have covered up everything. I'd also like you to sit down with our dispatcher. She's a pretty good artist, and if you can describe the woman you saw, we can show it around. See if anyone is missing."

"I would appreciate that," Ari said.

"And... you said you were planning to stay on the island for the rest of the week?"

Ari nodded. "We planned to leave next Monday morning."

"Okay. I'll let you know if we need you to stick around longer than that."

"Right. Thanks."

He looked at the ground again. "We'll find out what happened here. If it turns out someone killed a woman and then covered it up? I'll be the first in line to pin a medal to your chest."

Ari could only nod, following him back through the undergrowth to where they had parked the cars. Dale had remained on the road rather than compromising the crime scene. She gauged that things had gone wrong from Deputy Vaughn's expression. Ari shook the sheriff's hand, gave him a business card, and split away from him to join Dale by the car.

"What happened?"

"The body is gone."

Dale blinked. "Gone? What do you mean, gone?"

"I mean whoever slit that woman's throat must have come back and carried her away. The sheriff... he seems like a good guy, but he has nothing to go on. And no reason to believe that I saw what I claim to have seen." Ari looked down at her feet and dreaded what she had to say next. She'd sworn that the vacation would be all about Dale, all about their relationship.

"Ari, we said no work this weekend..."

"I know..."

"But I mean... God. You have to do something."

Ari looked at her. "You're not mad?"

Dale furrowed her brow. "Mad? Ari, some woman got her throat cut and her clothes ripped off. If you tell me you're just going to sit back and do nothing while these cops wait for evidence to drop in their laps, then I don't know who you are."

Ari cupped Dale's face and kissed her. "I love you."

"I know." Dale smiled. "That's why we don't need the whole week. It would've been nice, but..." She watched as the sheriff executed a three-point turn to go back to town. "The city needs you, Batman. You have to answer the call. I'll still be here when you're done."

"Okay. The sheriff wants me to go back to the station so someone can draw the girl. He thinks if we show it around someone might recognize her."

"Do you want me to drive you?"

"If you don't mind. Or I could drop you off at the cabin. But with a potential killer running around, I wouldn't feel comfortable leaving you alone out here."

Dale shuddered. "Yeah, I'm definitely coming with you."

She got into the car and Ari went around to the passenger side. She stopped before she got in and looked over the woods once more. Hiding somewhere out there was a killer, and Ari was going to do everything in her power to make sure he couldn't just vanish into the forests.

CHAPTER FOUR

ON THE drive back to town, Dale said she was going to the library to see if they had any back issues of the local newspaper that she could dig through.

"I want to see if this is completely out of the blue for this island or if there's a history of violence here. If this is the first attack of its kind in, like, fifty years, we'll have a better idea of who we're looking for. There might also be leads about who in town might be a suspect in this kind of crime."

Ari said, "Are you sure you don't want to be a detective?"

Dale winked at her. "This is the same stuff I always do. Digging through files so you can have all the information you need to do the real detective stuff. The only difference is that this time I have to do it in analog instead of digital."

She dropped Ari off at the station to work with the sketch artist and said she would swing by to pick her up when she was finished at the library. Ari saw the sheriff and deputy pull into the parking lot alongside the building and waited for them before she went inside.

The dispatcher was a young brunette woman named Lynne who

looked like she had stepped out of an ad for a fifties sock hop. She wore a barrette in her hair, a yellow-and-brown sweater and a matching skirt that reached past her knees. The sheriff had her fetch a drawing pad and pencil, and she sat with Ari at an empty desk to draw the missing victim. When she first sat down she thought it would be hard to remember details, but as soon as she closed her eyes she saw everything. She described the shape of the girl's face as best she could, then watched as Lynne started to sketch.

"I sort of expected they would have a computer program for this by now."

"Oh, they probably do," Lynne said. "But it's also probably not in the budget. And I work better like this, anyway. I can never manage to make a computer do what I want it to do, and 'good enough' isn't good enough for this kind of work."

Ari nodded. Slowly but surely Lynne managed to get the face down on paper. Ari had only seen her from an extreme angle with hair covering her face, but Lynne extrapolated from what Ari described and created a forward-facing mug shot. She described the woman's clothes as Lynne scanned the image onto the computer, and she typed out a description that would be listed alongside the image. When it was done she printed out a dozen copies.

"Do you think I could get one of those?" Ari asked.

Sheriff Drexler was sitting nearby with a cup of coffee. "Why would you need a copy?" Ari looked at him and started to answer, but he stopped her. "You'd only need a copy if you intended to investigate. You're a private investigator, and no one has hired you to look for this girl. Correct?"

"I guess, but..."

"But nothing, Miss Willow. We may be a small department, but we can handle this. We appreciate your help. If someone did kill a woman out there in the woods, odds are we would never have found her without you raising the alarm. So we're grateful for that. Now you just go back to your vacation and let us do our jobs."

She wanted to argue, but she knew she didn't have an argument.

"Okay. You're right. Can you at least let me know if you find anything?"

"We'll tell you what we can."

"All right. Thanks for your time, Sheriff. And for taking me seriously. I know you don't have a whole lot to go on."

He nodded. "Better to potentially waste a morning than risk letting one slip through the cracks. Enjoy your time on our island, Miss Willow."

"I'll try."

Ari walked out of the station and took a seat on one of the benches along the walkway. She took out her phone and sent Dale a text saying she was finished but added she wasn't in any hurry to get back to the cabin. If she got bored of waiting she would just walk the half mile and save Dale the trip.

The front door of the station swung open and Lynne came out. She spotted Ari and waved as she approached.

"Hi, Miss Willow. What are you doing out here?"

"Waiting for my girlfriend. She wanted to check something out at the library."

"Oh, okay." She crossed her legs and smoothed her skirt over the knee. "I was just on my way to lunch. We have some real good places in town. Burgers, salads, seafood of course."

Ari nodded. "I'll keep that in mind. Thanks."

"Sure." She paused. "You know, Tom's a good man. Sheriff Drexler? He's going to devote everything he can to finding this girl. But even so, I mean, there's only so much he can do when he doesn't have any proof that there was actually a crime committed. He can only go so far on faith."

"I understand. Truly. I'm grateful he's done as much as he has, frankly."

Lynne nodded. "Well. If there is someone out there who raped and killed a woman, I'd really want everyone pitching in. Every able body, you know?" She reached into her purse and placed a folded piece of paper on the bench between them. "Oh, you know, you should try Nancy's. Down by the ferry lanes, best sandwiches on the island. In fact I think I'll head there now. I hope to see you around, Miss Willow."

"Call me Ari. I'll keep that in mind. And thank you."

Lynne smiled sweetly, then stood up and walked to her car. Ari waited until she was gone before she picked up the paper and unfolded it. It was, as she expected, a print-out of the sketch. Ari had mixed feelings about taking it. On one hand she respected the sheriff's request to take care of the investigation in an official capacity. On the other, she made a promise to the dead girl. If she put herself in the sheriff's shoes - an unknown woman claiming to have seen a dead body she couldn't produce - she knew how much stock she would put into the search.

She folded the paper in half again and this time she spotted something written on the back in pencil. "Go see Bowie. Ask if she's seen anyone." There was an address and a rudimentary map that showed her where to go from the police station to reach it. Ari stood and tucked the paper into her back pocket. She texted Dale to tell her she was following a lead, gave the address where she could be found, and headed off in search of Bowie.

The address on the flyer led her to a sprawling green building with shingle siding and red accents on the windows. From the street the building was framed by the harbor, and from the parking lot it seemed to be crowned with evergreens. The parking lot was empty when she arrived, but Ari tested the front door and found that it was unlocked. She stepped inside a plush waiting area with a placard that told her to "please wait to be seated." The dining room beyond the hostess stand was empty, and the entire restaurant was flooded with harsh sunlight that made it look less elegant than she assumed it would look at dinnertime. A few candles and the delicate-looking lanterns on each table would transform the place into something incredibly romantic.

Ari stood at the entrance to the dining room and looked for signs of life. There was an open door to her left, and through it she could see a wall of wine bottles. Directly ahead of her was the kitchen, and a set of twin doors led onto an outdoor dining area on the patio.

"Hello?"

"Marco."

She turned toward the spiral stairs tucked away in one corner of the room. "Uh. Polo?"

A woman came halfway down, exposing her legs from the knee down, and bent down to look at the arrival. "Hi. Are you here for lunch or did you want to make a reservation?"

"I'm actually looking for Bowie."

"Ah." She straightened and came down the rest of the way. She was tall and lean, wearing a yellow T-shirt that accentuated her boyish figure. Her salt-and-pepper hair was cut in a sloppy shag, and she looked more like a lanky teenage boy than the middle-aged woman she actually was. As she got closer Ari could see her shirt was emblazoned with the word KENTUCKY over a faded cartoon landscape. "Name's actually Boo-we, like the Texan not the singer. Although I'd have preferred the singer." She grinned. "And you found her. How can I help you?"

"My name is Ariadne Willow. I'm a private investigator from Seattle." Ari took out the flyer and unfolded it. "Lynne from the police station seemed to think you might be able to help me find her."

Bowie took the paper and examined it closely. "Doesn't really look familiar. Lynne sent you to me because she knows that most people who come to the island usually come through here. You can have a romantic dinner, sit at the wine bar, and we have a lunch counter on the other side where you can get a mean grilled cheese. She must have thought this girl came by, but I don't recognize her. Sorry." She handed the paper back. "What happened to her?"

"I think she was murdered."

Bowie winced. "Aw, geez. Seriously? Here on the island?"

"I take it that sort of thing isn't common."

"Here? God no. We'd like to think it's absolutely impossible on the island, but humans are humans, I guess. Can I see the picture again?" Ari handed it over and Bowie studied it again, furrowing her brow this time and working her teeth against her bottom lip.

Ari said, "It might not be exactly right. A few of the details could have been imagined or remembered incorrectly."

"Hair's blonde," Bowie muttered, reading the statistics on the side. She put two fingers against her temple and rubbed slowly. Suddenly she snapped her fingers. "We deliver. Hold on. Can I text this picture to someone?"

Ari hoped it wouldn't get her in trouble with the sheriff, but she nodded. He planned to put the poster up all over town anyway, so it wouldn't hurt to have one more person see it ahead of time.

Bowie took a phone from her pocket, snapped a picture, and then typed out a text. "I'm sending it to our drivers. I'm not telling them the details, just asking if they've delivered to anyone who looks like this." She hit send and lowered the phone. "We only have two drivers, and we really don't deliver all that much. Maybe two or three orders every meal period? People usually like to come in, for the ambiance."

That was understandable. The place was lovely in the daytime, but she could only imagine what it was like at night. She took out her wallet and fished out a business card, noting that it was the second one she'd handed out during their no-work vacation.

"If anyone recognizes her, please give me or the sheriff a call."

"Will do." One side of her mouth lifted as she read the card. "Bitches Investigations. Really?"

Ari shrugged. "It brings us clients we don't mind working for and keeps away the ones we'd rather not deal with."

"I love it. I do. I'll definitely give you a call." She tucked the card into her jeans and regarded Ari. "So are you working with the sheriff on this? He doesn't seem like the sort who would bring in outside help."

"I'm working adjacent to him. I'm the one who found her, and I feel like I owe it to her."

Bowie nodded solemnly. "I understand. I'm sorry I couldn't be more help."

"It sounded like a longshot anyway." She held out her hand. "It was good to meet you, Bowie, despite the circumstances."

"You too."

They shook hands and, as Ari turned to leave, Bowie said, "Oh. Oh, wait. I'm getting a text." She took out her phone and read the screen. "Dylan thinks he recognizes her."

Ari couldn't help smiling, both at the good news and the driver's name. "Bowie and Dylan? Maybe you should consider changing the pronunciation of your name."

"We have a Mick, too." Bowie went into the wine bar, leaned over the counter, and came back with a yellow legal pad. She put it down on one of the tables and began sketching a map. "I would just give you the address, but you're from the city, so... uh, no offense."

"No, none taken," Ari said. "The map is definitely necessary."

Bowie drew quickly. "This is where Dylan said he took the food. He's not a hundred percent sure, but he said he's about sixty percent."

"That's good enough for me to check it out." Ari looked at the map and realized she was going to a cabin not far from the one where she and Dale were staying. She remembered the blonde woman on the pier and shuddered as if someone had walked over her grave. Had she seen the woman twice, once alive and then dead? Back home she would have said it was too big of a coincidence, but out here in the middle of nowhere was a different story.

"Thanks a lot, Miss Bowie."

"Just Bowie. I hope you find out who she is."

"Me too."

Ari left the restaurant and started across the parking lot. The quick blat of a car horn made her turn to see Dale was parked at the curb, and she jogged over and got into the passenger seat.

"Find anything?" they said at the same time. Dale gestured for Ari to go first, and she explained about Lynne giving her the picture on the sly and pointing her toward Bowie. She gave Dale the address and map, then said, "I think I saw the woman on the pier yesterday. When I went for my run, I saw another cabin about a mile or so away down the shore."

"On the shore? It might have been a lot more than a mile. It can look like someone is right in your backyard, but when you actually try to get there?" She looked at the map and started the car. When she pulled away from the curb she said, "But that is pretty close to the cabin. Maybe it was the woman you saw. Small world."

"Small island," Ari said. "Did you find anything at the library?"

"I did. The librarian let me look at their newspapers even though I don't have a card. I took out the past six months."

"Ambitious."

"It's every other week, so there were only twelve to go through. They all had police blotters, so I was able to dig through them relatively quickly. Mostly domestic disturbances, drunk and disorderly, property theft, vandalism. Some of the drunken brawls turned into assaults but the people involved were taken to jail and sobered up. No rapes, no murders. The sheriff may just be unwilling to admit it's possible on his little piece of paradise rather than covering anything up."

"I hope so. He seems like a good man. If I was in his shoes I'd probably shoot for wishful thinking, too."

They passed the turn-off for their cabin and continued south. Bowie's map told them to look for a gray mailbox, and Ari spotted it first. The access road was wider than theirs, and Dale navigated easily between the trees. Soon the road widened into a clearing and Ari saw that the cabin did indeed sit directly on the shoreline. The front of the house seemed bland and unadorned, and Ari realized it was because all of the ornamentation was on the water-side where it would be seen more frequently.

Dale parked next to an old Jeep with a ragtop. "What should we do?"

"You stay here. I'll go…" She craned her neck. The house was marginally more visible from the water than it was from the road, so it felt as if they were looking at the bland backyard. "Is this the front door, or do I go around to the other side?"

"Your guess is as good as mine."

"Okay. You stay here, I'm going to see if anyone is home."

"Be careful, puppy."

Ari squeezed Dale's arm and got out of the car. The clearing was ringed with sprawling madrone trees whose branches teemed with birds and squirrels. As Ari skirted the edge of the property she looked out at the water. The harbor did indeed look like the one where she'd seen the mysterious blonde woman the day before, and a similar boat was tied to the end. She stopped to look out over the water, attempting to see the spot where she had crouched next to the shore, but every cove looked the same to her.

Behind her, the door to the cabin slid open and she turned to see a blonde woman stepping out onto the back deck. She was tall and lean, and the word that jumped to the front of Ari's mind was "sleek." The woman wore a white dress shirt over a pair of shorts. The hem of the shirt overlapped the shorts, making it look as if she was only half dressed. Her hair was center-parted to frame an almost too-severe jawline, her widely spaced eyes and generous mouth making her seem out of proportion to herself. It combined to make a very attractive package.

She stopped when she saw Ari. "Oh. Hello." She crossed her right foot behind her right ankle and settled into the odd position like a bird perching on a wire. "Can I help you?"

Ari had no idea where to start. She wished she had brought the sheriff or Deputy Vaughn along just in case of this scenario.

"Is this about Penny?"

"Penny..."

"My sister." The fear was beginning to become apparent on the woman's face. "Did something happen to her?"

Ari said, "Can you describe her?"

"Why?"

Ari introduced herself again. "Was she wearing a blue windbreaker and jeans this morning?"

The woman's eyes widened slightly. "I don't know. She was gone before I woke up. But yes, she has a blue windbreaker. What happened?"

"I'm very sorry. But I think your sister was attacked this morning. She didn't make it."

She leaned forward, one arm extended for the railing, but Ari could see she wouldn't reach it before she fell. She darted up the steps and put her arm around the woman's waist and looked for somewhere to put her down gently, but instead she folded her legs underneath her and sat down right where she was. Ari crouched next to her and rested a hand on her shoulder.

"Your sister, her name was Penny?"

"Yes. Penelope Alton." She pressed the back of her wrist to her lips, staring blindly at the deck. "Where... where is she?"

Ari said, "That's sort of the problem. I found her in the woods not far from here, but when I came back with the police her body was gone."

"Gone...?"

"Someone took her away and cleaned up the crime scene."

She furrowed her brow and reached up with both hands to push her hair behind her ears. "Who... who would do that?"

"That's what I'm hoping to find out."

CHAPTER FIVE

ARI HELPED the stunned woman back into the house and guided her to the couch. The decor was an odd mix of magazine layout mixed with dorm room clutter, and Ari assumed she and her sister had just set up camp in a rental cabin. She sat the woman down and crouched next to her. "Do you need anything? Something to drink?"

She shook her head, still staring at her feet.

"Do you mind if my partner comes in?"

"Partner?"

"I'm a private—"

She closed her eyes and shook her head as if to clear the cobwebs. "Oh, right. Sure. Yes." She sniffled and pressed the heel of her hand to her eye. Ari gave her privacy by going to the door and stepping out onto the island-side deck. Dale spotted her and Ari waved her in, then went back to where the woman was sitting. A few seconds later, Dale arrived.

"This is my partner, Dale Frye. Dale, this is..."

The woman sniffled, then realized she hadn't given her name. "Oh. I'm Phoebe. Phoebe Alton. I'm sorry, I should have said…"

"It's okay." Ari looked over her shoulder at Dale. "Her sister Penny was the woman I found."

Dale said, "I'm so sorry."

Phoebe sniffled, and Dale produced a Kleenex from somewhere on her person and handed it to her. Phoebe managed a "thank you" and wiped at her eyes, while Ari looked at Dale in an expression she hoped conveyed gratitude. She sat on the couch next to Phoebe and waited until her sniffling subsided a bit before she spoke again.

"Do you and Penny live on the island?"

"No. We're visiting from, ah, I'm from Vancouver and she lives in California. It was Penny's idea." Her features seized again, as if she was holding back a flood of tears. "She wanted to surprise me."

"How long have you been on the island?"

"Four days. We were supposed to leave on Thursday."

"Did you have any run-ins, was there anyone who gave you a hard time or…?"

Phoebe shook her head. "We mostly just stayed out here. We're both cooped up in offices all day, so she want-wanted to just get out and enjoy nature." She hung her head again, tears pooling in the corners of her eyes before trailing down. Ari put a hand on her shoulder.

Dale said, "I should probably get the sheriff out here. Is there an address…?"

"There's a brochure on the fridge," Phoebe muttered, sniffling and dabbing at her eyes. "How could this happen? Someone killed her?" She looked at Ari again, as if hoping she had misunderstood. "Maybe it was an accident. Maybe she fell, or…"

Ari shook her head. "I'm sorry. She was… her throat was cut, and it looked like… someone had assaulted her."

Phoebe said, "Assaulted…?"

"Her pants were pulled down," Ari said, wincing at the implication she was making.

To her surprise, Phoebe's reaction was almost one of benign understanding. "Her pants were down?" she asked, sounding almost as if that was a silver lining. "Oh."

"There wasn't any evidence her attacker actually succeeded in... doing anything," Ari said. "Anything other than..." She flinched at herself and looked for Dale, who had just come out of the kitchen. "Is Sheriff Drexler on the way?"

"Yeah. He'll be here in a few minutes. He wanted to make sure you and I stayed put. He didn't sound happy."

"I bet he didn't," Ari said.

Phoebe looked at them. "Why would he be mad?"

"We're kind of not supposed to be investigating this."

"Oh."

Ari said, "You didn't have any confrontations since you came to the island? No one who might have gotten angry at Penny, maybe got into an argument with her and things got out of hand?"

"No. We didn't know anyone on the island. She just called me up out of the blue a few weeks ago and suggested coming out here. It sounded so amazing at the time, I couldn't say no."

"She chose the island?"

Phoebe nodded. "She found the island, found the rental, everything. She just wanted to get away from the city for a while." Her voice trailed off and she pressed the Kleenex against her eyes. "I lived so close by that she thought it would be nice for us to have the time together."

Ari heard the approach of Sheriff Drexler's car, followed by the slamming doors and shoes on the wooden deck. Phoebe lifted her head and tensed as Drexler gave a cursory knock and stepped inside. He gave Ari a withering, irritated glare before he looked at Phoebe.

"Miss Alton?"

"Yes. Phoebe."

"I'm Sheriff Drexler, this is Deputy Vaughn." He looked at Ari again. "Miss Willow. Odd to find you here. I believe you were told not to investigate this."

Ari said, "I couldn't just sit around and do nothing. And look, we have a name now. Penelope Alton. She's been missing since sometime this morning. Now you have more than just my word to go on. This is a real crime, despite the fact her body was taken away."

Drexler's expression didn't shift. "And we thank you for your assistance. Now if you'll excuse us, we have work to do here and we don't need you getting in the way."

"Wait," Phoebe said, putting a hand on Ari's arm to keep her from moving. "Wait, she found my sister's body. She identified her and found out where we were staying. I'm sorry, Sheriff, I have no doubt your officers are good at what they do, but I'm not exactly keen on the idea of kicking Ariadne off the case after she's done all the work."

Drexler looked down at the floor. "Ma'am, I understand that, but Miss Willow is a civilian."

"She's a private investigator. I can hire her, right?" She looked at Ari. "I can hire you to find who killed my sister."

"Um." Ari looked at Dale, then Drexler. "Technically. I suppose."

Phoebe said, "Do you have any female officers, Sheriff?"

Drexler shook his head. "No, ma'am, I don't."

"Penny could have been killed by someone she knew, and if that's the case then there's evidence to uncover. Someone is going to have to go through her stuff to see if there are any clues. I would prefer Ariadne conduct the search."

Drexler took a deep breath and let it out slowly. "Everything you find pertinent to the case goes through me."

"Absolutely," Ari said. "I've kept you informed so far even though I knew it would piss you off. Why would I stop now?"

He exhaled sharply through his nose and gestured for her to carry on. "While Miss Willow is searching your sister's room, maybe you could fill in some blanks for us."

Phoebe nodded. To Ari, she said, "Penny's room was down that hall on the left. It's the only door that's closed, I think."

Ari said, "I'll check it out. Thank you."

She stood up and stepped around Drexler to go down the hallway. The way he and the deputy tracked her with their eyes she knew they wouldn't have an easy partnership. She didn't much care what Drexler thought about her, but she doubted he would be as open with evidence he uncovered as she planned to be with what she found. Their joint investigation was destined to be a one-way street. The only important thing was finding Penny's killer.

Ari let herself into Penny's bedroom and closed the door behind her. The bed was unmade, and an open suitcase was sitting on the window seat. A cell phone plugged into a charger on the nightstand. Her pocketbook and purse were on the floor next to the closet. Ari crouched and checked to make sure Penny's identification was inside. The face on the driver's license was instantly familiar; she was much prettier in life than she'd been when Ari saw her, but the picture undeniably matched.

"Sorry, Phoebe," she said. "Sorry, Penny."

She put the pocketbook on the bed and picked up the phone. She could be absent-minded and leave her phone hither and yon, but Dale's was practically attached to her wrist. She wondered if it was out of character for Penny to leave the house without it, but it might depend on where she planned to go. She turned it on and crossed her fingers that it wouldn't be password-protected. The lock screen disappeared without hassle as she swept her thumb across the screen and she poked at the calendar app.

The week was blocked off for their island visit, with details such as the cabin's address and the contact details of the owner in case of emergency. She wondered if this fit the bill, since the death technically happened outside the home. There was an additional note - WFC - which appeared underneath the reservation details. Ari opened the calendar to that week and saw the initials came up a few more times associated with a numerical identifiers that she couldn't make heads or tails of. She used her phone to take a picture of the screen, feeling slightly odd doing it, but it was faster than taking notes. The rest of the phone didn't turn up any evidence of a significant other or conflicts at work. She found a myriad of pictures that featured a wide variety of people but no one popped up more than anyone else. She assumed they were friends and coworkers. A whole album was dedicated to "Pheeble", an apparent pet name she had for her sister. In the pictures where both sisters were together their family resemblance was very clear.

She moved on to the text messages. Several to her sister, some to work acquaintances listed by their surnames, and a few to someone listed as Evan. Ari clicked on Evan and scrolled up to mid-conversation. "Can you feel me sliding down onto~"

"Okay, so, Evan's a boyfriend," Ari said, quickly navigating away from whatever Penny had been about to describe in the text. Maybe he was just a friend with benefits or a booty call, but whoever he was Ari didn't see the point in perusing their phone sex to confirm their relationship. She went to the call log and saw she had quite a few conversations with Evan. Some calls lasted a few seconds, others went on for half an hour or more. The last call had been over twelve hours ago, and it had lasted almost forty-five minutes. Judging from the texts she had a good idea how the conversation would have gone.

She put the phone down, planning to hand it over to the police when she was finished going through the room. Penny was a stranger to the island, she had a boyfriend back in California, and she seemed to have a good relationship with her sister. Why would someone like that leave the cabin in the early morning hours, leave her phone, pocketbook, and purse behind, and head off into the woods? From her attire she wasn't out for a jog, and she'd been too far into the wild to be on a route.

There was a soft knock on the door and Phoebe stepped inside as Ari stood up. She smiled shyly, her eyes still red from crying.

"Am I interrupting?"

"No. I was about to come back out."

Phoebe came into the room. "I just wanted to officially hire you, just so the police don't too aggravated with you. I wasn't sure how much you charged..." She held up her checkbook, but Ari waved it away.

"We can work that out later. For right now, do you have a dollar?"

"Um." She patted her pockets and came up with a wallet. She took out a coin. "It's Canadian. Is that okay?"

Ari nodded. "It's actually worth more, I think." She took the loonie from her. "Consider us officially on retainer. I have a few questions, if you're willing."

"Anything. Anything I can do to help."

"Do you know an Evan?"

Phoebe's eyes widened and she put a hand over her mouth. "Oh, God. Evan. He's going to be devastated. I'm going to have to call him. I'm going to have to call... so many people..." She pushed her hands through her hair. "Oh. Um, h-he's her boyfriend. They've been together for... a while. At least a year. Thanksgiving was... yes. At least a year."

"Was everything good there?"

"As far as I know. I..." She made a face. "The first night we were here, I heard them talking on the phone through the wall. It sounded like things between them were, uh. Going... well..." She chuckled nervously. "I don't think you have to worry about him being involved. He wouldn't... leave her out in the woods like that."

Ari nodded. "Do you know what WFC might mean? She had it written on her phone for this week. It came up a couple of times."

"WFC..." She looked toward the window and thought for a long moment, her lips forming the letters a few times. "It might have something to do with her work? She's, she was, a physical therapist. She would help people who had been in accidents. Maybe she wanted to check in on someone's progress while we were here. I really can't think of what it would mean. I'm sorry."

"That's fine. You helped a lot, considering what you're going through. I'm going to give her phone to the police. Is that okay?"

"Yeah. I just need... can I get Evan's phone number off of there?"

Ari accessed the contacts list, and Phoebe wrote down the number. "He's going to be out of his mind... okay." She pushed her hair out of her face and closed her eyes.

"Hey." Ari put a hand on her shoulder. "This is a lot to take in. You thought you were on vacation, and now everything is blowing up in your face. There's stuff you have to do, and one item on that list is to take care of yourself. It's what Penny would have wanted."

Phoebe nodded. "You're right." She opened her eyes and looked at Ari for a long moment, holding eye contact until Ari felt vaguely uncomfortable. After a moment she said, "Are you gay?"

The question was so far out of left field that Ari thought she'd heard wrong. "I am. Is that an issue?"

"No. I'm not gay, but ever since I saw you I've felt something weird. I'm drawn to you for some reason. I trust you even though we met literally ten minutes ago. I don't know if it's instinct or the way you carry yourself, or if you just remind me of a girl I knew in high school. I thought maybe I was attracted to you but I don't think that's it. No offense."

"None taken. Dale's my partner."

"Your... oh! I see." She smiled and looked away, tears still glistening in the corner of her eye by her nose. "Well, you don't have to worry about me coming after you. It's just unusual for me to have this kind of instant connection with someone. There are two actual police officers out there that I trust less than this random woman who wandered into my backyard. It's confusing. But whatever the reason is, I'm glad you're on the case."

Ari said, "I'll do whatever I can to find the person who did this to your sister."

"Thank you."

"Right now I should go back out there. Oh." She took out her wallet and handed out yet another business card. She wondered how many she would have to give before their vacation was officially busted. "You can get in touch with me or Dale at that number any time. If you need to talk, Dale is a great listener."

"Thanks." She smiled weakly at the name of the agency. "Bitches. Penny would have gotten a kick out of that."

Phoebe led Ari back into the living room, where she handed over the phone to Sheriff Drexler. Phoebe announced that she had officially put the agency on retainer, so Ari and Dale were working as her agents. "You don't have to like it, Sheriff, but they're here and they seem to have done a pretty good job so far. I just want to make sure my sister has the best chance at justice."

Drexler said, "I understand how you feel, Miss Alton. We'll do everything in our power to work together on this. Would you like someone to stay with you?"

Phoebe looked at Deputy Vaughn without much enthusiasm.

Dale cleared her throat and stepped forward. "I could stay. I mean, we can't just dump this all on you and leave. Plus I hate the idea of leaving you out here all alone after what you just found out."

"Oh." Phoebe brightened at the suggestion. "I would be okay with her staying."

"Fantastic," Drexler said dryly. "We'll be in touch."

Ari hugged Dale goodbye, whispered in her ear to be careful, and got the car keys from her. "If you need anything..."

"I'll call."

"And I'll come running."

Ari kissed her goodbye and went out to find Drexler and Vaughn waiting by their car. She crossed the yard to let them speak their peace.

"We're not fans of this arrangement, Miss Willow. We don't have to deal much with murders up here, but we can hold our own. We don't need some civilian running around mucking things up."

"You probably don't deal with a lot of private investigators, either. I'm not a civilian, I'm a trained and licensed investigator. The difference is I report only to my client."

Vaughn said, "And answer to no one."

"That's not true. We have a very good relationship with the police back home. We do consulting work with them from time to time. This isn't a race to the finish, Sheriff. We're just two different tools working toward the same goal. We just want to find Penny Alton's killer and bring them to justice. Two heads are better than one, right?"

"I was thinking of the cooks and kitchens saying, to be honest. But there's nothing I can do now that she's officially hired you. What I will do is suggest you stay out of our way. If it comes down to arresting you for obstruction of justice, I'm willing to do that."

"Wow, and just a few hours ago you were going to pin a medal on my chest."

"You haven't found the body yet."

"Give me time."

Drexler opened his car door and folded himself into the seat. "That's what I'm worried about, Miss Willow. Time. The body has already disappeared. The more time that goes by, the more concerned I am that whoever killed her is getting farther and farther away from us. I hope we have time left on the clock, but it's not looking good at all."

He shut the door and Ari stepped back as he started the engine. As much as she didn't want to admit it, he had a point. The killer had come damned close to committing a perfect crime. Most people thought you had to wait three days to report someone missing, but that wasn't the case. Anyone could be reported missing as soon as their disappearance was noticed. That didn't mean the cops would leap on it with everything they had.

It could have been days before they even considered Penny had been murdered, and by then the killer could have been on the opposite coast with Penny's body sunk to the bottom of the Strait.

Penny's body might indeed be lost, but Ari was determined to make sure she didn't stay buried.

CHAPTER SIX

ARI DROVE back to where the road ended and walked down the trail to where she'd found Penny's body. The wind off the water had eliminated the majority of the blood scent. She knew she would still be able to find it if she went full-wolf, but she wanted to be on two feet just in case Penny's attacker was still lurking somewhere in the woods. Whoever had taken her was good, but no one could carry another person's dead weight through a wooded area without leaving some kind of trail. And if Penny had been running for her life, the forest would give evidence of that flight.

Ari stopped at the dead tree and envisioned the body again. Now that she had an idea of where Penny had been going - assuming of course she had been running for "home" - Ari had a better chance of backtracking her. Ari crossed the spot where Penny had fallen and tried to choose the most likely place for her to have come from. The trees to the right were too close together, and on the left there was a scattering of small bushes. Someone on the run would choose the path of least resistance, so Ari went with her instinct.

She moved slowly and kept alert for any signs of passage. A shoe print here, skids in the mud where someone had slipped, broken branches, bark stripped from a tree where someone had bumped into it on their way past. It took her a few minutes to find the right path but then she saw it: someone had taken a hard left turn and kicked up a wedge of stones.

Once she was on the right path it was easy to find out where Penny had come from. Ari turned west, away from shore and deeper into the wilderness. She had a mental map of this side of the island and imagined it as bell-shaped as she followed Penny's route. Occasionally the trees thinned enough that she could see the mountainous center of the island, and even though she had left the water behind she could hear the thrum of boat engines. The sounds of civilization might be muffled but they were definitely there. The island had seemed so small on the map, but now she could see how huge it really was. There was an entire forest crowded into a small amount of space.

After five minutes Ari crouched and inspected a spot of dirt where it looked as if someone had taken a fall. She hadn't noticed any mud on Penny's clothes, but she hadn't exactly had time to examine her very closely. The path was wider here, muddy in the center with small rocks bordering either side. It was much more traveled than the other paths, and it almost seemed as if it had been cultivated. She moved more cautiously as she followed it through the trees, stopping when she reached a clearing and stepped out of sight so she could observe without being spotted.

The clearing was currently empty, but it had a dirt road leading down to a long wooden dock. When she was sure no one was around she stepped out of cover and walked to the road. The trees closed in around the mouth of the clearing, and a wooden sign declared it Private Property - No Trespassing. Ari walked back down to the shore and stepped onto the dock. If Penny had crossed this wide open area while someone was chasing her, Ari had to think she would have taken the chance to run out onto the road. At least there she stood a chance of being seen by a passing motorist and less chance of getting tripped up by a bush or root.

Just to be sure she checked the opposite side of the clearing. Maybe Penny had been fleeing so desperately that she'd gotten tunnel vision and didn't realize how close to the road she was. She searched for nearly ten minutes trying to pick up the trail but she didn't see any evidence Penny had come through that way. She had to assume the pursuit began here, in the clearing, and Penny entered the woods in an attempt to lose her attacker.

She imagined Penny being here in early that morning, either alone or with someone. Maybe she'd gone for a hike and stumbled upon the property as Ari had. Maybe the owners had been there and decided they didn't take very kindly to interlopers. Ari tried to imagine it just after dawn, still shadowed by the trees, and saw Penny wandering out of the forest. And then... what? The men who were hypothetically at the dock invited her to have some breakfast, one of them got too fresh, and when Penny tried to run, he slit her throat?

Ari walked further out onto the dock and looked down the shore. The curve of the island prevented her from seeing the dock where Penny and her sister were renting, but if someone had a boat they could probably be there in a couple of minutes. If the owners of this little slip of land found out they were practically neighbors with the sister of their victim, there was very little to stop them from heading over in the middle of the night to shut her up.

Ari chewed her bottom lip and walked back to the road. Going through the woods, the clearing was about forty-five minutes away from Penny and Phoebe's cabin. She assumed that was about a mile by road, and maybe five minutes by boat. If she did start asking questions about how Penny died, she had to assume the killers might go after the surviving sister. That was if they didn't just go after her and Dale to try stopping the investigation in its tracks.

She sighed heavily and began the long walk back to where she had left the car. Whatever happened, she was going to have to take a faceless killer into account before she made her next move. She had to make sure it was safe for Dale, Penny, and herself before she got too involved.

Whatever happened, it was a hell of a way to start a vacation.

After Ari and the sheriff left, Phoebe went into the kitchen and began making tea and coffee. Dale followed her and, even though she didn't comment, Phoebe said, "I know. It's insane. I hope you want a cup of one, because I'm making them both. It's just what I do, I guess. I need to... make something right now. So even if you don't..."

"Tea would be great. Thank you."

Phoebe nodded and starred at the flow of water running from the faucet. After a moment she hung her head and closed her eyes. "I don't know how I'm ever going to do anything ever again. Penny was... she was the one who pushed me. She was the baby, but she was always pushing me to take the next step. Stop waiting for that guy I like and ask him out first. Apply for that job I don't think I'm qualified for. She was my coach. She was my hero. Even when she moved away all I had to do was call and she would whip me into shape. I just... I can't believe she's gone. I can't imagine a world she's not in."

Dale said, "I felt that way when my mother died. It seemed surreal that I couldn't reach out to her when I needed help. Or just someone to talk to."

"How'd you get over it?"

"I didn't. But I met Ariadne, and that helped. Ari didn't replace my mother, but she did give me someone to lean on when I needed it the most."

Phoebe turned off the faucet. "She just wanted to spend some time together this week."

"What did you guys do?"

"Ironically, not a whole lot together. She would go into town, and I'd stay here and read. But you have to understand our relationship. We could spend a whole hour in the same room together and not say a word. Or she could spend the whole afternoon out, and then we'd spend ten minutes talking about what we'd done before we went our separate ways."

Dale smiled. "I know how that can be. You're comfortable enough to just enjoy each other's presence."

"Yeah." She ran her fingers through her hair. "There are so many people I have to call."

"That can wait. Right now you need to take care of yourself." She looked at the two brewing drinks. "What do you want, coffee or tea?"

Phoebe chuckled. "Neither, really…"

"Okay. How about some milk? Or a glass of water?"

"Water sounds great right now."

Dale filled a glass and guided her back out into the living room. "I can't believe anyone would want to do this to her. Penny was always so sweet, and kind, and… and funny… the idea that anyone might want to hurt her is absurd."

"Maybe it wasn't someone who knew her. Maybe it was someone on the island. I did some reading this morning and it doesn't seem like a violent place. But you never know what might set someone off. I do know that Ariadne Willow is a hell of a detective. She won't give up. She made a promise to you sister and I know that she'll do everything in her power to keep it."

"You have a lot of faith in her."

Dale said, "She has certain secret weapons at her disposal. Nothing against the local police, but there's a reason people hire Ari. She's good at figuring out the clues and getting to the truth."

"Oh, my God." Phoebe's face had gone pale. Her eyes widened, and she suddenly sat straighter on the couch. "WFC. I know what WFC is. The initials in Penny's day planner, I know what they mean. Or… or I know who it is. Oh, my God."

"Who?"

"Wayne Francis Corbett." She looked around the room. "Does the island have a phone book? I have to know if he's here."

Dale stood up and went to the end table. She opened the cabinet underneath and found a very slender phone book. She thumbed through it as Phoebe leaned forward to cover her face with both hands.

"I don't see a Corbett listed. Why would your sister be meeting with him if he was?"

Phoebe bit down on her lips, turning her mouth into a sharp line. "Wayne Corbett was the rat bastard our mother worked for before we were born. She was a marine biologist, and she spent her entire damn life on these islands. Or rather under the water around these islands. She studied marine life, discovered two new species, and charted a decade in the life of an orca pod. When she presented her work, it was turned in under Corbett's name. He got the accolades and the grants. He got recognized for awards, and he never once acknowledged the fact he hadn't lifted a single damn finger. Mom spent years fighting to get her work recognized, but Corbett just dismissed her as a jealous intern. An intern. Her entire career dismissed, and her contemporaries thinking she's just some woman who fetched coffee for the people doing the real work."

"That's awful," Dale said.

"She eventually had to leave. She'd been working at a university on one of the islands in this archipelago, but after being shunned she couldn't bear showing her face. She moved to Vancouver and got a job teaching high school biology. It destroyed her. I could tell how much it killed her when she went to work every day. Corbett took away her passion for the work."

Dale said, "She couldn't prove the work was hers?"

"Corbett was established. All the work she did, all the grants paying for what she was doing, it went through Corbett. Donors made all of mom's work possible, and he was the one who got the donors to open their wallets. So it didn't matter if her name was on every report, it didn't matter if she woke up at four in the morning to go out on a boat in sub-freezing temperatures just to be there when a particular orca passed by. Everything her career meant, everything she had spent a third of her life building, suddenly snatched out from under her."

"She never tried to sue him?"

"She didn't have the means. Even if she wanted to take him to court, he would just use the university's lawyers to either offer a settlement or tie things up until our money ran out. She couldn't fight him." She glared at her water. "Her research got him a TV show.

The World Below with Wayne Corbett."

"Oh, right," Dale said. "I've... uh."

Phoebe smiled without humor. "That's fine. Everyone in this part of the world has seen it. He just looks pretty for the cameras while another generation of scientists does the actual work for him. It makes me sick to my stomach."

Dale said, "Why do you think his name would be in Penny's calendar?"

"I have no idea. But I know why she didn't tell me. If I knew he was on the island, I'd have..." She furrowed her brow and pushed out her lips. "Mom died a few years ago. We took her out on a boat to see the orcas when we knew her time was short. The family she documented for... for... ten years of her life. And she loved it, of course. She loved it, and she cried when she said goodbye to them. But when we were taking the boat back, I could see in her eyes that it was different. Just being on the water was painful to her. It reminded her of everything that fucker took from her. She couldn't even say goodbye to her friends without Corbett ruining it for her."

Dale wondered if Penny had known Corbett would be present when she rented the cabin, or if that information had come later. She might have found out when it was already too late to cancel or change the reservation, but then why leave the man's initials in her calendar?

"Can you think of any reason Penny might have wanted to meet Corbett?"

"I don't. I don't know how she could have met with him, looked him in the eye knowing what he did." She sniffled. "I never would have come here if I'd known. Maybe if I'd refused, Penny would still be alive."

"You don't think he killed her, do you?"

"I don't know. I know that he has an empire to protect. His whole career since taking the credit for what Mom did, his television show... he's a commodity now. He has too much to lose. If Penny confronted him and started dredging up the past, who knows what he might do to protect it?"

"If that's the case... then I think you need to tell Ariadne. Let her confront Corbett for you. He already destroyed your mother's life, and if he killed Penny... well, there's no sense giving him a shot at a clean sweep."

"I can't ask Ariadne to go into something so dangerous."

"Hey, it's what she does. As much as I might wish it wasn't." She smiled and put her hand on top of Phoebe's. "Trust me, Ariadne is good at this. She's the best, in fact. If Corbett is on the island, she'll find out if he was involved."

"And if he was?"

"If he was, then she'll make sure he doesn't get away this time."

When Ari got back to the cabin, Dale explained what Phoebe had remembered about Corbett, and his connection to their mother.

"And he's on the island?"

Phoebe held her hands out helplessly. "I don't know. Penny sure seemed to think he was, but I haven't seen any sign of him. Maybe when she would go out during the day she was trying to find him."

Ari thought about Bowie, the woman at the restaurant, and thought she might be a good source of information. "Okay. I'll look into that. In the meantime, I think I found the place where your sister was attacked. It's a fair distance down the road, but I think someone with a boat could pull up to your dock in a matter of minutes if they were looking to take you out as well."

Phoebe tensed and looked toward the windows. "Do you think that's a possibility?"

"I'm not sure of anything yet. But I know that you shouldn't be alone after everything you've been through." She looked at Dale, who gave the slightest of nods. "Dale and I have an extra room in our cabin. I know we're strangers..."

"No. Please, if you're... I hate to derail your plans..."

Dale said, "This is more important than our plans."

"Thank you. I would really appreciate that." She stood up and smoothed her hands over her thighs. "I'll go pack a bag."

Ari waited until she was down the hall before she turned to Dale. "I'm sorry to just offer like that..."

"Are you kidding? I would hate myself if she was out here by herself and something happened to her. Of course she can stay with us. We're on the same page here, Ariadne. I know what we planned and I know there's no way either of us could continue it with a clear conscience." She put her hands on Ari's shoulders. "We came out here for a reason. It's just a different reason than we thought."

"I'll give you a real vacation soon. I swear."

Dale smiled. "I'll take you up on that."

Phoebe came out of the bedroom dragging a suitcase and carrying a duffel bag over her shoulder. "Do you have a cell signal at your cabin? I guess I should use the rest of the afternoon calling people..."

Dale said, "I think it depends on the time of day, frankly."

"Okay. Uh. Oh... food."

Dale helped her pack some food from the fridge and Ari carried her bag out. They loaded her things into the backseat, and Dale got behind the wheel. As she backed up to take them back to the road, Ari turned in her seat to look at Phoebe. "Do you think Corbett is the kind of person who would kill your sister to keep this from coming out?"

"I don't know. I've tried not to think about him very much. It just seems like such a violent response. To slit her throat...?"

"He also tried to rape her," Ari said. It was blunt, yes, but she wanted to test Phoebe's reaction again.

Phoebe said, "Oh. Yeah."

Ari glanced at Dale, who either hadn't noticed the odd tossed-off inflection or just didn't want to take her eyes off the road. Maybe it was shock, maybe it was a reluctance to admit what had almost happened, but Phoebe seemed incredibly dismissive of the fact her sister had been found half-naked. She decided not to dwell too heavily on that until Phoebe had been given time to process the situation.

"It just seems like overkill to me. Rape and murder to cover up professional theft. Is stealing someone else's credit really a big enough deal that he would go this far to keep it from coming out?"

"The scientific community has a long history of screwing people over," Dale said. "Edison and Tesla, Watson and Crick with Rosalind Franklin. Lise Meitner discovered nuclear fission, and Otto Hahn got the Nobel Prize for it. There are probably a dozen other examples I can't think of off the top of my head, but it happens all the time."

Ari shrugged. "Yeah, but... people know about that. I might not have, but it's common knowledge, right? Even I've seen those 'Tesla was Robbed' T-shirts and I have no doubt it's more common with female scientists. It's shameful, but it's not some deep dark secret. If you did go public with what Corbett did to your mother, what would happen to Corbett?"

Phoebe said, "Probably a headline on a scientific news website. Maybe a magazine cover. There would be a brief blow-up, but outside of the research community there probably wouldn't be much of a ripple. After a couple of months it would be forgotten."

Dale pulled onto the road leading to their cabin. "He would still have his show, his prestige... his reputation might take a hit, and people might not want to work with him..."

"That wouldn't even be an issue," Phoebe admitted. "He's a TV personality now. He doesn't do research or publish papers anymore."

"Right. But the mainstream media would definitely care about a murder. He can't be stupid enough to not realize that. All he has to do is ignore her and keep doing what he's doing."

Phoebe said, "Depends on how mad she made him."

"You think she could make him mad enough to kill?"

"This is my sister you're talking about," she said with a weak smile. "I think she could make someone mad enough to declare war."

Dale said, "Maybe that's what she did."

Phoebe's smile faded as she looked out the window at the cabin. "Maybe so." She got out of the car, looked at the tree, and squinted to read the sign. "Willi's Bike-Eating Tree...?"

"Grandpa left a bike here," Dale said as she helped Phoebe with her bags. "And the tree grew around it. That's the family legend, anyway. Ari and I have already set up our things in the first bedroom, but you can take the second one."

Phoebe slung the strap of her duffel bag over her shoulder. "Thank you again. This is a lot of trouble for someone you've just met."

"Well, you don't know Ari. She's..." Dale chuckled. "Ari is an alpha dog. Always looking out for people even if they aren't a member of her pack."

Ari smirked at Dale as Phoebe turned to go back into the house. Once she was out of earshot, Ari said, "Cute."

"It's something I've been working on." She bumped her hand against Ari's wrist. "But I could tell something was bugging you. What's wrong?"

"Something's off about Phoebe's reactions. She's obviously traumatized about what happened to her sister, but it's all about the murder. The attempted rape doesn't even seem to faze her."

The wind had blown Dale's hair into her face, and she brushed it back behind her ear. "Maybe 'attempted' is the operative word to her. I mean, considering the fact her sister's throat was slit, she might just want to compartmentalize. I know that in her shoes I would be more focused on the crime that actually happened."

Ari nodded, but she didn't seem convinced. "Maybe. Can I have the keys? I think I know someone in town I can ask about Corbett."

Dale gave her the keys. "Be careful. If he gets wind that you're looking for him, he might try to cover his tracks again." She folded Ari's fingers around the keys and lowered her voice. "If you need the wolf, use the wolf."

"Absolutely not. Of all the promises I made you about this week that I've already broken, I'm going to keep at least one. That one is the most important."

"Forget the promises you made me. Make me one more: that you'll stay alive no matter what. And if staying alive means using the wolf, then you use it. Promise me, Ariadne."

"I promise."

Dale kissed her, then pressed a second kiss to the corner of Ari's mouth. "I love you so much."

"Stay safe," Ari said. "I love you."

Dale reluctantly let her go and started toward the cabin. Ari watched her go and then checked the time on her phone. It was mid-afternoon, so she hoped the restaurant where Bowie worked would be finished with its lunch rush by the time she arrived. She had a few questions she wanted answered, and she didn't want too many people overhearing when she asked them.

CHAPTER SEVEN

ARI REMEMBERED Bowie telling her there was a lunch counter at the restaurant, so she drove to the other side of the building. A parking lot separated the building from the wilderness and Ari hoped the three vehicles parked there meant that there wouldn't be much of a crowd. She parked near the door and headed inside. Two people were seated at the bar away from the cash register, and a group of four were in a booth on the other side of the room from the entrance. Only half the customers looked up as she entered, but their reaction caused everyone else to look.

She smiled nervously. "Hi..."

Bowie came out of the kitchen. She had put on an apron but was otherwise dressed as she had been that morning. She lifted her chin as a greeting and then said, "Willow, right? Something Willow."

"Ariadne Willow. Good memory."

Bowie shrugged. "It helps in my line of work. Have a seat. What are you drinking?"

"No, I'm not..." She almost said she wasn't hungry, but she actually hadn't eaten anything since dinner the night before. "I don't need a drink, but I'll take a couple of those grilled cheese sandwiches you mentioned if I could get them to go."

"Sure, sure."

"Thanks." Ari looked to her right and saw the two men at the counter were watching her. "How ya doing?"

They looked back at their food without acknowledging her.

"You'd think a tourist town would be more used to strangers."

Bowie smiled. "Strangers and tourists tend to come in at the regular times. You know, noon for lunch, seven for dinner, and twenty minutes before the ferry leaves. You're kind of in the twilight zone."

"Ah. Sorry."

"Nah, don't worry about it. Customer's a customer. I'll get on those sandwiches. How many did you want?"

"I'll need three, but could I maybe come back into the kitchen with you? There were some things I wanted to talk to you about, and two birds with one stone, and all that..."

Bowie frowned. "I guess. Don't usually let people back here, but it's not every day a private eye comes by asking questions. Come on back."

Ari sensed more than saw everyone making a mental note of what Bowie had just said. Fantastic. She followed Bowie into the kitchen. The room was incredibly narrow, crowded on both sides by appliances that probably should have been replaced years ago. Everything rattled and hummed, and the freezer conspired with the grill to create an uncomfortable tropic environment in the space where Bowie did her work. She stood in front of the grill and went to work on the sandwiches.

"Do you want French fries, hash browns, curly fries, or tornado fries?"

"What are tornado fries?"

She smiled. "I'll fix you some tornado fries." She buttered the bread and slapped it onto the grill. They had to raise their voices to be heard over the machinery, but Ari was confident no one would be able to hear their conversation out in the main room. "So what did you want to ask me about?"

"Do you know someone named Wayne Francis Corbett?"

"Oh, sure. Wayne Corbett. *The World Below*. He has a house here on the island."

That was one mystery solved, anyway. "Would you happen to know where?"

Bowie stepped back from the grill and looked at a spot on the wall. "I seem to remember it was on the north side of the town somewhere. I don't know the exact address. It's a helluva big place, though. You probably can't miss it if go looking for it. Why would you be looking for it?"

"It's complicated." Now that Ari could smell the melting cheese, she was starting to feel her hunger. She wished she had ordered something with meat in it. When the first sandwich was finished, Bowie wrapped it in paper and handed it to her. Ari thanked her and took a big bite, planning to speak around it until the flavor hit her tongue. Her eyes rolled back and she came very close to swooning. When she finally swallowed her mouthful, she said, "Oh, my God."

"Ya like that, huh?" She chuckled. "Yeah, it's pretty beloved around here."

Ari wished she had been paying closer attention to the prep. She took another bite and wondered if the other two would survive the trip back to the cabin.

"Corbett is friendly enough if you can catch him in town, but I wouldn't recommend going up there and trying to talk to him. He's got a gardener who kind of doubles as a security guard, bouncer, whatever. He's been known to rough people up. Mostly high school kids trying to get a picture in a celebrity's car, whatever." She looked at Ari. "Is this about the girl you were asking about this morning?"

"I found her sister," Ari said, tactfully not answering her question about whether Corbett was connected. "Her name was

Penelope Alton."

Bowie closed her eyes and shook her head. "Terrible. That's awful. Vacationers, I guess?" Ari nodded and Bowie twisted her lips into a disgusted expression. "Come out here to get away from work for a while... a place like this is supposed to be safe."

"Hopefully it still is," Ari said. "This might just be an isolated incident. Oh... one other thing," she said, hoping to disconnect her next question from their current conversation. "That address you gave me earlier. There's a private dock about two or three miles south of there on the same road. Our cabin doesn't have a dock or anything, and Dale wanted to get in a little boating if it was possible."

"Who is Dale?"

"Oh. My girlfriend."

"Oh, okay. Uh." She thought hard and then smiled. "Boy, you ask tough questions. Did it have one of those Private Property signs up on it?" Ari nodded. "Sometimes people put those up just so the tourists won't take over it. If you ask the sheriff and he can't find out who it belongs to, it might be a case of some abandoned dock getting taken over by whoever happened to find it first."

Ari said, "Okay." The second sandwich was done and Ari gestured for it. "Could I?"

Bowie handed it over. "Is the third one for your girlfriend?"

"We'll see how things go."

Bowie snickered. "Push comes to shove, I'll make you a freebie. Buy three, get one free."

"Sounds fair."

"Come over here and I'll show you what a tornado fry is."

The tornado fry turned out to be a full potato placed on a skewer, then sliced spirally and deep-fried. The final product was awkwardly large but delicious. Ari took two, along with two grilled cheeses to take back for Dale and Phoebe, then asked Bowie for a map of the town. She didn't trust the map on her phone the way Dale did. It was accurate up to a point, but a lot of the images on such a rural location were bound to be outdated or misleading. Then again, a paper map printed ten years earlier had its own flaws, but it was designed by someone who actually lived on the island. She would take local knowledge over Apple any day.

She did trust her phone for the internet, however, and the lunch counter had strong enough wifi for her to do a quick search. Google confirmed that Corbett had a home on the island. There was no map or address for it, of course. If they were back home she would just have Dale look it up. Even if it was unlisted Dale could find a legal channel to find out where he hung his hat. For now it looked like she was reduced to driving around and hoping she stumbled over the large estate Bowie had implied.

On her explorations she discovered that the island did actually have an airport, so Dale's offer to catch a plane hadn't been hollow. The town seemed to be exactly like any small town on the mainland, with the same movie theaters and a post office, convenience stores and bars. The only real difference was that its borders were stricter than most. She drove north and kept her eyes peeled for anything that looked like a celebrity's estate, but even so she almost overlooked it.

At first glance it seemed to be a high school, or some sort of private educational facility. There was a fence that had been carefully and expertly constructed so that it didn't clash with the natural feel of the area but would still deter anyone from just wandering onto the property. She parked across from the unadorned mailbox and looked up at the squat building atop a gentle knoll. There was a sprawling front yard, but the house sat high enough to afford the owner a view of the harbor.

She was barely parked there for five minutes when the front door opened and a man emerged. He wore a dress shirt with the sleeves rolled up and the button at his collar popped. Ari watched as he came down the driveway and approached her car. As he neared he made the universal "roll down the window" spin with his index finger. Ari complied.

"You know, that really doesn't make sense anymore. I don't think I've seen a car with a hand-cranked window since the nineties. It's like when people make the receiver for a phone with their thumb and pinkie."

"We're going to have to ask you to move along."

She smiled. "I'm just parked, trying to enjoy my lunch. Have you ever had one of these tornado fries? I can't imagine there's any real nutritional value, but damn."

"You're parked outside private property."

"Does what I say matter, or are these just prerecorded--"

He said, "Ma'am... move along."

"I guess that's a no. Just one question. Does Wayne Corbett live here?"

He smiled. "If you don't leave, I'll have to call the police to escort you off the property."

"Ooh. Sheriff Tom would not like that. Don't worry, I'll move along." She started the engine and he leaned back. "I met a guy like you a few years ago. He worked for a woman named Katherine Gavin. We had a brief relationship. Ended pretty poorly for him. I'd hate to think history was repeating itself."

"Move along, please."

Ari shrugged. "I guess we'll see what happen. Have a lovely day."

As she drove away she watched him in the rearview. His eyes didn't leave the car until she turned a corner and cut off his line of sight. Even then she could almost feel him watching her through the buildings. She sighed and let the facade drop. So Corbett had a guard dog. That was fine. She doubted his dog's bark was worse than her wolf's bite.

Somehow the rest of the food survived her trip back to the cabin. Phoebe had also neglected to eat since receiving news of her sister, and Dale donated her sandwich and tornado fry to her. As she ate,

Ari drifted just out of earshot and gently pulled Dale with her. "I looked around and I'm pretty sure I found out where Corbett lives. He has a big estate on the north side of town." She looked at Phoebe. "If he was involved, he was a long way from his safe haven when he killed Penny."

"Did you get a chance to speak with him?"

Ari shook her head. "He has a security guard. Remember Oliver Echols?"

"The man who shot me in the head? I have a vague memory of him, yes."

Ari cupped the side of Dale's head. Her hair had grown over the scar, a wound which had come inches away from stealing Dale from her mere days after they had finally found each other. "Corbett has a guy like him standing guard. I'm going to call the sheriff and let him know about Corbett's potential involvement, see if he'll let me sit in on a meeting. If not..."

"Alternate means." Dale nodded. "As long as you're safe."

"Promise." She kissed Dale's forehead and went back into the living room. "Phoebe? How are you doing?"

Phoebe touched her lips with a napkin before she spoke. "I don't know. I think it's going to hit me when I start calling people to tell them."

Dale said, "We'll be here if you need us. We usually don't cohabitate with our clients, so you're getting the full service treatment."

"I appreciate it. I honestly think I would have just... crawled into the bathtub and gone comatose if it wasn't for you two. Thank you."

"Whatever you need, we'll be here for you."

Phoebe said, "Okay. I suppose I should call her boyfriend."

"We'll give you some privacy."

They went into the kitchen, where Dale started making herself something to eat. Ari offered her one of the tornado fries but Dale gave her such a withering look that she put it down immediately. She left Dale to her food preparation and went outside to call the sheriff and fill him in on what she'd discovered. The phone rang twice before it was answered.

"Sheriff's office, this is Lynne."

"Hi, Lynne. This is Ariadne Willow, from earlier. I need to talk to Sheriff Drexler."

"Oh, of course. I hope you found somewhere to eat lunch."

Ari smiled. "I did. It was exactly what I was looking for. Thanks."

"Sure. I'll patch you in to the sheriff. Hold on just a second."

Ari waited as she was transferred, and the sheriff came on the line with a brusque: "Hello, Miss Willow."

"Sheriff. I wanted~"

"Were you snooping around Wayne Corbett's place this afternoon?"

Ari was thrown, her tongue tangling around the information she had planned to give. "Uh."

"His man Louis Fleming said he ran off someone who was lurking outside. He just wanted to be sure it got on the record in case you came back and tried to break in. Got your license plate number and everything. I didn't happen to catch it myself, but his description of your car seemed pretty accurate."

Ari grimaced and put her hand on her hip.

"Now, I told Mr. Fleming that his boss didn't have anything to worry about. I said you were just taking a little tour of the island and got star struck. That's what happened, right? You weren't scouting the place or something crazy like that?"

"Of course not," Ari said. "I was following a lead."

Drexler said, "A lead that took you to Wayne Corbett's house. Not bad for spending one day on the island."

"I actually got here yesterday."

"Twenty-four hours, then." His voice had acquired a hard edge. "I did some digging on you, Miss Willow. You went after Katherine Gavin. You were credited with finding Missing Melody. You were even involved with taking down Jacob Keighley for murder. Now it looks as if you've found another celebrity to go after."

She had to admit she'd never noticed the pattern to the clients, but it did look odd when they were all listed together that way. "I don't go after celebrities. I go after people who are breaking the law, or using their power to silence their victims."

Drexler said, "Look, Miss Willow, I respect the fact that Miss Alton hired you to investigate for her. There's nothing we can do about that. But I'm not going to have you going around harassing the people of this town."

Ari said, "So Wayne Corbett is definitely off the table?"

"Innocent until proven guilty, Miss Willow."

"It'll be hard to prove he's guilty if I can't investigate him."

Drexler sighed. "Do you honestly believe that he's involved in what happened?"

Ari considered sharing the Alton family's history with the sheriff, but at the moment she didn't feel too friendly toward him. "I'm just covering the angles."

"If you find something that justifies questioning him, tell me. I'll talk to him, we'll make it friendly and in no way litigious..."

Ari laughed. "Oh. Okay. I thought you were just worried about making him angry at the town, taking his tax dollars elsewhere. But you actually think he'll sue for harassment."

"Miss Willow, this hasn't gotten anywhere near harassment. At the moment he just wanted to give me a heads-up about a potential stalker. He's gotten a few over the years. If you show up again, it might be easier to just let him believe that and arrest you."

"You're that scared he might be involved."

"I'm scared that you'll convict him just because he's a celebrity. I don't know what made you sit outside his home this afternoon but

I'm certain it will not happen again. Am I clear?"

Ari stared at the trees. "Absolutely."

"Do you have anything else to tell me?"

Ari thought about the private dock. "Nope. I was just going to tell you about Corbett."

"I'm willing to work this case with you, Miss Willow, but I'm going to be the one in charge. If I tell you to back off, you are going to back off. Is that understood?"

Ari smiled and shook her head. "Stop asking me if I understand, Sheriff. There's no doubt in my mind what this conversation is about. I'll be in touch."

She disconnected the call and growled quietly, thumping the phone against her thigh before she turned and went back into the house. Phoebe stood up off the couch and said, "Hold on, she just came in."

Ari said, "What's going on?"

"Evan. Penny's boyfriend. I told him you were investigating and he said he might be able to help." Into the phone, she said, "Evan? I'm putting you on with her. Her name is Ariadne."

She took the phone and heard the sound of sniffling. "Evan? Hi. This is Ari Willow. I'm sorry that I have to ask for something at a time like this, but I think time is of the essence here. Anything you can tell me about Penny would be a big help."

He cleared his throat and she heard the rustle of Kleenex. "Yeah. Phoebe told me that Penny's body was... taken? Stolen?"

"We think whoever killed her also hid her body, yeah."

He sniffled again. "God. Monsters. Okay. Uh, okay, Penny was investigating that guy. WFC or whatever. Do you know who that is?"

"We have a pretty good idea. Did she say why she was investigating him?"

"Something about how he had destroyed her mother's career, so she was going to destroy his. She said that she wanted to sink him."

Ari said, "Did she say how she planned to do that?"

"No. But she did a lot of research. Every night, weekends. It started around Thanksgiving last year and just steamrolled. She was obsessed with the guy and I never even knew who he was. About a month ago she said she thought she had enough, so she set up this big week on the island where he was staying. He has a bunch of other residences, I guess? But this one is so touristy that it was easy for her to book a place. She invited Phoebe along because she thought it should be a family victory."

"You have no idea what she found?"

"No, but she was really excited about it."

Ari frowned and looked at Dale. "Okay. Thank you for your help, Evan."

"Oh, tell Phoebe that I'm going to call Penny's friends and coworkers. She's dealing with enough right now. I can at least take that off her plate."

"I'm sure she'll appreciate that. I'll be in touch if we need anything else. I'm very sorry for what happened, but I'm going to do what I can to bring her killer to justice."

Evan's breath hitched. "Thank you."

Ari hung up and gave the phone back to Phoebe. "He said he would handle the notifications of her friends and coworkers for you."

Phoebe's shoulders seemed to lift slightly. "Oh. That's very kind of him."

Dale said, "Did you talk to the sheriff?"

"I did. He's... looking forward to cooperating with us fully on this matter."

"Really."

Ari widened her eyes and smiled.

"Ah. Well... I know you ladies both ate, but I'm famished. So if anyone would like to join me for an early dinner, I'm getting it ready right now."

Phoebe said, "Actually I want to just go lie down, if that's all right."

"Of course," Dale said. "Anything you need, just let us know."

Phoebe thanked them quietly and then went into her room. Dale went into the kitchen to tend to her cooking, and Ari followed.

"So the sheriff, not a fan?"

"Corbett called to complain about me sitting outside his place. Apparently I'm not supposed to irritate the celebrities. As far as Drexler is concerned, Corbett is 'innocent until proven, well, let's not be too hasty in proving anything'."

"Wow. It'll be tough to make a case if you can't even talk to your prime suspect."

"I'll find a way." She looked at the stew Dale was making. "When you're finished eating, could you spend some time online? I want to see what you can dig up about Penny and Phoebe's mother."

Dale said, "Why? Do you think Phoebe lied about it?"

"Not at all. I just want to see how much you can dig up without your fancy programs. Penny's boyfriend said that she was investigating Corbett for months. It shouldn't have taken that long to find proof of what he did if he's not bothering to hide it."

"Maybe it's just not documented very well. Maybe Penny was a lousy detective, or just didn't know her way around computers. I'll take a look. Most of my really spiffy programs are on the computer back at the office, but I think I can work it out with what I have."

Ari shrugged. "Thank you. I wish we'd found a computer in Penny's room."

"She could have saved things to the Cloud." Ari stared at her without comprehension. "The Cloud. Come on, Ariadne, I've explained this to you a thousand times. You can save documents and files to the Cloud so that if you lose your computer the information is safe. You can just download it later from the..." She sighed. "Never mind. I'll ask Phoebe if she knows her sister's account names and passwords."

"Okay. Dig the Cloud."

Dale chuckled quietly. "Do you think she found more skeletons in Corbett's closet? Something the media really will care about?"

"Could be. A man who gladly takes credit for someone else's work and then builds a career off it? It's not a big leap to imagine he might do something else shady. The something else might just be enough to undermine his career."

"Here's hoping Penny has a big file marked 'The Smoking Gun'. I'll see what I can find"

"You can wait until after dinner tonight," Ari reminded her. "We are on vacation, after all."

Dale grinned. "You could've fooled me."

CHAPTER EIGHT

"THE STRAIT of Georgia is a massive inland sea, joining together British Columbia and Washington State through a shared ecosystem." The man on Dale's laptop screen was hiking up a trail, and at this point of his monologue he stopped to put one mountain boot up on a rock. Behind him a blanket of evergreens fell away to show the shining waters of Puget Sound behind him. He wore a heavy winter jacket, his gray hair cut short to make his face stand out more. His features were all large and rough-hewn, from his too-small dark eyes, his large nose, and his wide mouth. He turned to indicate the land around him as he continued.

"This glorious body of water with all its life and all its mysteries feeds hundreds, thousands!, of rivers and streams all through the Pacific Northwest. Over three thousand different species call this body of water home thanks to the unusual mix of fresh and saltwater, which creates a glorious bounty of nutrients for a wide variety of fish, mammals, birds, and plants. It's one of the most productive ecosystems in the world, but it needs our help to survive. It needs me, and it needs you, and it needs all of us working together to protect it."

He smiled, and it was easy to see why he was one of the most popular wildlife experts on television. "Thanks for joining me. I'm Wayne Corbett, and I'll see you next time." He walked off camera-right, and the credits rolled over the scenery.

Dale went back to the main page before the next episode could begin. Ari had finished her shower in time to catch the ending monologue as she changed into her shorts and a tank top, and she slid into bed as Dale closed the computer and put it aside.

"He seems like a good enough guy," Dale said softly. They were keeping their voices down because the sounds of Phoebe crying in the other room had finally faded. Dale hoped that she had managed to fall asleep at last. "Very charming and personable. There are times when he comes off a little smug, maybe..." She shrugged. "But he's definitely knowledgeable on the subject."

"He wouldn't have gotten where he is if he didn't know a little bit. Once he got high enough he stopped trying. It was easier to let other people do the heavy lifting. And that...? That could just be reading off a script someone else wrote for him. Anyone can be charming on a script."

"True. And it wouldn't be the first time a charismatic and beloved celebrity wound up having a dark side. But we can worry about that tomorrow. Come here."

"What?"

"You have been amazing about giving up your vacation and everything I promised you, but right now... I have nothing to investigate, no questions to ask, and I'm in bed with the most beautiful woman I've ever known. So for now," she pecked Dale's cheek, "while we're in this bed," she kissed the other cheek, "consider our vacation reinstated."

Dale smiled and kissed Ari's lips.

"You can do whatever you want."

"Absolutely anything?"

"Within reason."

"Dale grinned and kissed Ari harder. "Mm. You taste minty."

"Wait 'til you see what else I taste like."

Dale smiled and pushed the blankets down to their waists. She rolled over to straddle Ari, wrapped both arms around her, and kissed her harder. Ari put her hands in Dale's hair. Her thumb skipped across the hidden scar, moving on without pause to link her fingers together at the base of Dale's skull. Without moving from her position on Ari's waist, Dale moved her hands down and peeled off Ari's shirt, then reached down to push her shorts out of the way.

"Get those off."

Ari straightened her legs and pedaled until the underwear was around one ankle. She let it fell and get lost under the covers, and Dale kissed her chin, her neck, between her breasts, and then dragged her tongue the rest of the way down. Ari closed her eyes and hooked one hand under the headboard, lifting her hips so Dale could get a hand under her butt. Ari pushed the blanket out of the way and crossed her ankles on Dale's back. Dale sank down onto her stomach and teased Ari with her tongue before pushing it inside of her.

Ari arched her back and bit down on her bottom lip, squirming from the effort of not making noise. Dale moved her free hand to Ari's mound, stretched her thumb down to stroke Ari's clit, and hummed. Ari's toes curled and she rocked her hips from side to side. She pressed her head down into the pillow and tightened her grip on the headboard. She remembered the first time they'd been in the room, their actual first time, and how amazing it had been to know she was making love to Dale, that Dale was making love to her. Even now, after years of sharing her bed, it was still amazing to her that they'd found each other.

She came, twisting her body around without turning her thighs into a vice around Dale's head. She twitched in the aftermath, hands shaky as Dale kissed her way back up over Ari's stomach and chest, then nuzzled her neck and earlobe. She straddled Ari again, and Ari gripped her buttocks with both hands. Dale hitched forward and then sank back, setting the rhythm, and Ari picked it up. Her arms flexed as she moved Dale against her, turning her head until her lips opened against Dale's.

They both moaned, and Dale moved faster, resting one sweaty cheek against Ari's. "You," Ari gasped, unable to articulate anything else.

Dale moved her head so that her lips were resting against the edge of Ari's mouth when she said, "No. Us."

Ari smiled and kissed Dale in agreement. Dale came, arching her back and going tense before she collapsed on top of Ari. She took a deep breath and let it out slowly as Ari stroked her back, drawing shapes in the sweat as they caught their breath. Ari had settled in an awkward position and she shifted to avoid any soreness. She relaxed with her arms around Dale, already drifting off as her breathing slowed.

"Ari…"

Ari whispered, "She's asleep."

Dale slid her hand down Ari's bicep. "Puppy. Would the wolf be able to follow that trail? From where you found Penny to wherever she was killed?" Ari opened her eyes and looked at Dale in the darkness. "That much blood, and a dead body… I know you were able to track it somewhat, but if you had been in wolf form, you might have gotten further. You may have been able to find where they took her."

"Maybe," Ari admitted.

Dale pushed herself up. "I adore the idea of having a week, just you and me, just recuperating from everything we've been through. But the Ariadne I fell in love with is a wolf. Fighting that is fighting the person I love. Especially if the wolf is needed, and I think it is. The scent will be stronger tonight than it will be tomorrow or the next day. You have to do it now or you risk never finding her." She pecked Ari's lips and nose. "Go be the wolf, Ari. Go do what you have to do and, when you're done, I'll be here waiting for you. I'll always be here."

Ari sat up with Dale on her lap. "You know what you do?"

"What's that?"

"You make me understand marriage."

Dale grinned. "Yeah?"

Ari nodded. "Yeah. I never got the point, but... you make it clear." She kissed Dale. "I love you, Red."

"I love you, too." She climbed off, and Ari pulled her shorts and tank top back. She would wait until she was outside to change, leave the clothes on the back porch in case Phoebe was up getting a midnight snack when she returned from her run. "Be safe, Ari."

"Always."

Ari blew Dale a kiss and slipped out of the bedroom. She walked to the back door on the balls of her feet, carefully opened the door, and stepped outside. The night was brisk, and she shuddered briefly at the thought of being even briefly naked in the chill. Her breath plumed out in front of her as she ran over the topography of the island in her mind. The crime scene was a few miles south, so if she followed the shoreline—

"Hi."

Her entire body twitched to the left, away from the voice. Phoebe was sitting in an old rocking chair on the porch, her feet up in the seat and her bare legs hugged to her chest. She seemed to be wearing only a cable-knit sweater, one side of its collar fallen down to reveal a bare shoulder. The moonlight had painted her skin like marble, and she looked almost inhuman for a moment. Ari shuddered again and hugged herself against the chill as she faced her.

"Hi. We thought you were asleep."

"I tried. Then I thought I'd get some fresh air."

"I thought the same," Ari said. "No one tells you that a private investigator gets some screwed up sleep schedules. Usually around this time of night I'm staking out some seedy motel." She moved closer to the chair, her breath ribboning out from her mouth as she spoke. "I guess I don't have to ask why you're awake."

Phoebe looked out at the woods. "I kept worrying that if I went to sleep, I would dream about her. She would be back, and I'd wake up and have to face the reality of..." She brushed her hair out of her face. "I'm just worried about starting the pain all over again."

Ari leaned against the cabin's rough-hewn wall. "I get that."

"Do you have any sisters? Brothers?"

"No. I have Dale, though. If anything happened to her..." She caught herself before her voice broke. "It almost has. A couple of times, it's been really close. I saw a man shoot her in the head, and I watched her fall down, and for a few minutes I had to deal with the fact that..."

"My God," Phoebe muttered.

"But I got her back. I can't imagine what you're going through."

Phoebe said, "Penny was so unstoppable. We lived a thousand miles apart, but she could still convince me to do things I didn't want to do. It was like she was this force, you know? Even on the phone, even knowing she would have to get on a plane to slap me around, I was scared of her."

"Scared?"

"Not scared." Phoebe smiled. "When I say slap me around, I mean like sisters do. She pushed me to do things and when I doubted myself, she would cheerlead. I used to call her for pep talks. If I was scared she knew just what to say to get me on my feet so I could go on the attack." Tears rolled down her cheeks. "I have no idea what I'm going to do now."

"You're going to keep her with you. When you feel the need for one of those pep talks, her voice will come to you. It might not be the same, but it'll be a way to move on. You've probably gotten enough pep talks to fake your way through a couple."

Phoebe chuckled. "Yeah." She moved her arms to rest across her knees and looked at Ari. "Why do I feel like I know you?"

"I don't know."

"I'm never like this with people. I just met you today, you tell me my sister is dead, I... I shouldn't even be acknowledging your reality as a person. You should just be this thing in my line of sight. But I feel like I've known you forever. And I'm so grateful you're here."

Ari shrugged. "I'm happy we can help."

"If you were single I'd ask if I could sleep in your bed."

Ari had no idea how to respond to that. "Oh."

"I don't even like women." She sighed and closed her eyes. "Who knows. Maybe this is how I grieve. I latch onto the first person I see and create some stupid bond with her. For the record, you and Dale don't have to worry. Even if I did like women, I would never get between something as special as you two obviously have. You're so perfect together."

"Yeah, I think she fills in some of my rough edges."

"It's more than that. You're a team. I'd love to find someone like that, but it's not something you can just stumble into on some dating site. You have to get lucky."

Ari nodded. "I did. I think we both did, but... yeah. I got the sweet end of the deal."

Phoebe smiled. "Why does she call you puppy?"

Ari laughed. "That's a... a long story. Inside joke."

"Does it have to do with that?" She touched her throat to indicate Ari's collar.

"Yeah," Ari said. "And the name of the agency."

"Bitches," Phoebe muttered. "It's a good name."

Ari said, "Dale's idea. Like all good ideas in my life."

Phoebe smiled. "Maybe I'm attracted to you just because you're a really good person. I don't know a lot of people like you. Dale's the lucky one, I think."

"We'll beg to differ." Ari took a deep breath. "Okay... I think that's enough fresh air for now. Coming in?"

"In a minute."

"Okay." She paused at the door. "Penny would want you to take care of yourself. Whatever that means, she would want you protected and safe."

Phoebe looked at her. "Maybe that's why she sent you."

Ari smiled awkwardly, shrugged, and went back into the cabin. When she slipped back into the bedroom she saw Dale had already fallen asleep. She paused and looked at her, face relaxed and peaceful, her lips slightly parted to show her teeth. She reached out and brushed the hair away from her cheek. Dale stirred and Ari went still, not wanting to wake her yet, but Dale pressed her lips together.

"Mm, puppy." It was a sleepy murmur, but she repeated herself, more alert the second time. "Puppy...?" She opened her eyes and blinked at Ari, furrowing her brow. "Are... you..." She looked in vain for a clock. "Why are you back?"

"Phoebe was outside. She caught me."

"She *caught* you?"

"Not... changing. She caught me leaving the cabin. We talked. She's really shattered about her sister. I'm worried about her."

Dale brushed Ari's forearm. "Yeah. I think they were really close. It made me think about you, actually."

Ari smiled and bent to kiss Dale's fingers.

"If anything happened to you, Ari, I think... I think I'd be done. With Seattle, with everything. I'd probably have to move back home and start a whole new life."

"You could join the Amish."

Dale chuckled. "You joke, but a world without Ariadne Willow...? Yeah. I'd be fine shutting out that world and just, like, farming the land. Or I could be a pharmacist."

"I think you need schooling for that, babe."

"Oh." Dale blinked, her eyelids heavy and puffy from her interrupted sleep. "The point is, whatever I'd be after you would be a completely different person. I would have to be."

Ari said, "Same here."

"What would you do?"

"I don't like this game."

"I know. But humor me."

Ari sighed and put her head down on Dale's arm. "I'd be the wolf. There are *canidae* who do it. Spend ninety percent of their lives as wolves and only transform when it's absolutely necessary. It would help with my pain issues, I think."

Dale said, "It would erase who you are."

"So would losing you."

"Ari..." She lifted her head and Dale kissed her. "Something me."

Ari frowned. "I think you're falling back to sleep. You missed a word or two there."

"No. I mean..." She found Ari's hand to link their fingers together. "We don't want marriage, but we both know we're going to be together forever. And we both admit that being without each other would be such a life-changing event that we would both just erase the people we are now. I don't want to say 'marry me' because I still don't think that's for us. But... something me. Adopt me, for all I care."

Ari laughed. "I'm not going to adopt you. But I like the idea of some kind of vow." She kissed Dale's lips. "I'll anything-you-want you."

"Get back in bed and hold me until I fall back asleep?"

"Yes, yes, yes. A thousand times yes."

Dale chuckled as Ari got into bed, then gasped at her cold feet. She kicked at Ari, who squirmed away from her and nibbled her neck. Soon she warmed up, and Dale's breathing slowed as she fell back to sleep. After ten minutes or so, she heard Phoebe come back into the cabin and go into her room. Ari gave it another few minutes so Phoebe could actually go to sleep, then stroked Dale's upper arm and shoulder, her neck.

"Sweet dreams." Ari lightly kissed Dale's hair and slipped out of bed.

Phoebe took off her sweater and was about to climb into bed when she heard movement in the main room of the cabin. Someone, presumably Ari, crossed the living space and very quietly went back outside. Phoebe went to the window and moved the curtain aside just enough that she could see out but hopefully not enough that anyone could see inside. The moonlight cutting through the trees looked almost surreal, like a painting brought to life, but she couldn't see any movement.

She was about to let the curtain drop when she saw a burst of movement from the direction of the porch to the trees. It moved so quickly that it was enveloped in shadows before she could get a good look at it, but it almost seemed like a dog. Maybe an animal had gone up to the porch and Ariadne startled it by going outside.

Phoebe watched for another minute but the woods had become still and quiet. Whatever the animal had been, it most likely wasn't going to come back. And if Ari wanted some privacy, Phoebe was intruding on it by continuing to peep. She had already intruded on their lives enough, and she had no idea how she would even begin repaying their kindness.

Their generosity and willingness to help her made it even harder to lie. Or... no. She wasn't lying to them. Not exactly. She was withholding information that had no bearing on Penny's murder. Phoebe closed her eyes and said another silent prayer that she was right, and that it was truly unrelated. Ariadne would continue to investigate, and she would eventually find whoever did it. She could do that without all the facts. And if for some reason she needed to know more...

Phoebe decided she would cross that bridge when she was forced to. She let the curtain fall back into place and went to bed, crawling under the blankets and trying to find enough peace of mind to fall asleep, even if it did bring nightmares.

CHAPTER NINE

IT SEEMED to take the wolf a few minutes to realize where it was. Ari often thought of the wolf as a completely separate entity, but it was definitely just a different part of her mind. She was still herself when she was the wolf, she was just accessing a far deeper and more primal part of her consciousness. All the niceties of humanity were shed and she was left with only animalistic urges. Now, surrounded by woods without even a hint of civilization or urban landscapes, the wolf lunged forward into the trees.

She forced a bit of her influence onto the wolf, reminding it that there was a purpose to the run. She wasn't going to give up a warm bed and a loving girlfriend just to chase rabbits. She had to get back to the crime scene, but that was easier said than done. The island was a completely different place through the wolf's eyes. Scents and sounds blended together, a whole world of new experiences opening up all around her, and she couldn't blame the poor beast for being a bit distracted.

The wolf passed through the clearing where Phoebe and Penelope's cabin was, and the sisters had left enough of a lingering scent for her to pick up the trail. Ari went up onto the porch and snuffled around the door, the deck, the front porch, and the walk up from where the car was parked. Phoebe's scent was stronger, of course, but she also found a fading but still present trail for Penny. She raced off again, this time following the road so she would be more confident about finding the site again.

Whoever had taken Penny's body might have done a good enough job covering up for human investigators, but the wolf was not so easily fooled. Ari cut through the trees, up the rise, and stopped at the right place even before she saw the fallen tree she had been using as a marker. She put her snout to the ground and could smell where Penny had fallen, the blood and the various scents that came with death and decomposing. Penny had died messily and violently, and the evidence was clear as day for a wolf's senses. She could also smell a dozen other things: the sheriff, the deputy, all the other animals that had come through this clearing drawn by the smell of death, and most importantly she could smell men who had come to take the body away.

Two men, one more hygienic than the other, had wrapped the body in something - most likely a tarp - and then carried her south. Ari headed in that direction, only occasionally distracted by a wandering critter. Most wild animals were unsettled by *canidae*. She looked and acted like one of them, but she had the stink of humans all over her. They couldn't make heads or tails of what she was, so they gave her a wide berth.

She reached the clearing with the private dock and took the time to give it a full examination. She smelled a truck that had been leaking oil, a big stench of gasoline that hadn't even been apparent when she was in human form, and diesel. There had been a boat there recently. She was about to move on with her search when there was a sudden flash of lights across the trees near the road. She lifted her head, saw the truck pulling off the road, and darted into the woods.

The truck rolled to a stop at the dock and men emerged from either side. The passenger moved toward the woods where Ari was concealed and clicked his tongue.

"Leave it alone," the driver said.

"Ah, I just wanted to get a look at it. It looked like a wolf."

"There aren't wolves on the island. It was probably a fox."

"It was brown!"

The driver sighed, "Then it was someone's dog. Either way, you're going to get yourself bit. We don't have time to fuck around."

The driver walked down to the dock and lit a cigarette, while the passenger leaned against the truck. Neither of them spoke, but after a few minutes to passenger began to warble an old Johnny Cash song. Ari kept a safe distance away from the tree line, hunkered down out of sight but where she could see the men. The driver held his cigarette by his side, the red glow of the embers shining as he looked out over the water.

Ari heard the boat engine first. She looked out at the water and, a few seconds later, the driver told his partner to shut up with the singing. He walked out onto the dock as a small, unlit craft came into view. He flashed a signal from a light on his belt and the boat pulled in. He leaned out to grab a rope and with the men onboard he helped secure the boat to the piling. The passenger joined them out on the dock.

"Get everything?" the driver asked.

"Always do."

They unloaded something from the boat, and when the driver carried it up to the truck Ari saw it was a black duffel bag that was filled to bursting. The passenger and two men from the boat carried two bags each up to the truck and loaded them into the back.

The passenger said, "You guys ever hear of wolves on this island?"

"I told you, it was somebody's damn dog."

"There are wolves, I'm sure," one of the new arrivals said. "Some of 'em swim back and forth from the mainland."

The driver said, "Oh, that's bullshit. Dogs can't swim."

"Where on earth did you hear *that?* Of course dogs can swim, you ignorant motherfucker. I saw this video on YouTube where a dog jumped out of a boat and went after a shark."

"Oh! Well! If it was on *YouTube*... then I guess I'll just shut my mouth." He sighed. "Are we good to go?"

One of the men from the boat said, "Yep, you got everything. Same time, same place?"

"Same time, same place."

They shook hands and went their separate ways. The men climbed back into the truck, the driver taking the time to get one more drag off his cigarette before he flicked it toward the water. The men from the boat got back onboard, untied themselves, and shoved off before starting the engine. Both vehicles retreated, quickly getting swallowed by the darkness. Ari considered chasing down the truck to see where it ended up, but she knew that plan would only end in failure or capture. There was also the possibility the men might be armed and just shoot her rather than risk getting bitten. She waited until the sound of both engines had faded before she left her hiding place and sought out Penny's scent again.

Logic told her that they would have taken her out onto the boat and tied rocks to her body. Even if she floated back to shore, the water would have destroyed the lion's share of evidence. But as she searched near the dock she discovered that Penny hadn't gotten anywhere near the water's edge. Ari moved closer to the road and picked up the scent again.

That didn't make sense. Why would they risk taking her body anywhere? They could sink her in the harbor, take her out into the Strait to sink her there, or bury her somewhere in the woods. Moving her only increased their potential of getting caught.

Unless they wanted to make sure her body was as far away from this dock as possible. She was assuming one of the reasons they took her away in the first place was because they'd seen her find it. They knew someone would be coming out to look for her. So they wanted to get the body as far away from this place as possible so there wouldn't be any chance for it to be connected to the murder. Penny had been attacked here, in this clearing. Her clothes were torn off, she was stabbed in the neck, but somehow she managed to get up and ran away. She had run pretty damn far while losing blood, and...

Why hadn't she pulled her pants back up? The wolf huffed in frustration, forced to use its animal brain for logical thinking. If she was attacked and stabbed in the clearing, and if she had run away, why were her pants still around her knees when she finally collapsed? Were the stabbing and the attempted rape separate incidents? Could someone have come across a woman with a mortal wound and taken the opportunity to undress her?

Ari could still smell the truck driver's cigarette smoke in the air, and the exhaust from both vehicles hung heavy in the air. The chain of events was baffling to her and she wasn't likely to put it together out in the woods in wolf form. She sighed and stood up, shook out her fur, and retreated her consciousness.

Take us home, she told the wolf, *but feel free to take the scenic route.*

The darkness closed in on her vision, and the wolf took a moment to decide where to go before it took off at a dead run. She trusted her wolf to keep her safe, to keep out of sight, and to not spend the entire night exploring its new environs. She was prepared to be out for most of the night, however, and she wasn't surprised when her consciousness finally returned and she discovered the sky was more velvet-blue than black.

Got me home before the sun. Thanks, wolfie.

Her clothes were on the back porch, tucked behind the chair Phoebe had been sitting in earlier that night. Ari made sure the coast was clear before she ran across the lawn, using the wolf's snout to pull out the clothes. She held them in her teeth as she returned to the woods to transform. She focused on returning to her original shape and felt the shift inside of her. There wasn't a button she could push or a magic word she had to say. The transformation was just something she could cause to happen. It was a bodily function, like belching or farting. It could be controlled, it could be spontaneous, but there was always a measure of control. Tremors ran up her arms and she reared back as her paws transformed into hands.

She spread her fingers and then curled them into a fist as shockwaves of pain shot through her core. It felt as if her lupine pelvis was being twisted one way while her human frame twisted the opposite direction. She fell to the ground without thought of stopping her fall, hurting her shoulder as her body arched in pain. Her arms and legs were fully transformed, but her torso and throat were covered with quickly receding hair. Her skull snapped and, for a brief terrifying moment, it didn't snap back into the right position.

Ari sobbed with pain and terror as her body fought the change. It was worse than it had ever been, and tears dripped off her face into the mud as she finished transforming. Her entire body trembled, her hands up protectively over her face as the pain thrummed through her. Parts of her were numb and she was positive they had fallen off or been severed. She had flashes of trying to stand up only to find her arms were no longer part of her.

She had no idea how long she lay in the fetal position in the scree and crushed leaves, but very soon she was aware of Dale saying her name and then dropping down next to her. She grabbed Dale's arm, and Dale tenderly touched Ari's arms and side.

"What happened? Can you move?"

"The transformation," Ari gasped, scooting forward to put her head in Dale's lap. Dale folded herself around Ari and rocked her. "It's never hurt like that."

Ari was drenched with sweat. Dale dried it from her forehead and cheeks with the sleeve of her sweater. "Do you need me to carry you?"

She tried moving her legs and found that the pain dissipated as she stretched them out. She tested her hands by making fists. The movement was stiff, but the pain was manageable.

"I think I can walk," Ari said, "but can... can you help..."

"I can dress you."

Ari grimaced and looked away. Dale hooked her finger under her chin and forced eye contact.

"What are you doing?"

"I'm going to be an invalid. Soon, apparently. I can't do that to you."

Dale kissed her lips. "Get up."

Ari did as she was told. She got into her shorts and T-shirt, an effort that left her winded, and she leaned against a tree until she got her breath back.

"I think the wolf was angry I held it back so long. I think it wouldn't have been so bad if I hadn't been ignoring it for so long."

"Probably. But this is still a very bad sign, Ari."

"I know."

"We have to do something."

Ari nodded. "I know. But first we have to finish this case. Then we can focus on healing me." She held out her hand. "Help me stand?"

Dale took Ari's wrist and pulled her up. She guided Ari's arm around her waist while she put her own arm across Ari's shoulders. They had only taken a few steps when Ari slowed.

"Wait, stop."

"What is it? What hurts?"

"No. No, wait... is Phoebe in there?"

Dale said, "She was making coffee. Why?"

They moved slowly across the lawn. "I've been trying to think why Penny would run so far without pulling her pants up. If the attempted rape happened at the same time as the stabbing, she got pretty damn far with her pants around her knees."

"Maybe she was too busy trying to stop the bleeding."

"They would have tripped her up. Pulling her pants up would have been the first step to escaping. But what if I got it wrong? What if they stabbed her, and the fact that her pants were down was unrelated? What if she was taking off her pants herself?"

"As she was fleeing the killers? Why would she do..." Dale's eyes widened. "No. You're not suggesting she was a wolf, are you?"

Ari shrugged. "Ever since we met her, Phoebe's been saying she feels a connection to me." They had reached the deck, and Ari pushed the door open. Phoebe was sitting at the dining room table staring into a cup of coffee. Her eyes widened when she saw Ari's sweaty, pale face.

"Ariadne? Oh, my God, what happened?"

"*Canidae*," Ari said.

Phoebe blinked at her. "What?"

"*Canidae*. Does that mean anything to you?"

"Canadee? I..." She furrowed her brow. "Not... really. Like dogs?"

Ari said, "No. Well... yeah, I guess." She sighed. "Sorry. I had a theory, but I guess it didn't pan out. Sorry."

"It's okay. What the hell happened to you?"

Dale said, "She went out for a jog and fell down."

Phoebe said, "You poor thing. Let me get some ice."

"That's okay," Ari said. "It's more of a... bone issue. Falling down aggravated it. I just need to go lie down for a minute."

"Are you sure?" Ari nodded. "Let me know if you need anything."

"I will. Thank you."

Dale took Ari into the bedroom and gingerly lowered her onto the bed. "Lie down on your stomach." Ari was in too much pain to argue, grimacing as she stretched out on the mattress. Dale straddled her and began to massage her shoulders. Ari grunted and put her face into the pillow. After years of massages, Dale knew all the tightest spots and how to relax them with a few brief strokes of her fingers. Soon Ari's pain was on the retreat.

"You're good at this."

"After seven years, I oughta be."

Ari said, "Seven years... wow."

Dale smiled. "Seems like longer?"

"In a good way."

Dale bent down and kissed the top of Ari's head. "You should smoke. Or take a pill. Something."

"I will."

"Do you have any idea why it hurt so much this time?"

Ari said, "I was holding her down. She was punishing me."

Dale bent down and kissed Ari's neck. "Well, whatever the cause, you scared me."

"I know."

"We have to do something, Ari. If that had happened back home, if you had been out in some random park unable to reach a stash to call for me..."

Ari rolled over and took Dale's hands. "We'll figure something out."

"And if we don't?"

"Everybody's gotta die sometime." Dale recoiled, stricken, and Ari sat up to pull her close. "Hey... I'm sorry. I was just joking."

Dale pulled her hands away. "Well, don't. Not about that. Jesus, Ariadne."

"I'm sorry," Ari said again. She leaned in and let Dale close the distance between them. "We'll find a solution. Or Dr. Frost will, or Mom, or someone. The only reason I'm okay with joking about dying is because I don't have any regrets. I've loved you, and I've been loved by you, and every minute of these past seven years has felt like a gift. So I guess part of me expects it'll have to end eventually. If that ends with me dying..."

Dale flinched and slapped Ari's chest with the back of her hand. "Stop saying it."

Ari brushed Dale's hair back and kissed her eyebrows. "I won't say it again. We'll find a way."

Dale blinked away the wetness in her eyes and sniffled, then kissed Ari. After a few seconds she said, "I'm going to change the subject now."

"Deal."

"You really thought Penny was *canidae?*"

Ari sighed. "It fit. She was running from the people who stabbed her, and her pants were down. It would make sense that she dropped them herself in anticipation of changing into a wolf to get away, but I honestly believe Phoebe didn't recognize the word. I find it hard to imagine sisters as close as they were would keep a secret that big from each other."

"So we're left with a woman who was stabbed, ran for a mile through the woods, and in the process of fleeing started to get undressed."

"It must have something to do with the delivery I saw. Or the drop-off. Whatever that was, there's no way it was legitimate business. She might have seen it and they tried to keep her quiet."

Dale said, "So it might have nothing to do with Corbett at all."

Ari shrugged. "It makes more sense than a celebrity killing someone to cover up a fact you discovered on the internet after five minutes with Google. That clearing is where Penny started running, and it's where her body was carried after she was taken away. I have to find out who owns that dock."

"After you rest for a while. And take your pills."

"Yes, ma'am."

Dale kissed Ari's cheek. "No more jokes, okay. I really--"

"I know. I promise."

"Thank you." She kissed Ari's lips. "I'll take Phoebe to get some breakfast so you'll have privacy. Do you want me to bring you back anything?"

"Protein," Ari said.

Dale nodded. "Okay. Take care of yourself, puppy. I don't want to be an Amish pharmacist any time soon."

Ari smiled and lowered herself back to the pillow as Dale climbed off of her. Dale retrieved Ari's cannabis pills, got a glass of water, and handed them over. Once Ari had taken her medicine, Dale pulled the blankets up, tucked her in, and kissed her nose.

"We'll be back in about an hour. Rest."

"I will."

Dale left, and Ari closed her eyes. The massage had already worked wonders, but she was willing to give the cannabis a shot. Once Dale and Phoebe were gone she would even consider smoking a bit. She flexed her fingers under the blankets just to prove that she could, then rolled onto her side to get some sleep before she got back to the case.

CHAPTER TEN

ARI NAPPED for forty minutes, then got out of bed and smoked before she got dressed. The smell disgusted her, but she had to admit there were therapeutic qualities to the pot that helped ease her pain. Once she felt more or less capable of moving without falling down she put on her clothes and went out to find Dale's computer. She found a program that would do what she wanted it to do and began working out a timeline of what she knew.

By the time Dale showed up with her food, she was finished with her work and half-starved. "What took you so long?"

Dale said, "The wait at the diner was ridiculous. Forty minutes before we even got a seat."

"Tourist town, I guess." Ari opened the takeaway container and had to stop herself from tearing into it with her fingers. A night of running as the wolf had depleted her energy reserves and the pot had made her even more ravenous. She forced herself to use the plastic silverware from the bag as Dale examined the screen.

"What is this?"

"A timeline." She looked at Phoebe. "You can feel free to fill in any blanks about what you and Penny did on the island."

Phoebe stood next to the couch and sniffed the air. "Did... did you smoke pot while we were gone?"

"Medicinal," Ari and Dale said at the same time. Ari added, "For the bone thing."

"I wasn't judging. In fact, it would really help take the edge off. I'm barely holding it together, and I could use~"

Ari said, "Absolutely. There's a bag in our room, on the dresser next to the door. Help yourself."

"Thank you."

When she was gone, Dale whispered, "She wasn't lying. The drive to town, waiting for our table, even ordering. It was like sitting with a robot. But I could tell she was just following a script of 'normal behavior.' If she stops to think about what she's doing, she'll think about her sister, and then..."

"We'll just have to keep an eye on her."

Phoebe came back with a joint and sat next to Dale, who angled the screen so they could both see it. Ari scooted back on the couch and focused on her food, the Styrofoam resting on her thighs.

Dale turned the bullet points into a narrative. "Penelope and Phoebe Alton arrived on the island and proceeded to have a seemingly normal vacation. Penny would spend her days out of the cabin, activities unknown. Oh, and I checked her online account for anything that might have been saved to the Cloud."

"No 'Smoking Guns'?"

"Not even a Red Herring."

Ari looked at Phoebe. "I'd like to go back to your cabin and check her room again. If she was investigating Corbett she must have left some kind of journal."

"Absolutely. Whatever you need."

Dale continued. "On Tuesday morning, Penny left the cabin before Phoebe woke for reasons unknown. She traveled south, heading to a clearing with... wait, no, we don't know that."

Ari said, "That's where her... trail ends. There was no evidence she'd gone further."

"Right," Dale said, "but that doesn't mean it was her original destination. She might have gotten that far and seen something she wasn't meant to see."

"Good point," Ari said.

Dale made the correction. "Traveled south until she reached a clearing with a private dock. Observation revealed this dock is used for nocturnal exchanges between two men in a truck and an unknown number of men in a boat."

Phoebe said, "When was this?"

Ari stopped mid-chew and looked at Dale. "It was, uh, last night."

"You were out there last night? When?"

"After we spoke. I couldn't sleep, so I decided to go out, happened to see them."

Phoebe frowned. "So you... went out after I went to bed. I thought I heard you. And then you were outside again this morning? Did you sleep at all?"

"Sure. While you and Dale were at breakfast."

Phoebe started to say something else, but Dale stopped her with a wave of her hand. "Phoebe, I've been having this argument with her for seven years now. She's the sort of person who thinks a fifteen-minute nap is enough to get her through a weekend, then she falls asleep in the middle of a movie." To Ari, she said, "There were no identifying features on either vehicle? A name on the boat, some feature of the truck that might make it stand out?"

"Not even a bumper sticker," Ari said. "It was too dark to see any of the men. Maybe I could pick them out of a lineup if I heard their voices, but even then I wouldn't feel confident."

Dale said, "Mm. Okay, so we're presuming she saw the men with the boat and in the truck, she saw something that she wasn't supposed to, and… they chased her down."

Ari said, "That's where it falls apart. Did they stab her at the clearing and she got away, then succumbed to blood loss and passed out? That's what I'm assuming. That's why she was alone when I found her. They hadn't caught up with her yet. But the other scenario is that someone caught up with her, tried to rape her, then panicked when he cut her throat."

"And then went back to get his buddies to help him move the body," Dale said.

"I suppose that works." She looked at Phoebe who was chewing her thumbnail. "I'm sorry. We shouldn't be talking about this so bluntly in front of you."

Phoebe looked at her. "No. My sister was murdered. You don't have to be precious about that with me. I want to know what happened to her. I want to help however I can."

Ari said, "You deserve that much, at least. Right now I want to check out Penny's room, and I'll take a drive around town to see if I can find… something." She sighed. "A truck that matches what I saw, or someone who trips an alarm bell."

Dale said, "I can look at the public records and see if I can find out who owns that dock."

Phoebe sighed. "I guess that leaves me with calling the rest of Penny's friends that Evan didn't know about. Anyone want to trade?" She smiled sadly. "Joke."

Dale said, "I'll be here if you need someone to talk to. Or vent at, yell at, whatever."

"Thank you."

Ari kissed Dale's cheek and closed the Styrofoam box. "I'm going to head over to the cabin."

"What about your breakfast?"

"Gone. Ate it."

"When?"

"While we were talking."

"All of it?"

Ari shrugged. "I was hungry."

Dale sighed and rolled her eyes. Phoebe gave her the keys to the cabin and Ari told them she would be back as soon as she could.

Outside she stepped carefully off the porch and crossed the lawn slowly, gauging the state of her knees and hips as she went. Most of the pain was gone, but she still felt a twinge. She hoped she wouldn't have to run or even walk very far. When she got in the car she checked the glove compartment and took a pair of ibuprofen from the stash they kept there. She looked at the bottle and realized she had gone for it without thinking, and she tried to remember how many pain meds they had stashed throughout their apartment, cars, and office. She was afraid the time was fast approaching when she wouldn't be able to get through the day without pain management. She tried not to show fear in front of Dale, tried to joke about mortality, but every twinge terrified her.

At the moment all she could do was focus on the case. There would be plenty of time afterward to worry about her health. If the solution was finding some way to get rid of the wolf for good, or just fighting the change for the rest of her life, then that was what she would do. She wouldn't make Dale suffer through every painful shift.

If life was going to make her choose between Dale and the wolf, there was no doubt in her mind which one would come out on top.

Ari unlocked the Alton cabin and took a moment to make sure everything seemed undisturbed from their last visit. Confident that the killer hadn't dropped by, she went into Penny's room and began to do a more thorough search. Before she had been aware of the grieving sister right outside, not to mention having the pressure of two irritated cops waiting on her to finish. Now she had a bit more information and she wanted to see if that equaled more fruitful results.

She opened Penny's suitcase and went through the clothes and other sundry items. Chargers for various electronic devices, a vibrator, the bra from a two-piece bathing suit, a bit of jewelry... nothing that would shed any light on what she had been doing on the island. The drawers in the nightstand were similarly empty except for the essentials: a case for contacts, a pair of clunky backup glasses, an eReader, and a bottle of antacids. She checked under the pillow and the mattress and moved to the closet.

"If I was Penny," she muttered, "where would I keep track of my shady activities?"

Penny was going up against someone with a history of disputing facts, so she would want a hard copy of whatever she found. She would have written it down somewhere it could be irrefutably proven as evidence. Something she could sign and date, a journal or a notebook. Unfortunately there didn't seem to be anything like that in her room.

Odder still was the lack of a laptop or computer. Her phone was with the police, and maybe she had expected to rely solely on that for an internet connection. It seemed unlikely, though, that someone who came to the island with a plan to destroy someone's career wouldn't bring the evidence with her. Ari started to have the sinking feeling that Corbett had gotten into the cabin and removed anything incriminating.

She was searching the nightstand when her phone rang. She answered it with a cursory glance at the screen to see it was Dale calling. "Everything okay?"

"Everything's fine, puppy. Phoebe remembered something. Hold on, let me put her on."

A second later, Phoebe said, "Ariadne?"

"I'm here."

"I can't believe I forgot about this. Penny had an iPad. I was using it the night before... the..."

Ari said, "It's okay. Where is it?"

"It's in my bedroom. I don't remember where exactly."

Ari went into the other bedroom and found the tablet on the bedside table next to a charger. "I found it. Is there a password?"

"No, it should come on."

Ari hit the button and the screen lit up. Moments later she was on the home page, and she thanked Phoebe before hanging up. She sat on the edge of the bed and opened the notes section and found an entry marked WFC. When she opened it the first entry was "Wayne Fucking Corbett," and she couldn't help but smile.

"Ah, Penny. I think I would have liked you an awful lot."

The entry was full of information about Corbett's life, a miniature Wikipedia page about who he was and where he had come from. His parents were conservationists, and he got into science at a young age. He entered science fairs as early as second grade but rarely won. Penny had a few choice editorial comments to make about that fact but Ari skimmed over those for the time being. He eventually "failed upward" through the ranks due to his maleness and whiteness until he finally made a name for himself with research Phoebe and Penelope's mother had done.

Their mother was named Mariel Lyton. She was a researcher who had indeed dedicated her life to the Strait of Georgia. She was hired by Corbett in the eighties and used his money to fund her explorations. There were references to reports Mariel had written which were repeated verbatim in articles published by Corbett. According to Penny he had credited "a team of researchers" as "assisting him" with the data collection, but they were only listed by name in a large group index. As far as anyone was concerned, the work was a product of Corbett's work and the credit was his alone.

Mariel fought for proper accreditation, but her attempts were short-lived and ultimately came to naught. She resigned from the field and took a job teaching high school biology. "She was happy enough," Penny wrote, "but even me and Pheeble could see that she was depressed. Corbett didn't just take her research, he took the sea away from her. Everything she spent her life working toward was suddenly tainted by this man's theft. It would've been kinder to just shoot her and be done with it."

In the meantime, Corbett was becoming the go-to guy for Pacific Northwest educational programming. Ari remembered his show in the nineties, his mullet-like brown hair and leather jacket as he hiked through the woods to identify the creatures he stumbled across. Over the years he made the rounds from PBS, Saturday morning educational programs, Discovery Channel, Animal Planet, and the like. If one show got cancelled he had two more in the pipeline. He'd been famous across three decades, and all of it seemed to be built on work stolen from not only Mariel Lyton but everyone who had ever worked under him.

The note ended with what Ari considered to be Penny's mission statement. "I don't think he stole fame and fortune from Mom. I don't think she would even want to go the celebrity route. I believe her interactions with this man showed her that, in order to be a part of the world she loved, she would have to compromise and be treated as a non-entity. She was just a tool to the Wayne Fucking Corbetts of the world, and what she discovered would never be as important as what could be bought with those discoveries. Mom deserved to be recognized for her work, for what she did. And Wayne Fucking Corbett needs to be exposed for the fraud he is."

Ari said, "But where is your damn evidence?"

She scrolled back up and stopped at the section where Penny talked about her mother joining Corbett's team in the eighties. She wasn't entirely sure about the sisters' ages, but they seemed to be late twenties, early thirties. The notes didn't mention anything about their father. Ari had a sinking suspicion that Corbett was more than just a man who stole their mother's research. The timing worked out well enough that he might have actually been their father. If he fathered them and abandoned their mother to raise them alone, it would only be more reason for Penny to be gung-ho about destroying him. Then again, if there was no father in the picture, where did the name "Alton" come from?

She turned off the tablet and, even as she told herself she should turn it in to the police, she knew that she wouldn't. Even if the mysterious exchange at the dock turned out to be unrelated to Corbett, she didn't want to hand over her best connection to Penny's crusade just yet. Drexler might have the best of intentions, but she didn't trust him to go after Corbett with any real dedication. She had too many questions about how Penny Alton died, and Corbett was a big fat question mark right in the middle of it all. She didn't know how she could find the truth without talking to him, and Drexler made it clear he wasn't going to allow that to happen.

Ari got in the car, put Penny's tablet in the glove compartment where it wouldn't be readily visible, and went back to the road. She drove to town, bypassing the sheriff's office and Bowie's restaurant. She went directly to Corbett's house and parked in the driveway, nosing up to the gate before she stopped the engine and got out. The gate was more symbolic than an actual deterrent, and she was able to get up and over it without any problem. She was halfway up the driveway before Louis Fleming came out the front door.

"Miss Willow. Sheriff Drexler told us you might be back." He held up a cell phone. "I haven't called him yet, but I'm prepared to do so if you don't turn around and get back in your car."

"I'm not a crazed fan, I'm not some obsessed stalker..."

"Really? Because this is the second time in as many days I've had to run you off the property."

Ari said, "I'm here to talk about Penelope Alton. You may know of her mother, Mariel Lyton."

Fleming sighed heavily and rolled his eyes. "Mr. Corbett has said everything he wishes to say on that subject. If your intention is to dredge up ancient history, then I am absolutely convinced that you have no business being on his property."

Ari said, "You realize I don't have to talk to him, right? All I have to do is bang my head against your fence a few times, make a valiant effort to speak with him, and then I can make my report. Your boss knows how cable TV works. How many of those true-crime investigation shows would love to spend an episode on this case? A woman whose mother had history with Mr. Corbett is found dead on the same island where he has a house, and he hides behind closed doors when anyone tries to speak with him."

Fleming said, "When the proper authorities approach him with a question, he will be glad to speak with them. You..."

"I was officially employed by the victim's sister. If he wants to wait for the police to ask him downtown, that's his choice. But~"

The phone in Fleming's hand rang, and he looked at it for a moment before he answered. "Yes." He looked at Ari. "Are you sure? All right." He hung up and smiled tightly. "Mr. Corbett will see you. He's around back." He gestured to the side of the house with a dismissive flip of his hand. "You can just go around there. He'll be on the back porch waiting for you."

"Thanks," Ari said. "You've been ever so helpful. I'll mark that down on the comment card when I leave."

He glared at her, tracking her as she walked onto the grass to go around the house. The house only took up a small portion of the acreage; she could see tennis and basketball courts standing side-by-side near a garage large enough for three cars, although one bay was open to reveal a pristine boat within. The rest of the land was left untouched, a rolling carpet of green that stretched out from the fence to the first row of trees that marked a return to wilderness. Ari wondered if there was any fencing in the forest that would prevent the wolf from making its way back after dark.

She found Wayne Corbett on a back porch that was practically the size of a mall's food court standing at a barbeque with his back to her. The white smoke billowed across the lawn and blurred even the strongest scents of nature. He turned to see that she had arrived, flipped one of the steaks, and picked up a beer off the sideboard before he faced her. He was as handsome as ever, his brown mullet faded to an elegant silver and cut short. If anything age had made him even more attractive.

"Miss... Willow, was it?" he said with a smile. "It's nice to finally put a face to the name. And quite an attractive face at that."

Ari said, "Mr. Corbett. Thanks for agreeing to meet with me."

"Well, it seems like you weren't giving me much of a choice, were you? If I had Louis send you away, I think you would've just come back tomorrow and the next day. So why not cut to the chase, right?" He gestured at the grill. "Can I get you anything?"

She ignored her stomach's growl. "It's a little early for barbeque, isn't it?"

"It's never too early for some red meat," he said. "But I understand that you didn't come here to eat. You came here to talk about Mariel Lyton's girls. How is Mariel?"

"From what I hear, she died a while back."

He nodded and changed his expression to one of false sympathy, looking at the ground for a moment as if grieving. "That's a shame," he said. "And for one sister to lose the other... it's a damn shame. It really is. I don't know what the Alton girls told you about me, Miss Willow, but I'm well aware that I've been cast as their family's villain for thirty years now."

"You did take their mother's research."

He held his hands out to either side as if helpless. "As much as I hate to say it, that's the way things are done in the industry."

"Why?"

He stared for a moment. "Why are things done that way?"

"Why do you hate to say it? Seems to have worked out pretty well in your favor. Mariel Lyton was a high school teacher and you..." She gestured at the grounds. "You live at Neverland Ranch."

Corbett smiled. "This is from my television work. It has nothing to do with the research Mariel Lyton did with me."

"For you," Ari corrected. "And publishing her findings is what put you on the map in the first place, right? That's the reason people keep coming to you for television projects."

"They come to me because I'm experienced. I'm a friendly face." He offered her another smile. "People like me, Miss Willow."

Ari said, "Did Penelope Alton come to see you after she came to the island?"

"She did, actually. I didn't have a conversation with her. There was no point. She would accuse me of stealing her mother's work, I would try to explain how we operate, we'd go around and around, and in the end it wouldn't get either of us anything except frustrated. So I had Mr. Fleming send her away whenever she showed up."

"How often did she show up?"

He said, "Three times that I know of. Louis might have sent her away once or twice without bothering me over it."

"Do you think one of those times he might have decided to make sure she definitely didn't come back?"

Corbett chuckled. "You mean did he drive her out into the woods and stab her in the throat?"

"You find that funny?"

"I find it mildly amusing that I've been upgraded from a thief of intellectual property to a murderer. Next week someone will decide that I was involved in Benghazi or something equally horrible. This comes with the territory, Miss Willow. I'm very sorry that Penelope Alton died. I wish it hadn't happened and I truly hope her sister finds some kind of closure. But I assure you that I'm simply a convenient target for their blame. It's part of being a celebrity. People can hit you with as much hate as love. It's why I have a fence around my home and Louis keeping people away. Because of my history with their mother, they have decided to blame me for everything that goes wrong in their life. I'm a scapegoat."

Ari held his gaze to see if he would look away, but he never shifted. "I hope you'll be willing to speak to me again if I have any other questions."

He sighed and went back to his grilling. "Honestly, Miss Willow, if you come back again, that might constitute harassment. I'd have to call the sheriff."

"What if I could offer you something in return?"

He laughed. "And what might that be?"

Ari hesitated before she said anything else. The tease was out of her mouth before she fully thought out the consequences, but now she couldn't help but second-guess the choice. She knew the sort of man Corbett was, and she knew exactly what would make him clamor to help her. The question was whether she was willing to play such a big card with someone so slimy. Finally she decided she had no choice. If Drexler was threatening her with prison to stay away from Corbett, and if Corbett's guard dog was the hair-trigger she thought he was, there was only one way she could ensure she could get back on the property despite the can of worms it would open.

"*Canidae.*"

Corbett stopped with the beer halfway to his lips but didn't look at her. "The classification for canines? What about it?"

"I'm talking about the species."

He looked at her and smiled. "The myth, you mean? Werewolves, so famously written about in Karl Magnusson's insane ramblings and unpublished essays? Sorry. I don't do cryptozoology."

"Come on... guy like you, spent the past three decades wandering around the Pacific Northwest? You know they're more than just a myth."

"And you have proof?"

She lifted her chin and hooked one finger under her collar. "Where do you think I got this? I have all kinds of clients, Mr. Corbett."

He stared long enough for her to know he was intrigued. "What are you proposing?"

"I get to come talk to you whenever I want. We have a nice, civil conversation and you answer my questions without making me fight for them. Then, when this is all said and done, I'll tell you what I know about *canidae*. I did the research, you present your findings. Seems like your kind of thing."

He smiled, but she could see she'd hit a nerve from the way his eyes hardened. "What do you mean 'afterward'? Why not just tell me now?"

"Telling you now would give you a chance to weasel out of the deal once you had what you want. It's a great deal, assuming you're innocent."

Corbett chuckled and looked at his grill. "If they do exist, *canidae* are extremely secretive people. They wouldn't take very kindly to someone spilling the beans."

Ari shrugged. "I'll just tell you what I know and point you in the right direction. I won't actually be selling anyone out."

"That's a thin line."

"It's a gray area I think you'd be very comfortable in. What do you say? Seems like a pretty sweet deal for the scoop of a lifetime. This sort of exclusive is the sort of thing that could get you back to the lower cable channels."

"You know what, Miss Willow? I'll take you up on that offer. Even if I don't believe you actually know anything about *canidae*, I would be interested in hearing where you got that collar."

Ari said, "Okay. And if you wind up being guilty, I reserve the right to renege on my side of the deal. No offense, but I doubt you'll be able to film any Werewolves Exposed specials from prison."

"Fair enough. I look forward to it, Miss Willow. Are you sure you don't want to stay for a steak?"

"I'm sure. I should get back to investigating. Next time, though."

He smiled and nodded. "Next time."

Ari walked back around the house and found Louis Fleming by the gate as if he was standing guard. She smiled as she walked past him.

"You might want to talk to your boss. Next time I come here, I'll be welcomed as a guest."

"We'll see about that."

Ari got into the car and watched Fleming walk up the drive, then checked to make sure he hadn't gotten into the car to snoop. Penny's tablet was still where she had left it, and nothing seemed to have been moved around. She didn't know if she had accomplished more than exposing her investigation to Corbett and making an enemy of Fleming, but she was willing to take them as victories for the time being. As for her promise to tell him everything she knew about *canidae*... well, she could think of a few ways to back out of that when the time came, if the time came.

Her immediate plans involved going to Bowie's for something hot, fresh, and made of meat. She thought she had shown tremendous restraint at the smell of Corbett's grilling but now she definitely needed something to eat.

CHAPTER ELEVEN

BOWIE'S RESTAURANT was empty save for a pair of grizzled old men seated in a booth at the far end of the room. Neither of them looked up as she entered and took a seat at the counter. Apparently the novelty of her presence on the island had already worn off. There were several laminated menus tucked in between the ketchup and a napkin dispenser, and she took one to see what the place had to offer beyond tornado fries. Bowie came out of the kitchen and smiled. "Hey, my new favorite customer. I thought your girlfriend was just in here getting you breakfast."

"She was," Ari said, "but I guess I worked up an appetite."

Bowie chuckled. "Right on. Enjoying the vacation, I guess."

"Yeah. Yeah, we are."

"Uh-oh." Bowie faced her fully. "Is everything all right?"

Ari nodded. "Yeah. Things are completely fine."

Bowie smiled. "Can I call you Ariadne?"

"Ari."

"Okay, Ari. You work in a place like this, you get used to seeing the same faces day in and day out, usually around the same time. You work here long enough you start getting good at filling in the blanks. Something happened yesterday, right? A fight? Come on. Don't fight on your vacation."

Ari smiled. "It's not a fight. But you're good. I'll give you that."

"What are you having? I'll get it started and then we can talk."

Ari ordered the pork chops with a side of regular fries. When Bowie came back, she rested her elbows on the counter and motioned for Ari to come out with it.

"We didn't have a fight. I have... I'm..." She looked at her hands and tried to think of a way to sidestep the details. "I'm sick. I've been sick for a while, but it's been getting worse lately. I don't want to get into what I have, but it's bad. Potentially fatal. We have some remedies we've been using and they've worked, but lately the pain has been getting so bad that I'm worried they're not going to be as effective. And if we lose them, I'll be in agony. A lot."

Bowie softly said, "Is she feeling burdened?"

"No. The opposite, in fact. She takes care of me, she watches over me. Sometimes the pain is helped by massage, so she's always willing to give me a rub-down. I love her for that, but at the same time..."

"You think she deserves better."

Ari looked at her and slowly nodded.

"I got sick a few years ago. Breast cancer." Ari inadvertently looked at Bowie's shirt, remembering her first impression that she had a boyish figure. Bowie smiled and said, "Hard to believe, right? When I cut such a voluptuous silhouette? Yeah. Double mastectomy, the whole works. I had a girlfriend before I got diagnosed, and she stuck by me the whole time. She was a great supporter, a teammate, a cheerleader. And I fucking hated her for it. I hated her telling me I could get out of bed when I barely felt human, and I hated her for being healthy. I was just angry. I finally pushed her away for good. Victory was mine." She smiled and looked out the window. "Don't be a dumbass, Ari. She's there because she wants to be. She's helping you because she loves you. You aren't racking up a debt to her. Let her help."

"But if this does… if I don't get better, how can I force her to watch me die?"

Bowie said, "It's not your choice, Ari. She chose to be with you, she chose to stay, and she's sticking in there. Please don't make the same mistake I did."

"I'll try not to." She smiled. "Thanks, Bowie. Is this something you offer all your regulars?"

"Yep. Short-order cook and part-time confessional. I'll go check on your food. Think about what I said."

"I will. Thank you."

When Bowie went back into the kitchen, Ari reached up and stroked the collar she wore. She had bought the collar a year into their relationship for Dale to put on her, a symbol of their relationship. They'd discussed marriage but both agreed it wasn't something either of them wanted. They lived together and worked together, and while there were benefits to actually being spouses, neither of them felt the need to make it official.

In January Diana Macallan had pointed out the collar and asked what Dale wore in return. Ari told her that Dale didn't wear anything, and Diana thought that sounded a bit unfair. The time had definitely come to make amends for that oversight.

Ari was halfway to the car, full of pork chops and the thickest home fries she'd ever had, when she caught a whiff of something familiar. She stopped with her keys in one hand, casually scanning the parking lot and the street beyond. She zeroed in on a truck parked nearby as the source of the scent and was already approaching it when she realized it matched her memory of the truck she'd seen at the private dock the night before. She checked to make sure no one was around it before she continued walking. The odor that had attracted her was cigarette smoke, the same brand that the driver had been smoking the night before.

"Thank you, small towns." She memorized the license plate and peeked through the window. A plain white take-out cup, a floorboard full of trash, and on the dash was an old baseball cap with a logo too faded to read. The ashtray was popped out and had a butt resting on the lip of it, and Ari tried to remember the last time she'd seen a car with an ashtray built in. The reek of the cigarette smoke was apparent to her even through the glass.

There was every possibility that this was a different truck driven by a different person who just happened to smoke the same cigarettes as the man she'd seen the night before. When she crouched down to look at the tires she saw they were coated with dried mud and there was gravel in the treads. She had only been on the island three days and she could tell that it could have come from any one of a dozen places. Still, she lingered by the truck and formulated a lie to tell when the owner appeared. She walked to the bed of the truck and looked inside. Ropes, buckets, a ladder, a toolbox, and everything secured with bungee cords.

She didn't expect to find any remnants of Penny after so long out in the open, and she knew only a moron wouldn't have washed the truck after carting around a dead body, but she breathed deep anyway and was rewarded with the scent of human blood. A lot of human blood. A trace amount could be explained as an accidental cut or scrape, but this was strong. There had been a lot of blood spilled in the bed of the truck, and Ari couldn't imagine a scenario where it wasn't Penny Alton's.

"Help you with something?"

She recognized the voice even before she turned around, saving her the trouble of trying to match her hazy memory of what his body shape was. She smiled and tried her best to look nonthreatening as he approached. He wore a nice shirt over a pair of jeans, untucked, and he was carrying a bag of takeout from Bowie's restaurant. She hadn't noticed his arrival but he must have come in while she was eating.

"Hi. Sorry, I didn't mean to be a snoop."

He smiled. He had a wide face, thick eyebrows, and curly red hair that almost made him look comical. He was too broad at the chest to look like a clown, and there was something in his eyes that made the hair on the back of her neck stand up as he approached her.

"No problem at all. I never mind when a pretty woman checks me out."

She forced herself to smile. "I'm Ariadne."

"Now that is a beautiful name. I'm Jack. New to the island?"

Ari stepped aside so he could unlock the door. "I am. Well, a temporary resident. I'm visiting for a while with my friend." She put her hands behind her back and added a slight bounce to her step as she moved to stand closer to the curb. "So, I couldn't help but notice you have some sailing stuff in the back of the truck. You sail?"

"I dabble. Kind of hard to live on the island and not get out on a boat now and then, you know?"

Ari laughed out loud, swinging her hair over one shoulder. "Yeah, that's so true. I've been trying to get my friend to hire a boat or something, but she's being such a pain. I was kind of hoping that I could find someone who was willing to take me out." Her eyes widened. "Oh! Out on the water, I mean! Not... not like a date or anything." She lowered her chin and looked at him through her lashes.

The act was nauseating her, but Jack was buying it hook, line, and sinker. "Hell, I could take you out for a spin around the island. Might even see a whale or two."

"Oh, that would be so cool," Ari said, trying not to let on that she knew it was the wrong season for whales. "You sure it's not inconvenient?"

He ran his eyes down her body and she tried not to cringe. "For you, I'd make it work."

"Awesome. Let me see your phone, and I'll put my number in it."

Jack took the phone from his pocket and handed it over. Ari

turned it on and went to his contacts. "Whoops... hold on. This is different from my phone." She scrolled down and skimmed the names, looking for any that jumped out at her. "So what do you do on the island, Jack?" He answered her as she punched in her number, something about unloading trucks at the grocery store, and she finished looking at the names on his phone. She punched in her own number and smiled as she handed it back.

"So what do you do, Ariadne?"

"I work at a bank. Don't make me talk about it, I'll just fall asleep."

He chuckled. "I'm sure we could think of something else to talk about. I'll give you a call and we'll go out."

"Would we meet at the harbor, or do you have one of those personal docks like I saw when we were coming in?"

"Oh, I have a private dock." She smiled, glad her attempt to get him to brag worked. "You chose the right guy to snoop on."

"It certainly seems so! Wow. That's so cool. So, uh, maybe give me a call later tonight? I'll see when I can get rid of my friend and we can head out." She cocked her head to the side and ran her fingers through her hair. "I mean, I guess if we went out at nighttime, there wouldn't be a lot to see."

"Depends on where you look, sexy."

She laughed. "Oh, you're bad. I'll have to keep an eye on you!"

"As long as that means I can keep both eyes on you."

Ari laughed again, hating how shrill and fake she sounded but well aware of his reaction. "Okay. Well, I'll be waiting for your call. Behave yourself, Jack."

"Scout's honor."

She winked and walked away, remembering to look back over her shoulder as she went. She seemed to remember some flirting tip that told guys if the woman looked back it meant she was interested. So she looked back, caught Jack looking at her, and let her smile fade as she turned away from him. When she got into the car she quickly wrote down as many names as she could remember. None of his contacts were saved as Wayne Corbett or Louis Fleming, but there could be any number of people between a go-fer like Jack and the big boss. Still, she considered it a good sign that the only name she recognized on the list was Bowie, and that number had been categorized as "to-go."

In the rearview mirror she saw Jack reverse out of his spot and toss her a wave. She smiled and waved back, waiting until he was out of sight before she started the engine. She had no doubt that he'd been the driver, and there was a good chance one of the names she'd written down would match his passenger. She hoped she wouldn't have to keep her date with him, but if it gave her a chance to see their operation, she would grin and bear it as best she could.

Instead of driving straight back to the cabin, she drove through the southern-most part of town. Whoever took Penny's body had to have left it somewhere, and she doubted Jack and his partner in crime would want to drive farther than necessary with a body in the bed of their truck. She now believed they were the killers, but she still didn't know how or if Corbett was involved. Her theory was that they were just bagmen for whatever was coming on or going off the island. Boat drops in the middle of the night this close to the border usually meant drugs. She hadn't looked at a map but she thought the Boundary Pass was somewhere north of the island. It would be the easiest thing in the world to get on one island, pack up a boat, go dark, and drift across the border when the Coast Guard wasn't looking.

She passed a squat aluminum shack labeled Mike's Garage that she remembered from Jack's phone and drove slowly past. They seemed to be doing brisk business, three bays and two cars currently being worked on, and they had a small fleet of junkers lining either side of their driveway. For a moment Ari considered whether they might have hidden Penny's body in the trunk of an old car, but that was something the wolf could investigate later. It would pick up the scent of decomposing flesh no matter how tightly it was wrapped.

She eliminated any section of the touristy part of town as a potential hiding place. Even now she could see a parking lot of vehicles waiting for the next ferry to the mainland, and she knew that it would bring a whole new fleet when it finally arrived. There would be way too many people wandering around for any hiding place to be considered safe. She parked on the street that seemed to serve as the border between Visitors and Home Team and rested her hands on top of the steering wheel.

The body had to be dumped far enough from the crime scene that the body wouldn't draw attention to their private dock if someone happened to discover it.

The dump site also had to be far enough from the tourist center that some bumbling tourist from Kansas didn't trip over it on their way to take a picture of the harbor.

Ari took out her phone and opened the maps. Zooming in on the little island was difficult since it was too small for detailed satellite coverage, but she could still see little inroads and turnarounds even in the wooded areas. She could see where he could have stopped, dragged the body out, and then dumped her somewhere else. There were inlets where he could have put her in the water, or he could have gone inland to put her deeper into the woods.

She tried to put herself in Jack's shoes. It was early morning, they had picked up their nightly shipment of... whatever. Meth, guns, money, whatever was being exchanged. Then at some point they realized Penny had seen the entire thing. They chased her into the woods, stabbed her, and then dragged her back to the truck.

No. There was a window of opportunity where the body had been alone. So Jack stabbed her, then left her behind to go back to the truck. To get a tarp, to get Passenger to help him carry the body, to brainstorm if they should leave her out there.

The exchange happened in the dead of night. Why was Penny still there in the morning for Ari to find? The sun was up, the exchange should have happened already, and their paths should never have crossed. She tried to think back, tried to think if Penny could have died earlier, during the night. The blood was fresh, still wet. She furrowed her brow and chewed her thumbnail as she tried to work out the timeline. By morning there shouldn't have been anything for Penny to see. There should have been no reason for Jack and Passenger to kill her.

All Phoebe knew for sure was that Penny had left before she woke up. Ari considered the possibility that Penny had left in the middle of the night in order to witness the exchange. She had been out there at midnight or half past one or whenever, and she had seen the same thing Ari did: two men in a truck and two men in a boat. They saw her, killed her, and left her there to die.

"But she wasn't dead," Ari muttered around her thumb, squinting out the window but not focusing on anything but the picture in her mind. "They slit her throat and she... got up and started home. She was still alive. I didn't find her where she was killed, I found her where she dropped."

She put that down as a tentative fact. Maybe Jack and Passenger had been warned not to waste any time, so they eliminated the threat and went about their business. Took the money/drugs/meth/whatever to wherever they were supposed to. Then they reported to their boss - Ari was just going to assume that was Corbett until she had reason not to - and he might casually inquire if anything out of the ordinary had happened.

"Yeah," Ari imagined Jack saying, "some chick was snooping around. But we took care of her."

Corbett wasn't the sort to leave loose ends, and there's no way he would condone leaving a dead body out in the woods. So he sent Jack and Passenger back to retrieve their victim. For that to work, Penny had to have been alive when they left. Even if they had raped her before stabbing her, there was absolutely no reason for her pants to be around her knees. Ari couldn't get past that stumbling block. Stabbed in the neck, losing blood, in the middle of the woods, Penny had somehow found the strength to get up and attempt to walk home. Maybe she was disoriented or confused, maybe the blood loss had done weird things to her brain, but Ari still couldn't think of a situation that would have made her strip down.

Well. She could think of one reason, but she honestly didn't think Penny was *canidae*.

She sighed and decided the question was fruitless. Wherever Jack had taken Penny's body, the odds it was still around to be discovered were slim to none. Corbett would have gotten rid of it as soon as possible, especially once some out-of-towner started asking questions. She typed the notes into her phone and sent a backup to her Cloud as usual. When she got back to the cabin she would download everything to Dale's laptop and try to put it into a coherent narrative.

She had just reached for the ignition when she was startled by the blurting bark of a siren. She twisted in the seat and saw Sheriff Drexler pulling to a stop behind her.

"Great. This should go well." She rolled down the window as he approached the car. "I know I wasn't speeding. Am I blocking a bike path?"

"As a matter of fact, you are. But that's not what I wanted to talk to you about. Heard you made a little visit to Mr. Corbett's house this morning."

Ari said, "I'm actually an invited guest there now. Any time I want. Wayne and I worked it out. Did he call you, or was it Mr. Fleming?"

Drexler said, "It was Fleming. But whatever deal you struck once you were there doesn't concern me. What I'm worried about is the fact you went snooping after I expressly told you to leave him alone."

"He knows something about Penelope Alton's death. There's a history—"

He held up a hand to stop her. "I don't care about the history. I find it incredibly hard to believe that Corbett killed some girl because he knew her mama back in the day. I know Wayne Corbett, I've known him for years. This isn't about me protecting the city's tax dollars. I consider him a friend and at the moment my friend is being harassed by some private eye who doesn't know how to mind her own business."

"This is my business, Sheriff Drexler. I find it odd that you don't care about a woman who died on your island. She was assaulted, brutally stabbed, and nearly raped. It seems like that might be a bigger hit to your tourism dollars than the fact I'm bugging Corbett. You must have a newspaper in this town. How likely do you think it is they'll be as willing to ignore this as you are?"

Drexler looked at her. "I'm not ignoring Penelope Alton's death, nor am I trying to cover it up. It'll be in the weekend paper, you can bet on that. I'd like to have someone in custody by then~"

"Then let me help you."

"But," Drexler continued as if she hadn't spoken, "our job is complicated by the fact I have to keep fielding calls about you and tracking you down. Behave, Miss Willow. Go back to your cabin, enjoy your vacation, and let us handle this."

Ari said, "If I hadn't gotten involved, you would never have known there was a murder."

"Phoebe Alton would have come to us eventually," Drexler said.

"And if a hysterical woman came to you about her missing sister and offered no evidence whatsoever of foul play, would you have listened?"

Drexler didn't answer her.

"We both want the same thing, Sheriff. If Corbett has to have his feathers ruffled, wouldn't you rather leave that to me? I'm going to be leaving next week so it's not like he can hold a grudge."

"Enough, Miss Willow. Just pretend you're one of the thousand other tourists on the island this week. If you don't, I may have to take drastic measures."

"For instance?"

"Putting you in jail for the duration of your stay. You would be allowed to leave whenever you like provided you leave the island immediately."

Ari said, "What would the charges be?"

"Harassment, for starters. I'm sure I could think of others."

"I feel bad."

"That wasn't my intention."

"No, I feel bad because I kind of liked you when we met."

He glared at her. "I'm just trying to do my job to the best of my ability."

"You're threatening to arrest me for investigating this murder."

They stared each other down for what felt like a minute before Drexler said, "This is our home, Miss Willow. When you get finished running around looking for clues, you're going to go back to the big city like you said. But we'll still have to live here. I just want to make sure you don't rock a boat that you can't set right again. Invited or not, I don't want you going back out to Corbett's house. I'll arrest you for trespassing no matter what he says. Understood? The next time you have any questions for Mr. Corbett, come directly to the police station and tell me or Deputy Vaughn and we will present them to him in an official capacity. Am I understood?"

Ari said, "Are you protecting him?"

Drexler patted the top of her car. "Have a good day, Miss Willow. On second thought, have an uneventful day. I would hate for our next encounter to be acrimonious."

She watched him walk back to his car. Meth, money, heroin, weapons... something was coming ashore on the island in the middle of the night, and every interaction with Sheriff Drexler made her worry he wasn't as oblivious as she would have hoped. She knew he would wait for her to leave first, so she started the car and pulled away from the curb. He followed her back to the access road that would take her out of town back to her cabin.

CHAPTER TWELVE

ARI GOT back to the cabin and explained her run-in with Drexler. "I'm going to lie low for the rest of the day, go over my notes, see if I can come at this from a different angle."

She was still getting settled when Phoebe announced she was about to go crazy from cabin fever - "Literally a cabin, in this case..." - and Ari reluctantly agreed that she could take a walk. She didn't think Corbett was gunning for her. She truly believed Penny had been killed because of what she'd seen rather than what she'd dug up about their mother. He didn't have any reason to kill Phoebe. She took her phone with her and promised that she would be back in an hour. Dale said she was going to take a nap and, a moment after she went into the bedroom, Ari shut down the computer and followed her.

Dale had already taken off her sweater, standing by the bed in her bra and her arms still tangled in the sleeves. Her hair was wild from the static, and Ari stepped close and smoothed it down.

"Everything okay?"

"Yeah. I'm not supposed to be investigating that case anyway, and we have an hour before our houseguest gets back."

Dale smiled and tossed her sweater down. She wrapped her now-free arms around Ari's neck and smiled as she leaned in for a kiss. "Back to the vacation?"

"If you want." Ari bumped her nose against Dale's and then kissed her. Dale moaned and reached back to unfasten her bra. Ari started to unbutton her own shirt, but Dale stopped her. "What?"

"I want you dressed while I'm naked."

Ari smiled. "That's an unusual request..."

Dale stroked Ari's fingers. "Even before we were together, you were naked with me a lot. The wolf, the massages. It meant a lot to me, that you were letting yourself be so vulnerable. So just this once, take off my clothes, but leave yours on." She looked down at the catch of Ari's pants. "I mean, we can undo buttons and zippers for access, but..."

Ari silenced her with a kiss and undid her pants, slipping them down with her underwear. Dale stepped out of them and laughed as she was dumped onto the bed, her legs lifted into the air so Ari could peel off her socks. Ari kissed each ankle and eased her legs apart. Dale grabbed the collar of Ari's shirt and pulled her down, kissing her as Ari settled comfortable between her legs.

"You okay?" Ari whispered between kisses.

"Why do you taste like pork chops?"

"I stopped for lunch."

"After the breakfast I got you?"

Ari moaned. "If you're worried about the calories, I have a good idea how to work some of them off." She kissed Dale's grin, and Dale put her hands in Ari's hair as she lifted her hips to meet Ari's. The bed creaked under them, and Ari moved her lips to Dale's ear. She whispered to her, nipped her earlobe, and slid her hands down Dale's sides to hold onto her hips as they moved against each other. "Is it too rough?" Ari whispered.

Dale shook her head and curled her fingers in the material of Ari's shirt, pulling her tighter against her. She craned her neck to one side and Ari kissed her, licking from the base of her neck up to her jawline, and Dale squirmed underneath her with every thrust.

"Put your hands on my shoulders," Ari said, and Dale complied. Ari dug her knees into the mattress and moved her hand between them. She cupped Dale's sex, pressed against her with two fingers, and watched her face as she stroked. Dale parted her lips and touched her tongue to the corner of her mouth. Ari took advantage and kissed her, and their tongues met as Ari moved her hand in slow circles. Dale moved her hands to link her fingers on the back of Ari's neck.

"Wait, wait, wait," Dale chanted, pressing her lips to the skin just under Ari's eye.

"Are you okay?"

"Yes. Just hold... hold this..." She kissed to Ari's temple, both of them trembling as Dale caught her breath. Ari pressed her face against the hollow of Dale's shoulder and breathed deep. She could smell everything; Dale's perfume, her sweat, her shampoo, her skin cream and the soap she used in the shower, and underneath it all the undeniable scent of Dale Frye. She wondered if other lovers could be so precise about how their lover smelled or if it was a gift from the wolf. She pressed her tongue against Dale's throbbing pulse and Dale moaned helplessly.

"Now," Dale moaned.

"Now?"

"Make me come." Her fingers dug in at the base of Ari's skull and she arched her back off the mattress. "Ari, please, now."

Ari pressed the heel of her hand against Dale's mound and pushed her fingers inside. She bit her lip before she sat up and kissed Dale, taking her tongue into her mouth as her fingers flexed and stroked Dale to a shudderingly violent climax. Dale broke the kiss but kept her lips against Ari's mouth, gasping for breath as she began threading Ari's hair through her fingers.

"Puppy. How good is your sense of smell?"

Ari smiled. "I was just thinking about that. It's pretty good. Why?"

"I was just wondering." She kissed Ari's shoulder. "It's good enough that you tracked down Penny's body out in the woods. So I was wondering... uh... before we got together, I had girlfriends. And I enjoyed morning shenanigans with more than one of those girlfriends. So when I came in to work afterwards..."

"Yeah," Ari said. "Sometimes."

"Oh, God."

Ari chuckled and kissed Dale's lips. "I didn't mind. It was my problem, not yours." She bumped her nose against Dale's. "Usually I was just glad you were getting laid."

Dale chuckled. "Get off me. Lie on your side, facing that way."

Ari did as she was told. "Ordering me around now?"

"We're working against the clock." Dale spooned her from behind and wrapped both arms around Ari's waist. One hand went under her shirt, stroking her stomach, while the other unbuttoned her pants and wiggled its way inside her underwear. She kissed Ari's neck. "What do you want, Ari?"

"I want you to make me come." She reached back and rested her hand on Dale's hip, stroking the bare skin as Dale began to stoke her.

"What do you want?" Dale asked again.

Ari thought for a moment and then smiled. "I want you to fuck me, Dale."

She felt Dale's smile against her shoulder. "Whatever you say, boss."

Afterward they fell into a light doze which neither of them fought, Dale still naked but modestly wrapped in the sheet. She had her head on Ari's shoulder and one arm around her waist. Ari slept deeper than Dale due to her long night as the wolf, so she had to be roused by a gentle nudge. "Puppy... Ariadne, it's been over an hour."

"Mm." She opened her eyes and realized what Dale was saying. She lifted her head off the pillow. "Is Phoebe back?"

"I didn't hear her come in."

Ari reluctantly removed herself from Dale's embrace. She straightened her clothes while Dale scooted to the edge of the bed and got dressed. "I'm going to go look for her. Stay here, keep the doors locked, don't let anyone in unless it's me or Phoebe. Got it?"

"Yeah. Be safe, Ari."

"I will." She kissed Dale's lips and stroked her hair. "Did you see which way she went when she left?"

"Back toward her cabin."

Ari said, "Okay. She probably just went to get some things and lost track of time."

"Probably. I'll have my phone. I love you."

"Love you, too."

Ari still felt a tightening in her chest when they said that to each other. She had always tried to be sparing with that phrase in her past relationships, but even when she'd said it to other women, it didn't feel the same as when she said it to Dale. Saying it to Dale felt like offering part of herself, and hearing it in return felt like getting something bigger and better in exchange. And to say them here, in this room, where they had taken that first step... it meant something even larger.

She slipped her phone into her pocket and headed out through the back door. She cut through the woods at a jog, trying to remain optimistic. There was no reason to believe Corbett, Drexler, or whoever was really involved with the drop-offs would make a move on Phoebe. At the moment Ari was the one causing problems. They should sit back, let her chase her tail, and eventually send her away. The smart move would be to do absolutely nothing until the storm passed.

Then again, people who got into smuggling were by definition not exactly the greatest thinkers in the room. So she had to count on them acting rashly, without thought of consequence. There was every chance Corbett had decided to rid himself of the Alton sisters once and for all. She had every expectation that she was going to encounter a dead body at some point between cabins, bracing herself for the trauma of blundering onto a second crime scene.

To her great relief, there were no bodies to be found in the woods before she reached the cabin Penny had rented for the week. Ari slowed down as she approached the back porch, scanning the windows for signs of life.

"Phoebe? Are you here?"

She heard a noise behind her and turned. Phoebe was on the cabin cruiser, standing on the small square deck. She looked up and met Ari's gaze, then turned and went into the covered cockpit.

Something about her posture or her expression or a combination of the two set off alarms. Ari called her name again and ran to the dock, ignoring the water on either side. The engine came to life with a throaty gurgle, water churning up behind it as Ari came even with the stern. She inwardly cursed at herself for being so stupid when she leapt onto the small platform that jutted out from the rear of the ship, holding on for dear life before she had the courage to roll herself over the railing.

The hull seemed to shudder underneath her. She braced herself against the overhanging upper deck and reached for the cabin door. She was surprised to find it was locked when she could see Phoebe through the glass standing at the controls. Ari looked back and saw they were an uncomfortable distance from the dock now and getting further away. Soon they would be out in the harbor where the large sailboats and the ferry might pass through at any second.

Ari tamped down her fear and knocked on the door. "Phoebe! What are you doing?"

"I have to do this, Ariadne."

"Open the door so we can talk about this like normal people." And, she didn't mention, because standing on an eight-by-ten platform with nothing but a knee-high wall between her and the water was making her queasy. "Come on, Phoebe. Let me in. What's going on? What are you going to do?"

Phoebe kept her back to the door for another moment, then she killed the engine and turned around to unlock the door.

"Don't try to talk me out of this. You told me Drexler was preventing you from doing anything, so now I'm going to do something myself."

"What are you planning to do?" She stepped into the cabin where there was a modicum more safety. "I still think Drexler is a good guy. If I step back and stop antagonizing him~"

Phoebe said, "Do you know where my sister is, Miss Willow? Do you know where those assholes took my sister? I didn't think so." She turned back to look at the controls. They were drifted further from shore, and Ari could see other boats in the vicinity. Every single one of them looked as if they could cut Phoebe's cabin cruiser in half. Ari wiped her clammy palms on her jeans. Phoebe was oblivious to Ari's distress. "Penny deserves better than that. Mama deserved better than that."

"Phoebe, le-let's go back to shore, okay? We can talk about this with Dale. She's better at this sort of thing than I am. So..."

"No. I'm done talking, Miss Willow." She turned around and Ari could see a darkness in her eyes that hadn't been there before. "I'm going to go out and wait for that ship to come back tonight, then I'm going to follow them back wherever they came from. I'm going to find out how they're connected to Corbett and I'm going to take him down. I'm going to finish what Penny started, for her and mama both. I'm the only one left."

"Phoebe, that's incredibly dangerous. If they spot you..."

"They won't spot me. But you can't be there, Ariadne. I'm willing to risk myself, but not you." She grabbed Ari's upper arm with surprising force and shoved her backward. Ari almost tripped over her own feet as she was roughly escorted back out deck. "I can't turn back. If I turn back, I know I'll chicken out and I can't afford to do that. Penny gave her life for this. She deserves better but I'm all she gets."

Phoebe forced her to the side of the boat and, with a jolt of terror, Ari realized what she intended. "No. Hey... no, don't do this,

Phoebe. Please. Don't." Panic flooded her, worse than when the handful of times she'd actually been shot at. She grabbed Phoebe's arm with her free hand. "Don't do this. I'm terrified of the water. I can't swim. Don't put me in the water."

"The shore is right there," Phoebe said. "It's not deep at all. You can make it. I really am sorry, Ariadne, I am. But I have to do this. No turning back."

Ari swung blindly, adrenaline and fear taking over. She hit Phoebe on the chin, but Phoebe absorbed the blow and grabbed Ari's arm. Holding her by both forearms like a vice, Phoebe shoved her backward. Ari clutched at Phoebe's clothes, desperate for anything that would prevent what was about to happen, but it was too late. The cotton slipped through her fingers and Ari felt gravity take hold of her. She went under the water and every sound fled, her ears and mouth filling with water. In her panic, she felt the wolf crowd in, confused and terrified and trying to find a way to escape, but it was as trapped as she was.

She felt her arms and legs beginning to shift, but the panic attack robbed her of consciousness before she could see her full transformation.

Phoebe looked at the disturbed water next to her boat. She felt cold, and a widening hole of dread filled her chest as the bubbles diminished. Ari's warning that she couldn't swim echoed in her ears, along with the look of terror in her eyes when she hit the water. The dread dropped into her stomach as she realized maybe Ariadne had been sincere in her fright.

"Come on," she muttered, hands anxiously patting her sides. "Swim. Goddamn it, swim... the shore is right there. Swim!"

The bubbles continued to diminish, and Phoebe knew she didn't have a choice. Ari would drown if she didn't save her. She cursed under her breath and unbuttoned her pants, shoving them down as she stepped out of her shoes.

Dale's arms were around her. She felt warm and safe, but she was suffocating. Consciousness came back to her slowly as she realized where she was and what had happened. She was underwater, she was drowning, but someone did in fact have her in their arms. They were clinging to her from behind, arms locked around her chest, and in that moment Ari realized she was in wolf form. Her clothes were tattered, her jeans completely destroyed by the transformation from woman to wolf. The person pulling her to shore was female, and Ari knew that meant Phoebe. Phoebe now knew her secret. It was a small price to pay for life, however, and she was willing to explain everything once they were safely back to shore.

Phoebe surfaced with a gasp and Ari opened her mouth to take a joyous gasp of oxygen as she was carried back to solid ground. There was no beach to speak of, so Phoebe had to half-dump Ari onto the slippery rocks that served as breakfronts. Once she had her legs back under her she scurried to the muddy barrier between the rocks and the grass, dropping down and panting heavily. She heard Phoebe come out of the water behind her, panting and dragging herself across the mud as well.

Ari closed her eyes, bracing for the pain of transforming back, but it was surprisingly mild. She shivered violently for a few seconds after her joints all returned to their proper positions, still sopping wet as she wrapped her arms around herself and sat up. Her clothes were shredded but they would serve for modesty until she could get back to the cabin and change into something more appropriate.

"You're a werewolf," Phoebe said from somewhere to her left.

Ari nodded, still unwilling to open her eyes. She was grateful that Phoebe's tone was more curious surprise than complete shock. She felt like her entire body was clenched and, if she released it, she would be pulled back into the water. She also realized that some of the water on her face was tears, and she wiped them away.

"I guess we have a lot to talk about."

When she finally looked over at Phoebe her panic and shame faded in favor of a less complicated emotion: pure confusion. Phoebe was sitting a few feet away in the grass, still wearing her drenched white shirt. Curled in front of her, instead of a pair of naked legs, was a glistening silver-blue tail. The scales caught the sunlight and sparkled brightly, and Phoebe flipped the gossamer fin at the end where her feet should have been. She smiled shyly and sighed, reaching down to pat her hip.

"Yeah," Phoebe said. "I would say we do."

CHAPTER THIRTEEN

ARI TRIED to move her legs but, while the pain was much less than it had been that morning, she wanted to give herself a few minutes before she moved. Phoebe wasn't exactly in a position to get up and walk away either, so they sat together on the rocky shore. Ari looked out at the boat which was still drifting about a hundred yards away.

"The bone disease," Phoebe finally said. "The one that was hurting you. It's the transformation, right?" Ari nodded. "That makes sense."

Ari said, "Penny was trying to get to the water. That's why her pants were down. They cut her windpipe, so... what, maybe there was a chance she could breathe if she went underwater?"

Phoebe shrugged one shoulder. "I honestly don't know if that would work, but... yeah. That's what I assume she was doing. I'm sorry I couldn't tell you."

"No, I understand. You had no reason to expect I would believe you."

They lapsed back into silence. Ari looked at Phoebe's tail,

jerking slightly when she made the fin slap the ground. "So you can't just change back?"

Phoebe shook her head. "I'm still wet. It happens whenever we hit the water, and we have to dry off before we can get our legs back. It shouldn't take more than a few minutes."

"So whenever you get wet...?"

"No. We have to be submerged. I can shower and go out in the rain, but we can't take a bath without changing. I like changing in the tub."

"I can imagine," Ari said, having a flashback to Daryl Hannah in *Splash.*

Phoebe said, "You make a lot more sense to me now, too. The collar, Bitches Investigations, Dale calling you puppy..." She tilted her head to the side. "What is Dale?"

"Perfect. Normal." Ari smiled. "She's not like us."

"I see."

Ari bent her left leg and grimaced. It hurt, but not as bad as she had expected. She took her phone out of her pocket but, as expected, it was completely useless.

"Oh, shit," Phoebe said. "I didn't even think about your phone. Your notes from the investigation."

"It's okay. Dale told me what the Cloud was, so I put everything there. I can just download it to Dale's computer if I can't salvage this."

Phoebe said, "You can add the cost of a new phone to my bill." She ran her hands over her hips. "I should also profusely apologize for what I did. I had tunnel vision, and I'd decided that nothing was going to stand in the way of what I had to do. I should have listened when you said you were terrified of the water. Throwing you overboard was probably one of the worst things I've ever done to someone. I'm sorry."

"But then you came in after me. Consider us square."

"Thank you." She looked out at the boat and sighed. "I suppose

I should go out and recover it."

"Wait..."

Phoebe smiled. "I meant what I said, Ariadne. I know my plan was ridiculous. I just felt like I had to do something. I'll bring the boat back. I promise."

Ari said, "I'll go get some towels out of the house."

"I would appreciate that."

Phoebe rolled herself so that she was lying on her stomach, then with an unexpected elegance and grace, she propelled herself back to the waves using her arms and abdomen to move. Once she hit the water she spread her arms out to either side and vanished with a flip of her tail. Ari watched the waves for evidence of her passage but gave up after a few seconds. She stretched her legs and carefully stood up, testing her weight on her hips, knees, and ankles before she risked taking a step. She walked up to the cabin with the gait of the aged and infirm.

There were towels on the deck, and she looked out toward the boat as she gathered them up. Phoebe had just gripped the gunwale and pulled herself onto the boat, her tail coming out of the water with an elegant flip that tossed an arc of shining droplets through the air. Ari watched as she moved into the cabin and heard the grumble as the engine started up again. For a moment she doubted if Phoebe would keep her word, but she did in fact bring the boat around and began motoring back toward the dock.

Ari met her there with the towels, reluctantly climbing aboard to hand them over. Phoebe pulled herself up onto one of the bench seats and began rubbing the moisture from her lower body. Ari sat on the bench across from her.

"Does Corbett know that you're...?"

Phoebe shook her head. "Mom was like Dale. She met Daddy when she started working in the islands, and they fell in love. He kept his secret as long as he could but he finally had to tell her when she started talking about getting married, having kids. She didn't care. She just wanted to be with him. She spent time with him whenever she was on the island, but she wouldn't let him help her with her research. She wanted her discoveries to be untarnished." She smiled. "Ironic, huh? But eventually, I came along. Then Penny. He died before she was born, so she never met him. I did, but I don't really remember him."

Ari looked out at the water. "Your plan was to use the boat for the stakeout, then follow the smugglers underwater."

Phoebe nodded.

"That actually might have worked."

"Now you tell me."

Ari grinned. "It's still insanely risky. Hopefully we can think of an alternative plan." She glanced down and then quickly looked away when she realized at some point Phoebe's lower body had returned. "Uh, your legs are back."

"Oh." Phoebe pulled the hem of her shirt down and leaned forward to snag her clothes. Ari kept her eyes averted as she pulled her underwear and shorts back on. "I guess you don't like being called a werewolf, but I don't know the proper... *Canidae*. You worked out the fact that Penny was trying to change, you just thought she was trying to change into a wolf."

Ari said, "Yeah. I've met other shifters before. I know a police officer who can turn into a cat, I know a woman who can switch genders..."

"Whoa. That could be... useful..."

Ari grinned. "It was certainly interesting. But I've never met a..." She gestured for Phoebe to fill in the blank.

"We don't mind being called mermaids, or mermen for the guys. But we're officially called *naiads*."

"Right. Are there very many of you?"

Phoebe shook her head. "Those of us who are around tend to prefer the Mediterranean, the Caribbean, warmer waters than these. I'm a bit of a weirdo... take after my dad."

Ari smiled. "What happened to him?"

"He just got sick and died," Phoebe said. "The ocean isn't exactly the healthiest place to spend half your life these days. Pollutants."

"Right. I'm sorry."

Phoebe looked at her and stepped into her shoes. "Are you okay on the boat? We should get back on dry land now that I'm bipedal."

"I'm okay as long as we're just sitting here. But, yeah, since you offered. Dry land, please."

Ari helped her secure the boat, and then they walked together through the woods back to Ari and Dale's cabin. The walk was strenuous right after a transformation, and by the time they arrived she was leaning on Phoebe for support. Dale came out as soon as she spotted them. She hurried down the steps and ran to them, and Phoebe let go of Ari so Dale could take over for her.

"What happened?"

"Oh, quite a bit," Ari said. "Phoebe threw me off the boat."

"*What?*"

Ari put a hand on her stomach, trying to soothe the fire shooting out of her eyes. "It's okay. She's already apologized. We're fine now. While I was underwater I passed out, and the wolf took over."

Dale's anger turned to concern. "So she... knows?"

"She knows," Ari said. "But she evened things up by giving me a doozy of a secret about herself. Remember how we used to argue about whether there was an orca shifter? Someone who could change into a whale?"

"Yeah...?"

Phoebe said, "I've never seen or even heard of one. And neither have any of the other mermaids I've ever met."

Dale stopped at the base of the stairs. "Mermaid?"

"*Naiad*, if you want to be scientific," Ari said.

"Mermaid?" Dale repeated. She looked at Phoebe and smiled

awkwardly. "I used to have a decals in my bathtub shaped like you."

Ari said, "When? Last year?"

"When I was a kid," Dale said, slapping Ari's shoulder. They continued onto the deck and into the cabin. "I guess that explains why Penny's pants were down. I mean, assuming..."

Phoebe nodded. "She was a mermaid, too. And yes. I'm sorry I couldn't disabuse you of the notion she'd been raped, but there was no plausible explanation without telling our secret. I had no reason to believe you'd buy the story she was trying to get to the water so she could change into a mermaid."

Dale shook her head as she helped Ari down onto the couch. "A mermaid and a werewolf. I feel decidedly mundane at the moment."

Ari clutched Dale's hand, squeezed it, and brushed her thumb over the knuckles before letting it go. "Anything but mundane, babe."

Dale bent down to kiss the top of Ari's head and went into the bedroom. She came back with a blanket and a change of clothes. Phoebe went into her room to change while Ari got dressed on the couch. Dale took Ari's phone and put it in a bowl of rice, hoping that would help it recover from being drowned, then returned to the living room to sit on the couch.

"Are you okay? Serious answer, not the in-front-of-company answer."

"A little bit of pain, but not as bad as this morning. I think changing twice in one day helped this time, actually. The wolf doesn't feel like I'm neglecting it or ignoring it, so..." She shrugged.

Dale stroked the hair away from Ari's face. "I meant with the water. You were so anxious on the ferry, and you said you passed out. Not that I blame you. That would have been terrifying for anybody. But with your specific phobia..."

"I'm fine." Phoebe rejoined them in a fresh shirt which was once again long enough to conceal whether she was wearing shorts underneath. Ari nodded at her. "I guess this also explains your fashion choices. The less pants, the better."

"Oh. Yeah." She chuckled and tucked her hair behind her ears as she sat down. "Sometimes having legs and feet seems weird. Sometimes the fin seems weird." She shrugged. "Penny and I have been in and out of the water since we were babies so neither one feels weird." She wiggled her toes. "So have you met any other wolves?"

Ari laughed. "Oh, yeah. Quite a few. They're all around here if you know where to look, and what to look for."

"Mom said Dad told her there were more wondrous things in nature than we could ever hope to imagine. No orca shifters that I know of, though."

Dale grinned and patted Ari's thigh. "So what's the plan now?"

"Same as it was before. We spend the rest of today researching, putting together what we know, and hopefully it'll add up to something I can take to the sheriff."

Phoebe said, "Can we also discuss my idea? I know it's reckless and dangerous as hell, but I think it has a chance of working."

"What idea?" Dale asked.

"She thinks she can follow the boat to wherever it's coming from. Find the source of whatever is getting dropped off." Ari shrugged. "I thought it was far too dangerous in a boat, but if she's able to track them from underwater, maybe it's worth considering."

Dale shook her head. "Are you kidding? I think it's far too dangerous. She'd be exposing herself to the people who killed Penny. And maybe that was Penny's idea, too. She was lying in wait and they caught her. I'm sorry, but I'm voting against the idea."

Phoebe said, "When you put it like that, I guess I'm not so gung-ho about it myself. But we have to do something."

Ari said, "We know Penny found something that prompted this trip, something she was convinced would act as a smoking gun to bring Corbett down. Do you think it's a coincidence that she rented a cabin within two miles of the private dock? If Penny was able to find something incriminating then I'm sure Dale can find it, too."

"I'll try, but I can't promise anything. If I had my work computer

I'd be a little more confident."

Ari put her hand on Dale's leg and squeezed. "If you can't, then I'll just fire you and find someone who is better at this sort of thing."

"Aw, babe. I'm going to smother you with a pillow tonight."

Phoebe chuckled. "I don't know why Penny rented that particular cabin, but whatever her reasons, I'm glad you two rented the cabin next door. Maybe she set it up somehow, karmic energy or whatever. How else do you explain a werewolf renting a cabin next door to mermaids?"

Dale said, "I'm chalking it up to the fact there are far more wonderful things in the universe than anyone can imagine. No matter who our neighbors were, they were bound to be unique and amazing."

Phoebe smiled. "Well, while you two are doing your private investigating thing, I'm going to cook you dinner."

"You don't have to do that," Dale said.

Phoebe stood up. "I hijacked your vacation and I threw your girlfriend off a boat. I think this is the least punishment I could hope for. I'll go see what's in the kitchen."

Over dinner Ari and Phoebe shared stories about their respective selves. Ari explained some of the more interesting cases they had, with Dale eagerly pitching in with the story about waking up in the dog pound and getting crushed on by a poodle. Ari still didn't think the story was very funny, but Phoebe sided with Dale by laughing. When Dale hummed the opening strains of "Puppy Love," Ari threw a napkin at her. Phoebe decided to level the playing field with an embarrassing story of her own.

"So I was dating this guy whose sister had *The Little Mermaid* on VHS, and we were fooling around, and I decided he was going to be the first person I told about my... you know. I mean, he loved Ariel. I figured it might be a neat little trick, maybe a turn-on. I don't know. I was sixteen and just getting into sex. I thought it might be fun to be kinky." She sighed and crossed her arms in front of her on the table.

"So I got into the tub, let the change happen, and I called him in. He thought it was a costume at first, totally into it, but then he saw... well..." She leaned back and put the flat of her hand against the bottom arch of her rib cage. "The scales begin to taper off around here, and then it's smooth and silver-green up to my collar. He did not take that very well."

Ari snickered. "Yeah, I can see how that might be a little traumatic."

"It's always tough figuring out how to... you know, break the news."

"If you do it too early, what if it doesn't work out? And if you wait long enough to know it's the real deal, how do you get past the fact you waited so long to reveal the truth?"

Phoebe nodded emphatically. "Yes. Yes, exactly. How did you two get past that?"

Dale chuckled. "I thought I saw a dog being beaten up by a bunch of teenagers, so I went after them. I gave her my burger, took her home, and patched her up. I was going to go looking for Lost Dog posters in the morning or see if anyone had called the shelter looking for her. I went to bed and I left the dog sleeping on the couch..."

Ari said, "At which point I transformed back into myself. I didn't remember what had happened to the wolf, I was confused and disoriented, so I went to the bathroom and crawled into bed with who I thought was some woman I'd gone home with the night before. Back in those days I wasn't exactly picky about who I went home with. The idea that I might have just forgotten wasn't unbelievable at the time."

"Yeah," Dale said. "I bring home a stray dog and suddenly a naked woman is in my bed."

"Some people might call that a really good night."

Dale laughed. "As it turned out, yeah. We started our relationship naked in bed, then we were coworkers, and friends, and then..." She looked at Ari and smiled. "Eventually I tricked her into falling in love with me."

Ari said, "That's just what I let her believe."

Phoebe smiled. "Thank you both. For everything you've done for me. Ari, you very well might have saved my life by stopping me from doing something stupid. And Dale, you've made me feel like there might be a way to survive this week even though Penny..." She smiled tightly and shook her head. "Just... know that I appreciate everything you're doing. Finding who killed her almost feels secondary to... you know... keeping me sane."

Ari said, "Hopefully we can do both."

Phoebe nodded and stood up, but Dale stopped her from taking her dishes into the kitchen. "We'll take care of that."

"Are you sure?"

"Absolutely."

"Okay. Then I guess I'll just go on to bed. I might go for a swim later. Just a few quick laps, nothing dangerous, I swear. My momentary flash of martyrdom has passed, trust me. I'll knock on your door to let you know if I leave so you won't worry about me."

Ari chuckled. "We'd appreciate it. Good night, Phoebe."

"Good night to you, Ariadne. Dale."

When she was gone, Dale said, "Do you really think there's hope for catching Corbett?"

Ari shrugged. "I think anything's possible when you've got my back."

Dale grinned and leaned over the table to kiss Ari. "I'll do the dishes. You relax."

"If you insist."

Dale was only in the kitchen for a few seconds when she called Ari's name. Ari got up and found Dale standing next to the sealed container of rice holding Ari's phone. "Your phone is ringing. Feebly, but it's making the effort."

Ari opened the container and brushed the small pieces of rice away from the screen. "Shit. It's Jack."

"Ooh, your boyfriend?"

Ari ignored the teasing and grabbed a pen. She wrote down the number on the display. "Give me your phone. I don't want him to think I'm ignoring him."

Dale held out her phone. "You could always say you're playing hard to get."

"Remind me to spank you later."

"Ooh!"

Ari waited until her phone stopped ringing before she dialed from Dale's number. Jack answered on the second ring.

"Talk to me."

She rolled her eyes. "Hey! Hi! This is Ariadne. You just tried to call me, but my stupid phone got wet. It's sitting in a bucket of rice. Fingers crossed, you know. My whole life is on that thing. But I heard it ringing and I said, 'oh, shit, that's probably Jack thinking I'm playing hard to get.' Luckily my friend had a phone I could use."

He laughed. "I wasn't worried a bit."

"Cool, cool. So, uh. Were you... calling to tell me good news? I'm about to die of boredom out here in the boonies. My friend is so damn boring."

Dale stuck her rear end out and mimed a spank. Ari kicked at her.

"Well, I was thinking maybe we could go boating tomorrow. Early in the morning when everything is still kind of waking up, you know?"

"Oh, I bet that's real pretty."

"You don't know the half of it. I'm free any time."

Ari said, "How about ten? It'll give me enough time to have breakfast and, you know, pretty myself up for you." She chuckled.

"Ten sounds perfect. Should I pick you up at Bowie's?"

"Perfect. See you then. Bye-bye." She hung up and Dale let loose with the laugh she'd been holding back. "What?"

"Nothing. I just realized I would definitely not be attracted to the straight version of you."

Ari laughed and hugged Dale from behind. She wasn't too keen about going back out on a boat, especially not with a man she suspected of killing Penny, but if it helped bury Corbett, she would find a way to suffer through it.

CHAPTER FOURTEEN

ARI TOOK a bath to get all the harbor water off of her. She put Dale to bed, explained why she would be sleeping on the couch, and waited until Dale had fallen asleep before she slipped out of the room. She had only been lying and staring at the ceiling for half an hour when she heard the other bedroom door open and softly close. She looked over the top of her head and saw Phoebe tiptoeing toward the other bedroom. She was wearing a long button-down shirt and a pair of sneakers without socks.

"Hey. Don't knock."

Phoebe's shoulders hitched at the unexpected voice. "Ariadne," she whispered. "You didn't trust that I'd actually let you know when I was going?"

"It's not that," Ari whispered as she sat up. "Dale's sleep is disturbed enough by my shifting. I'm breaking promises to her left and right this week, but I wanted to be sure she at least got a good night's sleep. So I thought I'd wait out here for you."

"That's sweet." She came into the living room. "So she stays awake while you're out running around?"

Ari said, "On nights when I let the wolf run free, sometimes it takes me way out into the middle of nowhere. Then I change back and I'm sore, I'm naked, and I'm disoriented. Have you ever woken up naked in a place you don't recognize?"

"Unfortunately."

"Well, have any of those places been outside?"

"No," Phoebe laughed. "No, I can gratefully say that has never happened."

Ari said, "It happens to me at least a few times per month. When I wake up in a park, too sore to walk home, I find a stash with some Goodwill outfits inside. Then I call Dale and she comes to rescue me. She makes sure I'm safe. It's only fair that I lose a little sleep waiting up for you if it means she can enjoy an uninterrupted evening."

Phoebe smiled and started to turn away, but she stopped herself. "Can I make an observation that might be a little out of line? I mean, I feel like I've known you for years. And I guess now I understand why. Shifters know another shifter. But..."

"Go ahead. If I'm offended, I'll refuse to answer."

"Fair enough." She pressed her lips together, feet crossed at the ankles again as she considered her words. "When you talk about... 'the wolf'... you talk about it as if it's a completely separate entity. Something outside of you. But it's not. I'm not Phoebe and a mermaid, I'm... I'm just a mermaid. The mermaid is who I am in the water. The wolf is who you are when you let your wild side free. I know we only just met, but I think you're scared to admit that you and the wolf are the same thing. And I think that reluctance to accept it is one reason the transformation hurts so much."

Ari let that sink in for a moment. "I'm not sure how to respond to that."

"I'm not sure you have to. It's just an observation, and I may be totally off-base."

"I appreciate it. Dale..." She looked toward the bedroom. "She understands as much as she can, but sometimes I guess I need to hear it from someone who actually knows what it's like."

Phoebe nodded. "I was lucky to have my sister to talk to. I'm just trying to pay back what I owe you with some unsolicited advice."

"It's appreciated."

"Okay. I should go out. I shouldn't be more than an hour." She stood up. "And even if I happen to see the smuggler's boat, I'll keep my distance and get back here as soon as I can. You don't have to wait up for me. I'm sure Dale would appreciate her night of sleep better if you're in there with her."

Ari nodded. "I think you're right about that. Be safe, Phoebe. Thanks for the advice."

"Sure. Thanks for talking me out of my insanity."

Ari shrugged. "Sometimes we all just need an outsider's opinion to tell us we're being insane. Have a good swim."

"I'll try. Penny and I... one reason I was looking forward to this week was because we hadn't gotten to swim together as much as I'd like. I wish I'd known our last time in the water was going to be our last time ever."

"Who says it has to be?" Ari said. "Dedicate this outing to her. She'll be there with you in spirit."

Phoebe smiled. "I think I'll do that. Good night, Ariadne."

Ari wished her a good night and slipped into the bedroom as Phoebe left. Dale was curled on her side of the bed, one hand under the pillow and the other by her side. Ari slipped under the covers and gently moved Dale's hand so that it was touching her hip. Dale murmured in her sleep and instinctively rolled over, curling against Ari's side without waking up. Ari kissed Dale's forehead and tucked the blankets tighter around them.

As she drifted to sleep, she imagined she heard a splash in the distance as Phoebe returned to the water for one last swim with her sister, even if it was only in memory.

The next morning as they were getting dressed, Ari said, "I don't like the idea of you and Phoebe being out here on your own. I'm not saying you can't take care of yourselves, but~"

"We can spend the day in town," Dale said. "It will give us safety in numbers, and it will maybe help keep Phoebe's mind off her sister."

Ari said, "Hopefully. And hopefully I won't have to spend too much time with Jack."

Dale said, "What's the plan there?"

"I have to play it by ear. Even if I just manage to get in his truck, I might have some body odor to find Passenger with. Passenger is what I'm calling the other~"

"I got it." She stood in front of Ari, brushed her hands away, and finished buttoning her shirt for her. "Just don't get too much in character. I wasn't kidding when I said I wasn't attracted to Straight Ari. Definitely not my type."

Ari put her hands around Dale's waist and spread her fingers over Dale's rear. "Hm. I may need you to refresh my gay when I get home."

"I shall oblige." She brushed her lips around Ari's, then pressed a kiss to the corner of her mouth before slipping out of her grasp. "I heard Phoebe in the kitchen when I got up. I'm pretty sure she was making us breakfast."

"Bacon, eggs, toast, oatmeal, strawberry jam. She must have brought some of it from her cabin, because I know we didn't have any... oatmeal... what?"

Dale was staring at her with awe. "Your nose, puppy. Sometimes it's like dating a superhero."

Ari smiled and kissed Dale's neck as they left the bedroom. Phoebe was indeed at the dinner table and there were two plates waiting for them, but she hadn't waited before she started eating.

"Good morning. I hope you don't mind, but apparently cooking helps my brain shut down a little."

"Whatever works," Ari said. "How was your swim?"

Phoebe smiled. "Really good. I took your advice and imagine Penny with me. I could actually feel her swimming alongside me. It was a nice way to say goodbye."

After eating, Dale drove them into town and dropped Ari off in front of the police station. It was close enough to Bowie's that she could walk there in time to make her appointment with Jack, but first she wanted to try a peace offering. Lynne, the dispatcher-slash-sketch artist, was sitting at the main desk with a paperback novel. She sat up straighter when Ari came in, her initial smile fading as she turned to scan the room behind her.

"Miss Willow! Hi. The sheriff isn't exactly a fan of you right now. It's good to see you, though."

"You too. The sheriff might like me better after we have a conversation. Is he in?"

Lynne shook her head. "He's out for a little bit. If you're gonna talk about Mr. Corbett—"

Ari said, "No, I'm not investigating him anymore." At least not that day. "I was hoping he might know someone from town if I had a description. Kind of muscular, curly red hair, goes by Jack?"

Lynne wrinkled her nose, her top lip pulling up to reveal slightly oversized front teeth. "Jack Granger? You want to be the sheriff's friend, you won't mention that guy around him."

"Another friend?" Ari asked.

"Opposite. The last sheriff before Drexler? It was this big former Marine named Hurst. Hurst kept bringing Jack in on these misdemeanor charges and tried to get him to straighten up and fly right. Made him paint the whole building here, police and city hall both, and then he made him pick up trash on the side of the road. It seemed to take, but Jack was just scared of what Hurst would do if he fought back. He passed away, Drexler came in, and by that time Jack was an adult. He decided he was gonna take revenge for all the stuff Hurst made him do. The buildings he had to paint? Fresh coat of graffiti. All the trash he had to pick up off the side of the road, Jack and some of his buddies went around the night before trash pick-up day, stole some dumpsters from people's houses, drove up and down the main drag spilling it everywhere."

Ari said, "Sounds like public enemy number one. Why isn't he behind bars?"

"Couldn't prove it was him most of the time. Oh, of course, he'd come in acting all smug after it happened, but you can't jail someone on smug. Darn shame, too."

Ari smiled and started to ask something else, but the door behind her opened and she heard Drexler sigh. "Lynne, if you're gossiping again..."

"Not about Mr. Corbett. Honest. She wanted to know about Jackass Granger."

Drexler took off his jacket, pausing to swap a fragrant white bag from one hand to the other. He frowned at her. "What the hell do you want with Granger?"

"You told me to move off Corbett and I did. I think Granger could have done it."

"It would be a hell of a leap from littering to murder," Lynne said.

Drexler looked at her. "Don't you have somewhere to be? Somewhere you can't eavesdrop?"

"You're the one talking in front of my desk, Sheriff."

He sighed and motioned Ari past the front desk. He dropped the bag of doughnuts on Lynne's desk as he guided her to the back of the room.

"Jack is a menace, to be sure, but I don't think he's a murderer..."

Ari sighed. "Sheriff, if you're going to ban me from investigating him, too—"

"I didn't say that." He crossed his arms over his chest. "I suppose Lynne told you some of Jack's greatest hits? The spray paint and the harassment?"

"She didn't mention harassment."

He shrugged. "A couple of girls who had lapses in judgment and decided to date him started getting hang-up calls after they came to their senses and broke it off. He would leave things in their mailboxes, nothing we could officially tie back to him, of course, and none of them wanted to press charges in case that made him ramp things up. He would always eventually move on to his next target, so the girls would deal with it as long as they had to. It was easier."

"But?"

"But, I have a daughter. And if that asshole came anywhere near her, I'd want the sheriff to do something." He rubbed his bottom lip and then looked at her. "If you're focusing on Jack Granger, and if you really think he did this, I'll have your back."

Ari said, "So as long as you don't like the person I'm investigating, you're my number one fan." He glared at her and she waved off the comment. "Sorry. That was out of line."

"No, Miss Willow," he sighed, "it probably wasn't. I wouldn't have gotten so mad if you weren't making some sort of sense. Let me know if you need any help with Granger. He hasn't been violent toward any of these women, but if you're right he may have made the leap."

"I'll be careful."

She said goodbye to Lynne on her way out of the building and walked to Bowie's. She could see the appeal of living in a small town; the police station was centrally located, while Bowie's restaurant was near the harbor, and walking from one to the other gave her the chance to see a fair amount of the town. She could see herself living in a place like this when she and Dale were old and gray, retired from the private investigation game, doing whatever they were doing to fill their time.

Of course, if she was honest, she knew what they would be doing. She would be an invalid, either bedridden or in a wheelchair, and Dale would have to do everything for her. Feeding, bathing, getting her dressed. And the way things were going they wouldn't be old and gray before she had to give up the business. She flexed her hand, still feeling twinges of pain in her fingers from the transformation the day before, and she knew she would be lucky to still be working when she was forty at this rate.

She didn't have the luxury of focusing on that problem at the moment. The restaurant was crowded enough that she hoped Bowie wouldn't even notice her when she came in, but her hopes were dashed as soon as the bell chimed over her.

"Ariadne," Bowie said, nodding as she wiped off a place at the bar. "You keep showing up for lunch. You oughta come by here at night, see how I do romantic. That girl of yours will love it."

Ari looked around to see if anyone was paying attention. "Yeah, uh. Bowie, I'm kind of running something right now. If you could keep mention of Dale to a minimum..."

"Oh. Sure. Sorry."

"It's fine. And I'll be sure to bring her around before we go home. That's a promise."

The door chimed again and Ari turned to see Jack Granger coming in. He smiled when he saw her and said, "Hey, there's the girl with the pretty name."

Ari grinned. "Hiya, Jack. Right on time."

"Seriously?" She looked at Bowie and saw a look of disgust pass over her features. She looked at Ari, who tried to convey the fact she was conning Jack without letting him catch on. "To each their own, I guess," Bowie grumbled before she turned and disappeared into the kitchen.

Jack dismissed her with a wave. "Don't pay attention to her. She's hated me ever since I asked where she lost her titties." He laughed as if it were funny, and Ari held his stare before he trailed off into a series of weak coughs. "Hey, I... you know, it's just messing around, you know. I know what happened to 'em. I was, you know, trying to lighten the mood."

Ari knew he was only afraid he'd blown his chance with her, so she let him off easy with a shrug. She kept the attempt at humor on the back burner of her mind, just in case she needed more motivation to take the asshole down when the time came.

"I'm ready if you are," she said. "I can't wait to see what this beautiful town has to offer. Where are we going to go first?"

He put his arm across her shoulders and guided her out of the restaurant. "Well, I thought we'd do a spiral. Work our way out from the center, end up out in the woods... who knows what will happen once we're out there."

Ari said, "Why, Mr. Jack, are you planning to seduce me?"

He chuckled and tightened his grip on her shoulder. "We'll see what happens."

Ari held the smile, but inside she was grimacing at the prospect of spending most of the day with this man. So far she'd only managed five minutes and she was already looking for some kind of weapon. She reminded herself that suffering his antics would be a small price to pay if it meant bringing justice to Penelope Alton. She would just have to grin and bear it for as long as she had to before she found the evidence to bury him.

CHAPTER FIFTEEN

JACK'S RADIO was playing something Ari liked to call hick-rock; a guy with a drawl and a guitar with a twang, singing about taking a girl down to the 'crick'. She chose to listen to it rather than pay attention to what Jack was telling her. She had no doubt the town was interesting and had a very compelling history, but she also knew its story would be tainted by the person telling it. She would hear his opinion and his take on everything and that would color his facts. A little twang never hurt anyone.

There was one perk to getting his take on things. By serving as her tour guide, he was showing her the place of the island he frequented and, therefore, would be candidates for places he might have dumped Penny's body. She managed to hold up her side of the conversation without much trouble; there was very little effort required to sound like the vapid and bland woman Jack thought he'd picked up. She had forgotten what job she claimed to have, but he didn't seem overly interested in learning more about her.

"I only work part time at the grocery store. The rest of the time I pretty much do whatever people need me for." When they got in the truck he had pushed a baseball cap on and his curls erupted around his ears like twin puffballs. "If I need a little spending green I find someone who needs day labor, and if I'm good to go I just stay home and do whatever. That's called freedom, babe."

"Done anything cool recently?"

Jack shrugged one shoulder. "I dunno, it's all pretty much the same. You know, haul some trash for this person, move a couch for someone else. It's better than having a desk job. I would kill myself before I wore one of those neckties. You know they're basically nooses, right?"

"Right on," Ari said, scanning the buildings they passed. They were still in the heart of the town, which was identical to every small town she'd ever seen in real life or TV. They passed small businesses and town staples like a library and a bank. "Do you like the people you work for?"

"I mean, whatever," he said. "Some of them are better than others, some of them are huge a-holes, you know? They treat you like you're the hired help."

Because they hired you as help, Ari thought, but she bit her tongue. He rolled to a stop at a three-way intersection and waited for a crowd of tourists to walk by.

"See, tourists, though. I like the tourists. Every day you get a fresh shipment of ass that leaves the island in a couple days so you never have to see them again." He laughed and ran his eyes along the line of people as if sizing them up. "Girls from Nebraska and California and New York and Florida... we even get international flavors sometimes. I'm working my way around the globe and I ain't even had to leave home." He laughed and looked at her, apparently oblivious to the fact she was a tourist and they were allegedly on a date.

"Lucky girls," she managed.

He grinned and rolled through the intersection once it cleared. "I'm not making them do anything they don't wanna do. They want the hook-up as much as I do. I'm the mysterious island fling they don't talk about when they get home. They want it, and they need to get it out of their system, and I'm the guy they don't have to worry about running into at church, know what I mean?"

Ari turned to look out the window to hide her grimace. He reached over and patted her knee, and she had to resist the instinct to break one of his fingers.

"Don't worry, though. Just because I've had other girls doesn't mean you're not special. You've probably been around, too, right?"

"Oh, yeah. I've had a couple girls."

Jack guffawed. "Ooh, boy, you're a live one, huh?"

"You know, Jack, I'm getting kind of thirsty. I don't want to stop the tour yet, but is there somewhere we can get a soda or something?"

"Yeah, there's a place right up here. Sure you don't want to go to my house? I got beer, soda, juice..."

"Yeah, I want to see the island."

"Okay, sure. Sure."

He pulled into the parking lot of the gas station and told her he would be right back. He didn't bother asking what she wanted, but she didn't care since she had other priorities. As soon as he shut the door she had opened the glove compartment and began digging through the parking violations and receipts crammed into the tiny space. There were a lot of invoices scrawled onto the back of envelopes - "unloaded six bags of cedar chips to M. Davidson's back yard, helped spread it out. 2 hrs, $30/hr. $60 paid" - and only discovered that he grossly overcharged for his mediocre services.

She looked up saw Jack was in line with a half-dozen other customers, his back to the door. She dug a little further and found several more receipts that had been rubber-banded together. She peeked at the bottom of one and saw the signature of one "W F Corbett."

"Jackpot." She tucked the wad of receipts into her back pocket and reached under the seat. Her fingers came to rest on a cool, flat piece of leather, and she knew what it was even before she pulled it out. The blade of the hunting knife had almost definitely been cleaned even if it hadn't been used to kill Penny, but there were deeper scents that no cleaning could get out. She glanced up to check Jack's progress through the line before she brought the knife out and held it under her nose. She closed her eyes and breathed deep to let the wolf dissect the smells.

Dirt, sweat, skin. Grime... oil... blood.

Blood. She opened her eyes, shoved the knife back under the seat, and sat up in time to see Jack coming out of the store.

He climbed into the truck and held out a bottle of Diet Coke to her, keeping the can of Red Bull for himself. She took the bottle with a tight smile but didn't say anything. She had taken for granted all the times Dale bought her coffee despite not liking the smell, all the little things Dale just knew about her without asking. He pulled out of the parking lot and drove toward the harbor.

"Are we really going to spend the whole day just looking at stuff every tourist sees? I mean, cool, you guys have a movie theater. But if I'm getting the personalized localized tour, I want some inside scoop. Gossip, you know?"

He grinned and took a swig of his energy drink. "All right. You want dirt? I got some dirt for you. You ever watch that show, *The World Below?*"

Ari stared at him. "Sure."

"The guy who hosts it has a house on the island. I could show you where he lives."

"You're kidding! Wow, that's so cool!"

He nodded. "We got all kinds of celebrities who come here. You know, chill out and get away from the press and everyone hounding them. They come to places like this because people in small towns know how to protect someone's privacy."

Ari decided not to point out that he'd just offered to show her Corbett's house. "That's so cool," she said again. She was running out of Valley Girl slang. "So when you say you work for random people, does that mean you work for celebrities?"

"Sometimes, sometimes." He bobbed his head up and down,

trying to play it off as nothing. "You know, they're people just like anyone else. But you want to see the real interesting side of town... just you wait." He took the next right turn and headed north.

By that point, Ari had a decent grasp of the island's layout. It was a horseshoe shape with a harbor in the center. Their cabin was on the western arm, there was a resort on the eastern side, and the town was at the arch. Jack was driving them north and out of the comforts of town. Soon the cluster of businesses and restaurants gave way to homes with large lawns, and then those faded into businesses that looked as if they had gone out of business years ago. Before long there was nothing but rolling hills of grass to their right and sparse trees to the left. The pavement gave way to dirt, twin tracks separated by a hump of grass, and soon even that faded to almost nothing.

"You're taking me out to the middle of nowhere, huh?"

He smiled. "Don't worry, girlie. You're safe with me."

Ari moved her foot back and felt the sheath of the hunting knife. It was good to know where it was, and better to know she could get it before he could.

Eventually the trees thinned out again and revealed the coastline. Ari couldn't help but gasp at the sight of water stretching from one side of the world to the other, a huge expanse of extraordinarily still blue waters that were occasionally interrupted by waves and odd movement below the surface. Orca whales, she guessed, or some other variety of sea life. Even with her aversion to all things aquatic, the sight was tremendous. On the horizon she could see sprawling green landmasses of islands. The sight was quite literally awe-inspiring, and she hated that she was sharing the moment with someone like Jack Granger.

He parked and opened the door, motioning for her to get out as well. "It's beautiful out here," she said. A few hundred yards down the coast she saw a small shack. It was impossible to tell from such a distance what its purpose had been, and now it was an abandoned and isolated building in dire need of a new coat of paint. Ari wondered how long it had stood there empty. She had a sinking feeling in her gut that she knew what purpose it served now, and why

Jack had brought her here.

"You bring a lot of girls out here?"

"Some," he admitted. He looked out at the water with his hands linked on top of his head. "I'm not saying they're not special, you know. I just think everyone should get a chance to see it. A lot of tourists just follow the arrows. They don't really take the chance to explore. You said you wanted to see the secret parts of the island, well here we are."

Ari looked toward the small house again. "What's over there?"

"Nothing. You see that over there?" He pointed at the islands across the strait. "That there is Canada. Somewhere out in the middle of all this water America stops. That's crazy, huh? You go down on that beach and you're as far as you can go without leaving the country."

"Wow." Again she was impressed in spite of herself, and again she wished she was sharing this moment with Dale. Or anyone else, really. She looked at the house and started toward it. "What did that house used to be? It looks cool."

He said, "It's really not. Hey." He grabbed her arm and pulled hard enough to hurt. She turned and looked down at his fingers, then looked into his eyes. He let her go and smiled. "Sorry. Sometimes I don't know my own strength. It's just, ah, kids? With BB guns. They shoot out the windows so there's a lot of broken glass up there."

"I can be careful."

"See that tall grass? Snakes."

Ari looked at the grass and thought it was a probable warning, but she was now curious why he was so adamant about keeping her away from it. Her fingers twitched at the possibility she had found Penny's final resting place.

"I can't just take a peek?"

"I wouldn't."

The playfulness was out of his voice by then. She fell back into character and shrugged as she turned to face him. He smiled to cover his warning.

"You know, you're the most beautiful girl I've ever seen on this island."

Ari laughed. "Right."

"No, you are. I'm damn lucky you were looking at my truck and not someone else's." He leaned in to kiss her and Ari rocked back on her heels.

"Whoa. What are you doing? I thought we were just getting to know each other."

He sighed and looked down at his feet, nodding and then shaking his head. "Right. Okay. Sure." He sighed heavily, almost angrily, and looked out at the water. It was the sigh of someone who expected to be given something for free and was annoyed he would have to work for it. "I guess... could I take you to dinner? We could go to Bowie's. She's not just a lunch counter, you know. She has a whole dining hall."

Ari had wasted too many romantic island moments on this guy, and she was going to save one for Dale. "We can have dinner, but not at Bowie's. I don't think she likes me too much."

Jack grinned. "Come to think of it, she's not exactly a fan of me, either. Okay. There are other places we can go. I guess I can't call you since your phone is... what happened to it?"

Ari growled and rolled her eyes. "Dropped it in the tub. Such an idiot. I hope the rice saves it. But yeah, um. Do you still have my... friend's number on your phone?" She nearly screwed up and called Dale her girlfriend.

He checked his phone and said, "Yep, there she is. I can just call you on that?"

"Sure."

He put the phone back in his pocket. "Well, I guess I should get you back to town. Girls need a lot of time to get ready for big dates, right?"

Ari smiled despite the fact doing so hurt her face. "Yeah.

Women do, too."

"Girls, women." He shook his head. "You don't hear men getting all fed up about being called boys, do you? So sensitive. We don't mean anything by it."

Ari almost argued with him, but she didn't see the point. Besides, at least for the time being, she wanted to stay on Jack's good side. She had a feeling there were more answers to be found in the isolated little house by the seashore, the last American house before the edge of the country. She resisted looking back at it as she got into the truck. She didn't want Jack to even suspect her interest in the place. But now that she knew it existed, and she knew this was Jack's hideaways, every instinct she had told her that the little shack was where she would find Penny Alton.

Jack dropped her off at Bowie's and Ari borrowed the phone to call Dale for a ride back to the cabin. The person behind the counter told her that Bowie had gone home for the afternoon, so Ari was spared having to explain what she'd been doing with Jack Granger. Part of her was disappointed. She genuinely liked Bowie and she didn't want her to think Ari was the kind of person who would cheat with a scumbag like Jack.

Dale picked her up and spent the drive back to the cabin describing her day with Phoebe. "A lot of walking around and just enjoying the sights. We might have seen every knick-knack and tchotchke on the island by the time we were done. A lot of times I felt like I was a surrogate sister for her. I hope I was able to help."

Ari reached over and massaged the back of Dale's neck.

"How was your day?" Dale asked.

"You remember how you said you didn't like straight-me?" Dale nodded. "Well, I'm not exactly a fan of her, either. But I think I found a lead. A couple of them, actually." She took the receipts and invoices from her back pocket and removed the rubber band from them. "Some work orders for Corbett. They're all intensely vague. Most of them say 'packing items, relocating supplies,' stuff like that."

"Sounds like code for smuggling," Dale said.

Ari nodded. "That would be my guess. It's not enough to take to the sheriff yet. And he was so pleased I had moved on to investigating Granger."

They pulled into the clearing and Dale parked near the bike-eating tree. Ari opened the door, but Dale put a hand on her thigh to stop her.

Ari close the door again. "Everything okay?"

"Yeah. But this is private. Could you do one thing first? Get out of the car, go over there, and spin the bicycle wheel. While you're spinning it, say your name out loud. Can you do that?"

Ari furrowed her brow and gave her a confused smile, but she nodded. She got out of the car, gripped the wheel, and began spinning it counterclockwise. "Ariadne Willow," she said. She looked over her shoulder and saw Dale was smiling, so she walked back to the car and got in. She shut the door and chuckled. "What was that all about?"

Dale said, "There's a story I never told you about that bicycle. When I was a little girl, Mom told me the bike was trapped in time. That meant the past, present, and future were all the same to the bike because it was touching them all at once. She held me up and told me to spin the wheel and say my name out loud. She said one day I'd come back here with the person I was going to marry. I would have them spin the wheel and say their name, and we would hear ourselves through time. And even though we wouldn't know it, when we heard those names again, we would understand how important it was. And we would never let each other go."

Ari smiled and took Dale's hand. "That's beautiful."

"She used different pronouns," Dale said with a shy smile. "But... I mean, I think the gist is the same."

"I think so, too. You should have had me do it as soon as we got here."

"I almost did. But I wanted something special to mark the occasion, and it wasn't ready until today. When we first decided to come up here, I had an idea. I sent it ahead so they could work on it." She looked at the cabin. "Obviously I didn't know it would be in the middle of all of this, but I thought we could take a second and salvage one small bit of our vacation."

Ari smiled. "The suspense is killing me."

Dale reached into the backseat and retrieved a small blue bag. She sat it on her lap and pinched the top closed with her fingers. "You bought the collar for me to put on you. That was the symbol that we were... together. It meant so much to me when you bought me that collar. You told me to put it on you and I've... I've never felt so loved. So I decided that it was past time to buy something for you to give me."

Ari laughed and covered her eyes.

"I'm serious."

"I know," Ari said. "I'm sorry. I'm only laughing because I had the exact same idea. I just couldn't think of a way to bring it up without sounding like 'Go buy yourself something pretty."

Dale grinned nervously. "Well, I did think of something. I-I hoped you would put it on me the way I put on your collar."

"I would be honored, Dale."

She smiled and opened the bag, holding out to Ari. Ari reached in and took out a bracelet, holding it in the light so she could see the details. It was two different colored strands twined together, one slightly darker than the other, curling in an almost teardrop shape.

"Okay..."

Dale said, "The last time you got a haircut, I saved a lock of your hair. And when you're the wolf... sorry, puppy, but you shed. When we cleaned out my apartment I found a lot of stray hair. So I gathered it up, the longer strands, and I... uh, there's, uh, this lady in town. She makes jewelry from hair. So I had her string them together. That's a bracelet made of your hair with the wolf's hair. Joined."

Ari teared up. "Dale... this is absolutely... this is perfect. Thank you." She leaned across the console and hugged her. "This means so much to me."

"I wanted to show you that I'm not just here for you. I'm here for the wolf, too. Even when she's hurting you, I know she's a part of you. So I love her, too." She kissed Ari's cheek and sat back. "So put it on me...?"

"Yes, of course." She sniffled. "Uh, which... left or right?"

"Left."

Ari figured out the clasp and put it on her. "This is spectacular, Dale."

"I remembered the lady from when I was a kid. I just crossed my fingers that she was still working. Lucky for me."

"Lucky for us both," Ari said. She bent down and kissed Dale's wrist. "I'm going to treasure this. Thank you so much."

"You're welcome." She turned her hand around, her palm against Ari's, and embraced her. They knew they would have to go inside soon, or else Phoebe might become concerned, but for the time being they were content to just hold one another in the dark of the car.

Chapter Sixteen

DALE OPENED her eyes and groped for her phone to see what time it was, only to remember it was in Ari's satchel. She rolled onto her back and saw Ari had fallen asleep instead of "just lying here with you until you fall asleep." She scooted closer and kissed Ari's neck above and below her collar, then walked her fingers over Ari's stomach until she stirred. "Puppy, get up. You fell asleep. Time to go."

Ari grumbled and moaned, then stroked Dale's arm. "Right. Sorry."

Dale smiled. "Don't be. It's kind of a nice change, me waking you up for once."

Ari chuckled and sat up. Her satchel was next to the bed and she checked it to make sure she had everything. Her own phone was still in its restorative rice bed, so she was borrowing Dale's. It was nestled in her folded jeans and a shirt. The bag also carried her wallet and shoes. She made sure she had everything she needed and then stood to strip out of her pajamas. She took a deep breath, rolled her shoulders, and looked at Dale.

Dale winked at her. "If you need anything at all, call Phoebe's cell."

Ari nodded. "I will."

Dale pulled her legs up under the blankets and wrapped her arms around them. Normally she hated watching Ari's transformations but this time she wanted to watch. With all the pain Ari went through changing from one to the other, she felt she owed her to act as a witness. Ari closed her eyes and took a breath, rolled her shoulders, and exhaled slowly. What happened next was so fast that she couldn't tell what the first step was. Suddenly Ari had fallen forward, her arms resting on the bed as she dropped to one knee. She twisted her head on her neck and her fingers dug into the blankets. Her hair had fallen into her face but she flipped it back to reveal her lower jaw was now drastically pronounced, her nose misshapen. Dale flinched at the sight, but Ari's skull twisted and settled back in the shape of the wolf's head. Her back legs scrambled and she hopped up onto the bed, sides bellowing out as she caught her breath.

Dale picked up the satchel and looped it over Ari's head. She fastened the secondary strap across her chest, made sure it wouldn't get in her way.

"There you go, puppy. Come on..."

She got out of bed and Ari trotted after her. Phoebe was sitting on the couch, and she smiled apologetically before she looked at Ari.

"I hope you don't mind. I wanted to see her off, wish her luck..."

"Of course."

Ari walked up to Phoebe and put out her right paw. Phoebe chuckled and took the paw, then crouched in front of Ari.

"Even if you don't find my sister's body, I want to thank you for everything you've done and everything you've sacrificed for her." She hugged Ari's neck. "She would have really loved meeting you, Ariadne. Be safe."

Dale reached down and stroked the back of Ari's head. "That goes double from me, puppy. No unnecessary risks."

Ari turned her head and licked Dale's palm. Dale smiled and led

Ari to the front door. Ari bumped against Dale's leg, looked up at her, and then darted out into the night. Dale hugged herself, wishing she had put on a jacket or sweater before she came out of the bedroom. Phoebe was standing just behind her and watched over her shoulder as Ari ran down the trail back to the road.

"She's a beautiful wolf. I didn't really have a chance to appreciate it the last time I saw her, but she's gorgeous."

"She really is." Dale crossed her arms and touched her bracelet, stroking the braided hairs like a talisman as she sent Ari all the good thoughts she could spare. "Come on. If you're planning to stay awake until she calls, I have some tricks that help fight off drowsiness."

They went back inside, but not before Dale said a quiet prayer that Ari would be safe.

She stopped in the woods, catching her breath and taking a moment to get her bearings. The wolf had never known wilderness like this. Everywhere she could run in Seattle was industrialized, paved over, fenced off, and tamed. This was true wilderness. Even with the town nearby the night was almost completely silent except for the sound of water and the rustle of wind through the leaves. She heard other animals in the woods but they steered clear of each other as best they could. At one point she encountered a deer that started to run, but then stopped and stared as if trying to figure out what she was.

Just keep going, beautiful, Ari thought.

The deer either understood what Ari wanted or simply had pressing business elsewhere, because it turned and was gone in a flicker of its small white tail. Ari continued on her way, cutting to the north before she reached town. It probably would have been a much shorter journey to follow the outer coast of the island, but she didn't want to risk getting lost in the wild. It was easy enough to get turned around in daylight, and she had a feeling night would be a thousand times worse. It was safer to go back and retrace the route Jack had taken in his truck.

The town was a mile from their cabin, and it was just over two more miles to the shack. She knew the wolf would appreciate the exercise; she never really got a chance to stretch her legs in the city. She remembered Phoebe's advice and tried to think differently. The wolf wasn't the one appreciating the wide open woods; it was all her. She was solitary, and she was one creature. When she let go, when she "let the wolf off the leash," she was just surrendering to her own desires.

She ran on, keeping the road to her right so she would be less likely to get lost. In the dark everything looked utterly different. The space between buildings looked black as the deepest caves, but the sky above was so clear that the moon gave her enough light to see. She took a few detours, chasing scents and letting the wolf explore a bit before reminding herself she had a mission to do.

Eventually she reached the clearing. A quick scan of the area revealed she was alone but she still remained in the trees where she wouldn't be seen as she transformed. When it was done she dropped onto her butt in the grass, panting heavily as the pain shot up her arms and through her hips. She closed her eyes and tried to coast through the worst of the pain, teeth clenched as sweat rolled down the sides of her face and dripped off her chin.

"Fuck," she growled, shaking off the tremors that ran through her. She was still hurting but she had a finite amount of time to snoop around. She took off the satchel and quickly got dressed, feeling more human once her shoes were on. She pushed her hair back and fashioned it into a loose ponytail before she pushed herself up against a tree. She was able to walk and, as she walked, the pain in her knees and ankles subsided. She kept her breathing steady as she crossed the clearing where Jack had parked the truck. Dale had included a flashlight in the pack, and she shined it ahead of her to see the suddenly ominous and foreboding shack up ahead.

She gave the building a wide berth as she circled it, her light trained on the ground for signs of any recent disturbance. She saw footprints in the dirt leading up to the entrance, even though the door looked as if it hadn't been opened in years. The windows were caked over with dirt and sediment, and she wondered if that was a byproduct of being so close to the water or if Jack and his cronies had done it to discourage anyone from looking inside.

There was nothing to indicate a hasty burial on the grounds so she moved closer and almost immediately picked up a whiff of decomposition. She put her hand flat against the door and pushed, but it was locked. She could feel a bit of give, though, proving it was most likely on its last legs. She knew Sheriff Drexler would want her to back off and call for help and, if she did, he would tell her to walk away and wait for someone to come check it out.

"But no matter how good my sense of smell is, it's inadmissible in court," she said. "This is private property and they'd need probable cause for a warrant."

She turned sideways and slammed her shoulder against the door. It wobbled, so she did it again, then gave it a solid kick. The door splintered at the hinges and sagged drunkenly where the lock hung tightly to the doorframe. She moved it carefully, not touching the knob in case there were fingerprints, and moved the door out of her way.

"Oh, no, I tripped and fell," she muttered in a monotone.

The remnants of the lock mechanism were bright gold, with only a few scratches where it had been scraped by the tongue.

"Okay, why would you put a brand-new lock on a falling-down building?" Her nose had already told her the answer, but she wanted to delay as long as possible. Part of her wanted to believe Penny had somehow miraculously survived, that her body had disappeared from the woods because she got up and reached the water. She was out there in the Strait breathing through gills and looking for a way to patch up the wound in her throat and everyone would be happy.

Cobwebs formed an oddly gorgeous sculpture overhead as she entered, only a few strands dangling low enough to get caught in her hair. She swept them aside with her arm as she examined the interior of the shack. Three sawhorses against the opposite wall held up a piece of plywood which in turn displayed a fine array of empty liquor bottles. On the far wall was a pair of mattresses stacked on top of one another, and the walls around the bed were marked with dozens of names and dates.

On the floor next to the bed, wrapped in a tarp that had been tied at the neck, waist, and ankles, was Penelope Alton's body.

Ari knelt next to it and was surprised to feel tears burning her eyes. She had come to really like Phoebe and, through her, she felt as if she knew Penny. She resisted touching the body for fear of contaminating evidence and she wiped away her tears before they could drip to the ground. She thought of Laura Gavin and how she had failed her. She'd been there to witness Laura's last words and to see her take her last breath.

"I'm sorry, Penny," she whispered. "Sorry I didn't get there a little earlier."

She remained a moment longer, sitting vigil or whatever a religious type might have called it. Whoever had dumped her body in this shack obviously hadn't cared about her, and she deserved to have someone give her a moment.

Finally she stood and wiped away her tears, sniffled, and went to stand by the door. She could see a fair distance down the main road and she would be warned well in advance if Jack or Passenger came back to check on their little dump site. She wiped her eyes and dialed the police station, resting her head wearily against the jamb as she listened to its buzzing ring in her ear.

A woman she didn't recognize answered. "Police, this is Louisa, what can I help you with?"

"I need to talk to the sheriff."

"Sheriff's already gone home, hon. Deputy Stockton is the one on-call. Want I should give him a ring for you?"

Ari said, "Wake the sheriff up. He'll want to be here for this. Tell him if he needs Penelope Alton's body to start taking this case seriously, I can tell him where to find it."

Silence from the other end, then finally: "Hon, will you hold on for a second?"

"I'm not going anywhere."

She heard a click as she was put on hold, and she slumped against the wall. With the door kicked in she knew there was no way she could hide her presence if Jack or another of Corbett's goons showed up, but at the moment she didn't care. She almost wanted them to come so she could take appropriate vengeance for what they had done. For the moment she just stood with her back against the wall and waited for Louisa to get the sheriff on the phone.

After what felt like ten minutes but was probably more like two, there was a click on the line. "Miss Willow?" the night dispatcher said.

"I'm here."

"Where are you?"

Ari gave directions to the shack as best she could, using the same landmarks she used to navigate.

"Okay, I know exactly where that is. Lord. Okay. Sheriff Drexler says to stay put, and we're sending someone out right now. Just wait right there, okay?"

"I'll be here."

She hung up and looked at the phone for a moment, then dialed Phoebe's number. Dale answered on the first ring.

"Ari?"

"Hey. Everything's fine. Is Phoebe there?"

"You're on speaker," Dale said.

Phoebe said, "I'm here."

Ari said, "I can't talk long. I just wanted to let you know that I found her."

She heard the sound of Phoebe crying, and then Dale softly said, "Well done, puppy. She's trying to say thank you, but..."

Ari said, "I'll let you take care of her. I'll call again when I can."

"Okay. Love you."

"I love you, too."

It was less than a minute after they hung up that Ari saw the flashing red and blue lights of the police car, followed by the actual vehicle itself coming around the curve. It was followed by a dark van Ari assumed was the coroner or medical examiner or whoever would be in charge of a scene like this. The police car stopped a fair distance away from the shack and a blinding spotlight snapped on. Ari squinted into its glare and heard the cop car doors opening.

"It's inside--"

"Put your hands on your head and get down on your knees."

"Seriously? I'm the one who called!" She moved her hands to the top of her head and laced her fingers together. "My name is Ariadne Willow. I'm a private investigator."

The cop approached with his gun drawn, but aimed at the ground. "We know who you are, Miss Willow. Sheriff Drexler told us all about you. He wants to keep an eye on you while we're sorting this out." He holstered his gun and stepped behind her, then pulled one of her arms back.

"Oh, you've gotta be kidding me," Ari said as the first cuff went on.

"You're not under arrest. You're only being detained."

She thought about arguing but she could tell it wouldn't get her anywhere. She let the deputy fasten the handcuffs without further comment.

"The body is back there?"

"Yeah."

"All right. Stay here."

Ari snorted and shook her head, looking out at the black water. There was enough light that she could see the waves but little else, so she turned her head to the sky and waited for the deputy to confirm her gruesome discovery.

CHAPTER SEVENTEEN

AFTER THE scene was cleared, the deputy allowed the coroner to go inside and take over. A second car arrived, its lights joining the first to make the clearing look almost festive as the officers conferred in the triangle of vehicles. Finally one of them walked over to where Ari had been left waiting and motioned for her to stand. She had moved from a kneeling position to sitting cross-legged on the grass, and standing with both hands behind her back was far more complicated than she expected. The deputy gripped her elbow and helped her up, then walked her to his car.

"My bag," she said.

He picked up the bag and looked through it to make sure there was nothing from the crime scene. It was a quick search since the bag was empty, and he put it in her hand so she could awkwardly carry it.

"Where are we going?"

"To the station. Sheriff wants you there all nice and cozy."

"Do I at least get a phone call?"

He said, "Once we're there."

She let him put her in the backseat and slumped down. The shack had been surrounded with crime scene tape, and Ari could see that someone had set up spotlights that lit the inside of the shack like a lighthouse. She could see the shadows of the small team examining the area as the deputy got behind the wheel and started the engine.

"Her name was Penelope Alton," Ari said.

"We actually don't know that for sure."

Ari said, "Oh, come on..."

"I didn't look under the tarp. Did you?"

I smelled her. I know her smell. "No," she said.

"We'll sort it all out in time."

"Right."

She dropped her head back against the seat and closed her eyes for the ride back to the station. The deputy parked behind the building and helped her out of the car. It was late enough, or much too early depending on how one looked at it, that there was no one on the street to watch her being led into the building in cuffs. They bypassed the booking room, and she was spared the indignity of fingerprinting or a mug shot, but he took her to a row of cells and unlocked one of them.

"Seriously? I can't just wait out in the front room?"

"Nope. Sheriff doesn't want you slipping away or getting into stuff. We can't afford to have someone babysit you, so... in you go."

She sighed again and shook her head as she went into the cell. "You're not going to process me?"

"You're not under arrest."

She laughed. "You have a weird way of proving it."

"Turn around."

She did, and he unlocked her cuffs. "Just sit tight and the sheriff will let you out when he's ready."

"I can still make a phone call, right?"

"You have a phone?" She patted her pocket. "Make all the calls you want."

He locked her in and disappeared down the hall. Ari took out her phone and sat on the edge of the cot. Dale answered slower than last time, but Ari assumed she had still been comforting Phoebe.

"Everything okay there?"

"Depends on who you ask," Ari said. "The Sheriff had someone bring me down to the station so I'd stay out of his way."

Dale said, "He what? You're..."

"I'm not under arrest. They said that a couple of times." She looked at the bars. "But I did get cuffed, and I'm sitting in a jail cell, so the difference seems kind of semantic right now. And they did let me keep the phone, so there's that. I just didn't want you to worry when I didn't come back tonight. The sheriff will probably let me out in the morning."

"Let me know when and I'll come pick you up."

"I will. You might even get to sleep in."

Dale laughed. "I wouldn't know what to do with myself. I'll see you in the morning."

"Okay. Love you."

"Love you."

Ari hung up and swung her feet up onto the cot. She didn't expect to sleep, but after a few minutes she realized there wasn't much else for her to do in the cell. She crossed her feet at the ankles and rested her hands on her stomach. She had been "detained" before, usually for vagrancy during her time on the streets, and she'd never been able to sleep in the cell. This time was different. She'd found Penny's body, and she knew Dale was coming to get her. Those two facts put her mind at enough ease that she was able to drift off quickly into a deep and dreamless sleep.

The door opened loud enough to wake her, and Ari was sitting on the edge of the bed when Sheriff Drexler appeared in front of her cell. He looked older than he had the day before, and he had a fine dusting of fuzz on his jaw and the top of his head. He looked at her with extremely tired eyes and she knew that he'd added 'woken from a deep sleep' onto her list of sins.

"Miss Willow. I've seen you more this week than I've seen my girlfriend."

"Sorry about that."

He unlocked the cell door. "Well, your girlfriend brought the victim's sister down to identify the body. We should have confirmation soon. Donny, that's our coroner, confirmed she was killed by a knife wound to the throat, just as you reported. No overt signs of sexual assault, but she's going to make certain of that before she says anything official."

Ari nodded. She wished she had known the whole story before she reported the attempted rape, but there was nothing that could be done about it now.

"Am I free to go?" she asked.

"Not quite yet. I want to have a discussion with you about how you found the body. I assume Jack Granger was involved."

Ari said, "I pretended to go on a date with him. He took me out there to see Canada, but he got jumpy when I tried to get closer to the shack. I thought there might be a reason for that, so I went back after dark."

"Deputy Robbins said there wasn't a vehicle at the scene."

"I walked."

"You walked. Two or three miles, over unfamiliar terrain, in the dark, to a place you had only been once before."

Ari said, "How else would I have gotten there? Swam?"

He stared at her. "You're hiding something, Miss Willow. I don't think you're involved in this girl's death, I don't think that at all, but I do think there's more that you're not saying. I can't for the life of me imagine why."

"I'm not holding back anything that affects the case in any way, I assure you."

Drexler ran his thumb over his bottom lip and motioned for her to follow him out into the main room. Lynne was on duty, and she looked up as Ari was brought out. She smiled, waved, and quickly dropped her hand when she saw the expression on Drexler's face.

"I would hope this goes without saying, Miss Willow, but you are not to go anywhere near that crime scene. It's two miles outside of town, so I'm asking you to not go within a mile and a half of it. We have our guys going over every inch of that place for evidence Jack Granger is most likely the one who left the body there. We don't want anything, anything at all, to get in the way of finally convicting this asshole. So please, please, Miss Willow. Keep your goddamn distance. Am I clear?"

"I won't go anywhere near the crime scene."

"The shack." He aimed a finger at her. "Say you won't go near the shack."

Ari chuckled. "Wow. You really don't trust me, do you?"

"Have you given me any reason whatsoever to trust you?"

She sighed and held up her hand with her fingers extended. "I won't go within a mile and a half of that shack. You have my word. Despite what you might think, and despite my behavior this past week, there are people who would take that to the bank." She held out her hand to him. "I'm an honorable person, Sheriff Drexler."

He looked at her hand. "The main reason you've been such a pain in my ass is because you made a promise to someone who was already dead. That tells me a lot about who you are." He shook her hand. "I'll take your word for it, Miss Willow. Don't make me regret it."

She nodded.

"Now. If you'll excuse me, every officer I have is running around trying to keep a lid on this."

"Right. Uh, you said Dale brought Phoebe Alton into town to identify the body. Are they still around?"

"I saw Miss Frye outside when I came in."

"Thanks." She walked out, smiling at Lynne when she passed the front desk. "Good morning, Lynne."

"Morning, Miss Willow. Want a doughnut?"

"I... will, actually." Her instinct was to refuse, but she had missed breakfast. Lynne opened the white box on the edge of the desk and held it out so Ari could take her pick. "Thanks."

"Sure. These aren't Krispy Kremes or anything fancy like that. They're better. Homemade from a bakery here on the island. Enjoy."

Ari smiled. "Can I take one for my girlfriend?"

"Sure! Go ahead. I saw her on the way in! The redhead sitting outside the forensics building? Cute! Very cute!"

"Yeah, I certainly think so." She wrapped a napkin around two chocolate doughnuts. "Thanks."

Lynne shrugged. "Least I can do after the sheriff made you spend the night here. At least now we can claim we offer a complimentary breakfast."

"I guess you heard why I was here."

"Yeah. That poor girl. Do you really think Jack did it? I mean, he's a scumbag, but a murderer?"

"I don't know much yet, not that I can prove. Hopefully either the sheriff or I can connect the dots and make sure he goes down for it."

Lynne said, "Good luck to you both!"

Ari went outside and looked to the south, then the north. Dale was sitting on a bench halfway down the block watching people go by. Ari approached from a wide angle, coming up on her from behind so Dale wouldn't see her coming.

"Excuse me," she said, "I just got out of prison and I was

wondering if you had a business opportunity for a hardened convict."

Dale looked up and smiled. "Well, gee, you look harmless enough. What were you in for?"

"Poisoning doughnuts. Oh, speaking of which... I got you breakfast."

Dale smiled and took one. "So did you have to wear the orange jumpsuit or did they have classic black-and-white striped?"

"Neither. I just wore street clothes."

"Oh. Any big bad cellmates?"

Ari shook her head. "Just me."

"You're really harshing my prison fantasy buzz, baby."

"Oh, really? I'll keep that in mind."

Dale smiled and took a bite of her doughnut. Ari picked at hers without actually eating much of it. Eventually she stopped trying and looked down at the bracelet on Dale's wrist. In the sunlight she could more easily discern between the human strands and the lighter wolf hair. She reached over and brushed her thumb over it, again awed that Dale had the foresight to put together such an amazing tribute. Any fool could buy a diamond ring, but this was something precious. She focused on it to settle her mind. Dale ran her thumb over the back of Ari's hand.

"Are you okay? It couldn't have been easy finding her body twice."

"The second time was less traumatic." She decided not to tell Dale about the tears until they were in a more private situation. "She was bundled up so I didn't have to... see. But yeah. It was a little rough. The one I'm worried about is Phoebe. Is she still inside?" She looked toward the building that she could now see had a very subtle marker identifying it as the Office of the Medical Examiner and Morgue.

"Deputy Vaughn took her to see the sheriff. He wanted to have a conversation with her about this whole mess. I think he wants to convince her to fire you."

Ari said, "Good luck to him." She checked her watch. "I'm going to sneak in and have a look around."

"Sneak in where? The morgue? Ari..."

"I only promised to stay away from the crime scene. This doesn't count."

"The sheriff is going to have your hide."

Ari shrugged. "I'll tell him you have dibs."

"You know what's ironic?" Dale said as Ari started to walk away.

Ari stopped. "What's that?"

"The first time I brought you to this island, it was so you wouldn't be falsely arrested on a murder charge." She looked over her shoulder and smiled. "You have a way of messing up all my plans, puppy."

Ari bent over the back of the bench and kissed Dale's lips. "Yeah, but I make up for it with better plans."

She went up the front walk and let herself into the building, a cool and dark place that felt like it was hermetically sealed to block any outside noises. The floors were buffed to a bright sheen, the walls were bare except for a few framed sepia photographs of the island, and Ari felt a reverence she normally reserved for churches. She supposed it was only natural for a morgue to have a certain gravitas, but it seemed this town had really done it right.

Small silver nameplates on the wall pointed her in the right direction, and she saw that Autopsy Theater was down the hall to her left. Her footsteps sounded hollow and heavy as she walked down the hall, pausing before she pushed open the swinging door and entered a dark prep room. Windows along the opposite wall looked into a sterile environment where Penelope Alton was lying shrouded on a table. Ari went to the window.

"You're not supposed to be in here."

Ari jumped at the sound and turned to see someone standing by the sink. At first glance she thought it was a man, tall and slender, blonde hair cut short and slicked down across the forehead, but the features were unmistakably feminine. She wore horn-rimmed glasses, a white dress shirt, and a black tie that was tucked into a slate-gray vest. Her sleeves were rolled up past the elbows and her hands glistened from washing them before she began her work.

"Hi. Sorry. I'm Ariadne Willow. I'm~"

"The private investigator from the mainland. I've heard about you. Everyone on the island has heard about you. You're the one who found her. Twice. I saw you last night. Getting arrested. Sorry. I'm glad you're out of jail now. I'm Donny, Donny Sapp."

Ari was unsettled by that, but she shrugged it off. "I don't want to get in anybody's way. All I'm interested in is finding out who is responsible for Penny's death."

"The sheriff seems to think it was Jack Granger."

"I think he was the killer, but I also think he was ordered to do it. I think he was trying to protect something a lot larger. Do you think he's capable of running a drug smuggling operation?"

Donny adjusted her glasses. "Jack Granger? Uh. No. No, not exactly. He's an errand boy if anything. A follower. Not a leader." She pressed her lips together. "Sorry. I feel like I'm talking very fast. I... don't... talk to a lot of humans. Uh, living..." She squeezed her eyes shut for a three-count. "Living people. I don't talk to living people very often."

Ari said, "That's fine."

"But, um, as I was going to say, um. I believe in cooperation. I believe that two heads are better than one in situations like this. I believe the sheriff m-may have certain... biases that could affect his investigation. He's a good man. Don't get me wrong. But... if I were to mention a few things, facts, in response to your inquiries, I don't think he would be too mad. Not that he has much of a choice. I'm the only doctor he has." She smiled, showing too much teeth, and seemed to realize it was unsettling. She lessened the smile and chuckled nervously.

Ari tried to put the doctor at ease. "So... Donny's an unusual name for a woman."

"Oh. Actually it's Dionne. I go by Donny because it's easier for people to pronounce. And spell. And I look like a man."

"I wasn't going to say anything."

"It's okay. It's not like it was an accident."

Ari grinned. "Okay. Inquiries... what evidence did you find at the scene?"

"I didn't personally find much, but there was a crew who gathered a lot of garbage and detritus. Beer bottles, condoms, snack food wrappers. It seemed like there was a fair amount of sexual depravity occurring in that little shack. I know that I saw evidence of quite a few visitors, despite the cobwebs and general aesthetic of abandonment. Beyond that I couldn't say how many people were involved in leaving Miss Alton there."

"Has it always been abandoned?"

"No, no. No. But for years, at least. I don't know what it used to be, but now it's a popular spot for local high school kids to go and neck. And, well, Jack Granger. I suppose mentally he still counts as a high school kid. I was about to begin my examination. You're welcome to stay and observe. The sheriff may have qualms about you hearing details before he does, but that can't be helped if you're in the room as I make the observations. I tend to think out loud while I work."

Ari said, "I would appreciate that. Thank you."

"Like I said, I believe in cooperation. I think if investigators shared their evidence more often there would be a smaller percentage of unsolved cases on the books. Teamwork. It's all about teamwork." She nodded and reached to adjust her tie, then remembered she had just washed her hands. "Ah. Right. Did I touch my glasses while we were talking?"

"Uh, a couple of times, I think."

"Drat. Okay. I'll wash my hands again, and then I will begin."

Ari nodded and Donny went back to the sink. Ari looked through the glass at Penny's covered body and hoped it held clues that would help her bring Jack Granger down. With the right leverage, she had faith that she could follow him up the branch to Wayne Corbett. She was still convinced he had something to do with the whole mess currently entangling the island, but without evidence she wasn't going to convince the sheriff.

"Okay," Donny said. "Wish me luck."

Ari nodded and said, "Luck," then watched as Donny went into the theater to begin her work.

CHAPTER EIGHTEEN

SHERIFF DREXLER opened the door, looked at Ari, and hung his head as he pushed the door shut behind him. "Willow. I should've known you would be here."

Ari said, "It's not the crime scene, nor is it the shack. I haven't broken my promise."

"Technically you're right. But I'm going to be very glad to see your taillights when you leave this island." He stood next to her and looked into the theater where Donny was still at work. "Has she found anything yet?"

"I don't know. She seems to be singing something."

"Simon and Garfunkel. At least that's who it was last time. For weeks I couldn't hear 'The Boxer' without getting queasy from remembering." He crossed his arms and watched the doctor work. "We don't get many murder cases here. Last one was three years ago, and that was just about as open and shut as it could be. Bastard was practically standing over the body with the gun when we rolled up. I didn't want to believe you when you came running in saying we had one, and then the body up and vanished. I think maybe part of me... a very small part... wanted you to be wrong. And it was easier to believe that if I ignored you."

Ari looked at him. "Is that an apology?"

"No. It's also not carte blanche for you to run around doing whatever you want without consequences. But you've gotten us this far, and I appreciate that."

Donny stepped up to the other side of the glass and pressed a button. "Sheriff Drexler, I've examined the wound and I thought you would want to know that I've determined the weapon is a fixed blade approximately six inches long with a non-serrated edge."

"Thank you, Donny," Drexler said. She nodded and went back to her work.

Ari said, "Jack Granger has a knife like that in his truck."

"In plain sight?"

Ari pursed her lips and shrugged. "He invited me into his truck and left me alone in it for a few minutes. He had to assume I might snoop."

"Especially if he got to know you." Drexler said, "Where was the knife?"

"Under the seat."

"I suppose you could've dropped something and while you were groping around..."

Ari shrugged. "I am a butterfingers."

"If I arrest him and this goes to trial, I'm going to expect you to testify."

Ari nodded. "I'd be more than happy to put this guy away. Whatever it takes."

"Okay. Come on. Let's go see Mr. Granger about a knife."

"You're letting me come with you?"

"If I don't, you'll probably go anyway and get there before I do. At least this way I can shoot you if you start pissing me off."

Ari smiled. "I told you I'd grow on you."

As they left Ari realized Donny had left the intercom on as she began singing an Elvis Costello song under her breath.

Outside the morgue, she explained to Dale where they were going. Dale wished her luck and said she was going to take Phoebe back to the cabin so she could lie down for a while. Drexler didn't tell her to get in the backseat, so she slid into the front seat of the police car. Drexler looked over at her as she scanned the various devices and screens on his dashboard.

"First time in the front of one of these?"

Ari said, "I plead the fifth."

He said nothing and pulled away from the curb. They passed Dale's car and Ari lifted her hand to wave. Dale mouthed 'good luck' and formed the 'I love you' sign with her fingers.

Ari didn't know why she expected the neighborhoods of the island to be different from the mainland, but as soon as Drexler turned onto one of the streets, she could have been in any one of the bedroom communities around Seattle. He drove her past the nicer homes, across a bridge that spanned a drainage ditch, and soon the houses on either side of the road became drabber and more decrepit. He parked half off the road, the car tilted dangerously into a roadside ditch, and climbed out onto the slope. The gravel crunched under Ari's shoes as she walked around the back of the car.

"Granger's house?" she said.

"Yeah. His truck isn't here, though." He looked up the road as if he expected to see Jack driving up to greet them. "He might be lying low if he heard we found Penelope's body."

Ari said, "There's a chance he would be willing to see me." Drexler looked at her and she shrugged. "We were supposed to go on a date last night, but I put it off. I could call and see if he's willing to reschedule for right now. The other option is staking this place out and hope he doesn't get spooked when he sees you waiting for him."

Drexler considered her plan. Finally he nodded. "Call him. See if he'll agree to meet."

Ari took out her phone and dialed Jack's number. She paced away from the car, then turned and walked back as it rang in her ear. She was about to give up when he finally answered.

"Hello? Ariadne?"

"Yeah, it's me. Listen, sorry about last night. My friend and I are spending the day apart, so I thought if you wanted to spend a little while together, I'm free. We could grab lunch or... you know, whatever. Play it by ear."

He was quiet for a moment and then said, "Yeah. That sounds good. Where do you want me to pick you up?"

Ari gave Drexler a thumb's up. "How about we meet at Bowie's? I know she doesn't like us, but it's kind of becoming our place, you know?" She noticed that she had hooked her thumb in the belt loop of her jeans and was scuffing the gravel with the toe of her shoe. She was positive straight women didn't act like this when they talked to men, but for some reason playing the part made her act like a smitten teenager. "I was thinking maybe we could get a picnic and head back out to the beach you showed me yesterday. The one with the view of Canada and that cool shack?"

Drexler made a cutting motion across his throat but dropped his hand when he realized it was too late. Ari didn't care; she wanted to see how Jack would react when it was brought up.

"Sounds good," he said. "Give me fifteen, all right?"

"I'll be waiting for you, sexy." She hung up and pocketed the phone. "I need to be at Bowie's in fifteen minutes."

Drexler motioned for her to get back in the car. "How did he react when you mentioned the shack?"

"He didn't. He sounded off, though. Like he had just woken up or he was distracted by something. He might know something's wrong even if he doesn't know I found Penny's body."

Drexler drove her to Bowie's and parked on the evening

restaurant side, out of sight from the lunch side. They hashed out the plan on the drive: Ari would wait outside for Jack to arrive, invite him in to order their picnic, and Drexler would be waiting at a booth by the door. Once Jack was inside Drexler would block his exit and invite him to the station for a conversation about his knife.

Ari was in place near the front door when Jack's truck pulled up. He didn't park but instead pulled lengthwise across three empty spaces. Ari smiled and waved, but he kept the engine running and motioned her to come closer through the windshield. She hesitated and walked up to the passenger side window.

"Hey. Come on in, we can order some lunch."

"Why don't you get in? We can go for a drive."

Ari struggled to maintain her smile. "You don't want to have a picnic?"

"I want you to get into the truck."

The humor had faded from his voice. Ari risked looking back toward the restaurant, but she couldn't see through the glass.

"Mr. Corbett wants to see you."

Ari looked at him again. "Corbett?"

"He told me to pick you up. You want to see him, get in the truck. Right now."

She felt she didn't have any options, so she opened the door and climbed into the truck. Jack faced forward, grumpy and irritated as he pulled out of the parking lot. In the side mirror she saw Drexler come outside to watch as the truck drove away. Ari fastened her seatbelt and looked at Jack's belt. She couldn't see the knife, but it could have been on his other side or tucked into his boot. If he was smart he had thrown it into the harbor.

"So. You do a lot of work for Mr. Corbett?"

"You already know I do. Just be quiet. I said he wanted to talk to you. I don't."

Ari said, "So you figured out I'm not really interested in you?"

He slapped his hand on top of the steering wheel and gripped it hard enough to turn his knuckles white. "Mr. Corbett says you're gay."

Ari shrugged, grateful she would be able to drop the act. "Sorry for misleading you."

Jack huffed and shook his head. "I don't want to talk to you. Mr. Corbett's going to say everything that needs to be said."

The rest of the ride passed in silence. Ari watched in the side mirror to see if Sheriff Drexler was in pursuit, but she never saw his car. Corbett's front gate was open so Jack could pull straight in, but he stopped and got out of the truck to close the gate behind him. As soon as Jack was outside Ari bent down and groped under the seat for the knife. As she suspected, it was gone.

"Looking for the knife?" Jack asked as he climbed back into the cab. "Yeah, it's not there anymore."

Ari said, "Jack, you're in enough trouble as it is. Whatever you're doing here isn't going to help matters. The sheriff~"

"I thought I said I didn't want to talk to you anymore."

He drove her up to the house and motioned for her to get out. She wished she had some sort of weapon, or something she could fashion into a weapon. She followed Jack to the back porch again, where once again Corbett seemed to be cooking something on the grill. Thick clouds of white smoke rose from the hooded machine, accumulating under the overhang before being caught by the wind and trailing up into the sky. Whatever he was cooking smelled burnt. Worse than burnt, it smelled charred. She wrinkled her nose and waved a hand in front of her face.

Corbett was sitting at a steel-frame patio table with two empty glasses and a pitcher of iced tea in front of him. Seated to his right was Louis Fleming.

As she approached, Corbett pointed at the grill. "Jack, would you please tend to the steaks?"

"I think they're a little well-done," Ari said.

Corbett smiled and gestured for her to sit across from him. He wore a pale yellow Hawaiian shirt and white cargo pants, his feet bare under the table. He sat up straighter as Ari pulled out the chair across from him, and he smiled.

"Welcome back to my home, Miss Willow. I hope Jack didn't frighten you too much. I told him not to take no for an answer when he brought you here."

"No trouble," Ari said.

"Good. Jack was here when you called this morning. It seems we had a little... security issue that came up overnight and Jack wanted me to take care of it. Would you like some tea? I think I have some lemonade in the house if you'd prefer that."

Ari said, "It's a little late in the year for iced tea and lemonade, don't you think?"

"I don't believe in that. I don't believe in restricting a favorite drink to a certain time of the year. I say if you want something, take it."

"Dangerous philosophy."

He smiled. "From time to time." He poured himself a glass. He offered one to Louis, but he declined with a slight shake of his head. "I asked Jack to bring you here because it seems there's been a rather gruesome discovery on our little island. Penelope Alton was killed on her body was found up on the northern shore of the island. Terrible thing. I knew Penelope when she was little. Did you know that? I worked with her mother, and those little girls were always running around and getting into things." He smiled wistfully at the memory. "Horrible about what happened."

Ari said, "Yeah. Horrible." She looked at Jack, who had diminished the plume of smoke to a light curtain of white-gray.

"I'm going to tell you what happened Tuesday morning." Ari looked at Corbett. "It's a simple story. Jack and Penelope ran into each other in town. I don't know if she was legitimately attracted to him, or if she was just using him to get closer to me. You would know about that, wouldn't you?" He grinned. "Either way, poor Jack thought her interest was genuine. He took her out into the woods and started getting amorous with her. She fought back and he tried to subdue her with a knife. He just wanted to scare her a little. But in the struggle, she got cut. He let her go, she ran, and by the time he found her, she had bled out. He came to me for help and of course I told him to do the right thing. Instead he tried to cover it up as best he could. I think we've seen that his best was hardly good enough."

Ari said, "Why was he here this morning?"

"He went out to check on the shack, as he has every night since he left the body there, and this time he saw a bunch of police surrounding the building. He came here to ask me what he should do. I advised him to go directly to the police and turn himself in."

"No." She narrowed her eyes. "You told him to pick me up and bring me here so you could lay everything out for me. Why?"

Corbett leaned forward. "This is the official version of what happened, Miss Willow. It closes the book on this little episode. Jack goes to jail for what he did, Phoebe Alton is mollified, and you can go back to enjoying what's left of your vacation with your girlfriend. Phoebe has closure, and everyone is happy. Especially the sheriff. He's wanted to pin something on Jack for a while. Can't do much better than a murder charge."

Ari crossed her arms. "You said that Jack came to you for help right after he killed Penny. But the last time I was here, you covered for him."

"I was still hoping he would do the right thing on his own. I hoped I wouldn't have to turn him in. But now, there's little choice." He sighed. "Jack has disappointed all of us. It's time he faced the consequences for his actions."

Ari took a deep breath. Now that the smoke had dissipated some, she could smell something pungent underneath it. Louis' phone chimed and, after looking at it, he stood up and walked away from the table. Corbett watched him go.

"That would be the front gate alerting him that the sheriff has come after you. Jack's going to turn himself in and this whole nasty ordeal will be behind us once and for all."

Ari said, "All tied up in a neat little bow."

Corbett shrugged. "The truth is tidy, Miss Willow. Lies are where things start to get messy. Now, if you want to catch a ride with the sheriff when he takes Mr. Granger to prison, you should probably get a move on." He stood up and finished his iced tea in one swallow. "But I haven't forgotten our deal. I kept up my side of it, even though you never had cause to visit my home. I want to know everything you can tell me about the *canidae* myth. It should be a very interesting conversation."

"Yeah. I'm sure it will be. Have a nice day, Mr. Corbett."

"And the same to you." Ari walked back to the corner of the house, and Jack fell in step beside her. She looked over at him and saw a half-dozen conflicting emotions playing out over his face. "You're taking a dive, aren't you? I mean, you definitely killed Penelope, so you deserve to be arrested for that. But Corbett's throwing you under the bus. He's trying to stop the investigation before it gets started. Tell me what he's hiding. What happens at that dock? Drugs? Guns?"

Jack stopped and crowded into her personal space. "You think I'm giving away my freedom for nothing? Mr. Corbett wanted me to shut up, and I'm going to do what he says. I have my reasons."

Ari said, "You can make another deal with the sheriff. A better deal."

He didn't telegraph his punch, he simply shot his arm out like a piston and slammed his fist into her gut. Ari dropped to one knee, struggling to inhale as he loomed over her.

"This all would've gone away if you had kept your big nose out of it. I wouldn't be going to jail, and Mr. Corbett..." He inhaled and let the air out slowly. "If the sheriff wasn't sitting outside the gate, I'd go back there and get some of the things from Mr. Corbett's barbeque, and I'd show you what I thought of your meddling."

Ari glared up at him, still too breathless to speak. He sneered and walked away, and she sagged against the side of Corbett's house as she clutched her stomach with one arm. Jack didn't look at her as he walked away, his hands balled into fists at his sides. He was a murderer, Ari believed that without hesitation. But she also knew he was a scapegoat. Corbett wanted her and the sheriff to give up and leave his operation alone and he was willing to kill for it.

She and Dale had two days left in their vacation. The smart and safe thing would be to walk away, let the island continue as it had been for years.

Unfortunately she'd never been a fan of the safe, easy thing. She straightened, grunted at the pain in her abdomen, and weakly followed Jack to the waiting police car.

CHAPTER NINETEEN

ARI STAYED at the police station while Jack was processed, sitting at an empty desk behind Lynne's station. When Drexler came back out she stood up and moved to intercept him before he reached his office. He saw her coming and stopped. "Jack has been printed and photographed, and Deputy Vaughn is taking his statement right now. This afternoon he'll be officially charged with the murder of Penelope Alton."

She refrained from mentioned they had met the newspaper's deadline. "Sheriff, you're going to hate me for this, but~"

"The case isn't closed?" He sighed and nodded. "I happen to agree with you, Miss Willow. Jack Granger was gift-wrapped and thrown in our faces. I show up on Wayne Corbett's property and he hands me a troublesome young man who is ready to confess? I'm surprised he didn't leave him on the front step with a bow on his head. The knife is in Jack's truck, and I believe it belongs to him and that it was used to commit the murder. I don't believe he took her out to the middle of the woods at the crack of dawn and tried to rape her." He rubbed his face and looked toward Lynne, then lowered his voice. "The case is officially closed with the department, Miss Willow."

She closed her eyes and felt dread closing in on her.

"But am I correct in assuming you're still under the employ of Phoebe Alton to find out what really happened to her sister?"

Ari perked up. "I am. I'm on the case until she's satisfied with my conclusion."

"If you want to waste your time investigating a closed case, be my guest. If you need any assistance, in an unofficial capacity, of course..."

"I'll let you know." She took the receipts out of her back pocket and held them up. "These are receipts from Wayne Corbett to Jack Granger. I found them in the glove compartment of his truck. Since you've impounded it to look for evidence of Penny's murder, you would have found them anyway. They prove Jack and Corbett have a professional relationship. I think that whatever the real motive for Penny's murder was, it involves that dock. And I think Corbett is the one behind all of it."

Drexler nodded as he shuffled through the receipts. "I'll keep these handy. Just in case. And I won't stand in your way, but I do want to be updated from time to time on what you're doing. I can have some rogue investigator running around the island without answering to me. Understood?"

"Yes, sir. Thank you."

He nodded and went into his office. When Ari passed the front desk, Lynne reached out and grabbed her arm. Her eyes were wide, and her lips had parted in an expression of genuine surprise. When she spoke, her voice was an awed whisper.

"He apologized to you!"

"What? When?"

"Just now!"

Ari looked toward the closed office door. "Was I here for that part?"

"I've worked for that man since I was in high school, okay? Trust me. That's as close as anyone's gotten to an apology after they've pissed him off as much as you did. You're... like... a god."

Ari grinned. "Nah. I just know how to play the alpha dog."

Lynne smiled. "You're neat."

Ari winked at her and left the building. She knew that taking down Corbett would be an uphill battle, but she didn't have to start from scratch. There had to be some truth to the lie, and that truth was that Jack Granger was Penny's murderer. His motive was wrong, though. Penny had only been half-naked because she was trying to get to the water in a last-ditch effort to survive. She had been attacked because she saw the exchange.

It occurred to her that with Jack in prison and his truck impounded, Corbett would need a new driver. Maybe the mysterious Passenger would be promoted to Driver, or Louis Fleming would get recruited. He didn't exactly seem like an errand boy but desperate times called for desperate measures. She gave up on speculating who would fill the void. There was every possibility Corbett had an entire stable of people he could call on for the job.

She took out her phone and called Dale to give her an update. She left out the part about being punched in the stomach, as she knew it would only make her worry, and asked about Phoebe.

"She's been in her room since we got back. I tried to get her to eat something but she wasn't hungry. I'll try again in a little while." She paused. "I can hear her crying. It's awful, Ari. I wish there was something I could do, but losing your sister..."

Ari said, "I know. I'm glad you're there for her."

"Are you coming back?"

"Not yet. I may be gone most of the day, actually. There's something I need to check out. Do you know what would smell like..." She thought back to the pungent odor she'd picked up under the smoke at Corbett's house and tried to categorize it. "Sewage, rotten eggs, and... bleach?"

Dale thought for a while, and then Ari heard the sound of typing. "Something disgusting, that's for certain. All three mixed together?"

"Yeah. I smelled it at Corbett's house. Both times I've been there, he's had the grill going. This time he wasn't even really pretending to cook something. He had some meat on the grill, but it had to have turned to charcoal by the time I showed up. I think he was trying to cover up the smell, but he didn't count on my nose."

"No one ever does, baby," Dale said. Suddenly her voice became excited. "Oh, wait. Sewage, rotten eggs, and bleach. Ari, you might have been smelling a meth lab."

Ari raised an eyebrow. "Meth? That makes sense. If he's moving meth across the border, it would be a big operation. Big enough to kill someone who had stumbled over the exchange."

"It would definitely be big enough to destroy Corbett's career if it came out," Dale said.

Ari said, "Without question. Okay, I'll call you later."

"Bye, puppy."

Ari walked to Bowie's restaurant. The lunch crowd was out in force, and Bowie was behind the counter in a t-shirt advertising something called Professor Blastoff. She looked up as Ari entered and her eyes widened, then she motioned for Ari to come around behind the counter. She placed a plate in front of a customer, listened and nodded at something he said, then gripped Ari's elbow and guided her back toward the kitchen.

"Do you do this will every new arrival to the island, or am I special?"

"Uhh. You're interesting, I'll say that." She crossed her arms and looked out into the dining room for any imminent needs. "I can't talk much because I have the rush going, but what the hell is going on? You come in, you have your gorgeous ginger girlfriend bringing you breakfast, and then you're going on dates with Jack Granger and dragging Sheriff Drexler around with you... what the hell is going on?"

"Well, since it's going to hit the papers tomorrow, Jack Granger just got arrested for killing Penelope Alton."

Bowie's eyes widened even further. "Get the hell out. Is the sheriff going to make it stick?"

"He confessed."

"Holy cow. So your whole thing with him yesterday was like a sting?"

Ari nodded. "Believe me, if I was going to give heterosexuality a try, I'd go for someone a little less onerous than Jack Granger for the experiment. I was trying to find evidence tying him to Wayne Corbett. I think he's up to something big, I just need to find the connection. I guessed you would be the one to come to for inside information. Is there a big drug problem here in town?"

Bowie furrowed her brow and crossed her arms. "Uh. Well, I'm sure there are drugs. There are drugs everywhere. Pot's legal now..."

"Right. I think Corbett's upgraded to meth. Have there been any problems on the island with it?"

"I... I don't know. Look, I don't want to talk about that sort of thing."

"Look, Bowie, the only person in any danger will be me."

Bowie chuckled nervously. "And me, if anything happens to you and that girl of yours finds out I was involved. It's one thing to help you take out a bad egg like Granger. Getting him behind bars helped the island."

"This will help the island, too."

"By getting us press as the meth capital of the Pacific Northwest? I don't know, Ariadne."

Ari said, "You care about the people of this island, Bowie. Corbett is using them like a shield. When Sheriff Drexler got close, Corbett threw Jack Granger at him like a fattened calf. Jack is a murderer, but Corbett either threatened him or coerced him into surrendering so the police would stop digging. He'll do whatever he has to if it means protecting his operation."

Bowie looked down at her feet. When she spoke again her voice was meek. "Corbett probably promised to give money to Jack's father. He's been in the hospital for a while now. Medical bills. That's probably how he got Jack to turn himself in."

Ari nodded. "Okay."

"Most of the meth that's cooked here goes out to Canada. But some of it sticks around. There's a resort on the eastern side of the island. You probably saw it when you were coming in. A lot of deals go down there. With all the tourists who come to the island, there's a built-in customer base. They buy their shit, get on a boat, and go back to wherever they came from. Corbett probably has people working the ferry lanes, hanging out at the resort, you know... working around the shops down there. Are you thinking you can get one of them to turn on Corbett?"

"That's the plan, yeah. Catch them in the act, then the sheriff can offer them a deal to hand over their supplier."

"I doubt you'll have much luck. You really think he'll send his people out today? Jack's cooling his heels in a jail cell, you're coming at him with all your guns a-blazing..."

"Damn, you're right. I'll think of something else." She looked at Bowie. "You're not thrown by the idea Corbett might be smuggling drugs. You knew, didn't you?"

She winced. "Oh, hell. Everyone on this island knows, or at least suspected. Where do you think he gets the flunkies to deal for him? High school dropouts or people too lazy and stupid to hold down real jobs. We only have two real industries on this island: tourism and Wayne Corbett. He supports local businesses. He bought a few shops downtown when they were about to go bankrupt and he kept them afloat until the owners could get back on their feet."

Ari said, "So if he goes to jail..."

Bowie shrugged. "The island might go down with him. Or it might not." She sighed and looked out at the people in the dining room. Someone held up an empty mug and she motioned she would be there in a minute. "We're resilient, we can fight if we have to. Maybe having Corbett as a guardian angel made us complacent for a few years. And I guess if we can't survive without dirty money, then maybe we don't deserve to survive."

"You'll still have the tourists."

Bowie smiled and nodded. "Yeah." Someone else motioned for her. "Ah, I have to go. I'm swamped. But hey." She put her hand on Ari's arm. "Forget what I said about the whole... everything, okay? Yeah, Corbett might be helping the economy, but that shit he brings in is destroying the people here. He needs to be taken down. We'll survive, or we'll adjust, or... just do what needs doing. Okay?"

"I will."

Bowie went back to work and Ari headed out. She did remember seeing the resort from the ferry, but she didn't want to make the trek out there on foot. She also wanted to stop by the cabin and check in with Dale and Phoebe to make sure everything was okay with them. With any luck Corbett would think he had gotten away by offering up his sacrificial lamb, but he wouldn't know for a while if the plan had worked. Ari agreed with Bowie that he would likely suspend his operations at least until Jack was officially charged and the story had broken. Hopefully that meant they would have a detente until morning.

That gave them the rest of the day to figure out how they were going to take him down.

CHAPTER TWENTY

WHEN ARI got back to the cabin, Dale was on her computer at the dinner table. Ari went straight to the kitchen and got a glass of juice, and Dale joined her as she drank it. "Hey. Did you walk all the way from town?" Ari nodded, and Dale rubbed her upper arm. "You've really been pushing yourself this week."

"I need a vacation from this vacation," Ari said.

Dale smiled but wasn't amused. She tightened her hand on Ari's shoulder and massaged the tense muscle. "You're going to be feeling this next week, puppy."

"Next week I won't have to worry about Corbett getting away with murder." She took Dale's hand to kiss the knuckles. "I'm fine right now. The last transformation I went through didn't hurt as bad as I expected, and Phoebe gave me some tips that I think will help in the long run."

"You push yourself this week and promise to take it easy next week. But next week comes along and you get another case, and you push yourself a little further. What happens when you get to the edge, Ari? One day you'll push yourself so far you won't be able to come back."

Ari said, "What happened to being here for me?"

Dale frowned. "I'll still be there for you. Ariadne, if you end up being a forty-year-old quadriplegic who can't even feed yourself, I'll be there for you. But if there's a way for you to avoid that pain, if there's something you're doing that's putting you in more pain, then you're damn right I'm going to say something."

"I was born without the wolf," Ari said, "but it's part of me now. I can't change that. I wouldn't change that."

"I wouldn't ask you to. I just think you need to be more careful."

Ari started to argue, but then she took Dale's hand to squeeze her fingers. "I'm scared, Dale. I'm scared of being a forty-year-old in a wheelchair who can't even get out of bed without help. I'm scared that in a couple of years your entire life is going to revolve around keeping me alive. If that happens..."

Dale tried to pull her hand away, but Ari held tight.

"If that happens..."

"No. Stop."

"If the wolf breaks me, I want you to do something about it." She looked into Dale's eyes. "If it gets to that point, I don't want to just exist and I don't want to be a burden to you. Hopefully we'll both be able to see it coming and we can make a plan, but–"

Dale put her arms around Ari's neck and kissed her lips and her cheeks. "I don't want you to suffer." She rested her cheek against Ari's. "I'll do what has to be done. When the time comes and there are no other options."

"Thank you."

Dale nodded and kissed Ari's neck. "But we'll keep looking for a solution until then. And part of that is being smart about how and when you transform. I'm not saying shun the wolf. We got a scary look at how that can backfire on us. But... Ari..."

"I know." She kissed the tip of Dale's nose. "I trusted you with my business. I trusted you with my heart. Why not my health? I love you."

"I love you, too. Have you eaten today?"

"Uh..."

"That means no, or not enough. Either way, there's stuff to make a sandwich in the fridge." She patted Ari's hip and stepped out of the embrace. "Help yourself."

"You're not going to make it for me?"

Dale snorted. "Keep dreaming, lady. I'm not your maid. I'm your secretary and your masseuse and your business manager, I'm your cheerleader and your girlfriend and your drug supplier, your research assistant and your psychiatrist, I am your coffee maker... but I'll be damned if I'm your sandwich-maker." She laughed as Ari dipped her and placed a kiss on both her cheeks.

"You forgot the most important thing you are."

"Hm?"

Ari kissed her lips. "You're Dale. That's all. Just Dale."

Dale grinned. "Well, that's certain a time-saver."

Ari made herself a sandwich and carried it to the table. Dale sat in front of the computer with Ari seated to her left. "Right now we need to focus on how to get Corbett. Drexler said he considers the case closed, but he made it clear that he won't stand in the way if I keep investigating."

"I've spent the day looking up the police records for the past two years. There's been a marked increase in drug arrests. Before it was legalized two years ago, most of the possession arrests were for pot. Since then it's been meth."

Ari said, "Corbett making his mark on the old hometown."

"Seems that way. I kept track of the people who were arrested with intent. I figure those will be the people Corbett uses to distribute, and since they got jail time for helping him, they might be more willing to turn against him."

"Great idea," Ari said. "Was Jack Granger on the list?"

Dale shook her head and passed the notepad to Ari. "No, but

maybe that's why he was still working up until this morning. If we can find some of the people on that list, we might be able to learn more about his operation."

The bedroom door opened as Ari was skimming the list. Phoebe had changed into a pair of shorts and a baggy sweater, her hair mussed from tossing and turning. She pushed it out of her face and smiled.

"Hello, Ariadne. I thought I heard your voice."

"Sorry. I hope we didn't disturb you."

"No, I wasn't asleep. Any news?"

Ari said, "Yes, actually. The man who killed your sister is in jail." Phoebe gripped the back of her chair and closed her eyes. "Jack Granger was arrested this morning and he gave a full confession. That part of this whole mess is over, at least."

"Thank you." She sniffled and smiled sadly. "Thank you so much. I can't believe you got him. I can never repay you for what you've done."

"It was our pleasure."

Phoebe took the seat across from Ari and looked at their work. "You said 'that part' of this whole mess is over. You're trying to find a way to stop Corbett."

Ari said, "We're doing what we can, yes."

"I want in."

Ari looked at Dale. "You don't have to do that."

"Yes, I do. In fact, that was one of the things I was thinking about. You may have caught her killer, but she still has unfinished business. She came to this island to take Corbett down. I want to help finish that. Now, I appreciate you stopping me from going after the boat half-cocked without a real plan. You made me sit down and think about whether it was really a good or a smart plan. Now that I've had time to reflect, I think it's not only good, I think it's necessary. We have to know where that boat is coming from if we want to cripple Corbett. We have to know where the drugs are going. Penny must have been trying to do the same thing, but I have something she didn't. I have backup."

Ari and Dale looked at each other.

"I don't know why Penny kept me in the dark. Maybe if she hadn't she would still be alive or we would both be dead. Either way, I can't just sit back and let you take all the risks. I have to finish what she started. For her, for our mother, and because it's the right thing to do."

Dale said, "You're positive you can follow them without being spotted?"

"We used to do it all the time just for fun, even during the day. We would chase boats and occasionally let them glimpse us. We got really careful so no one could get a picture of us. We got to play, and tourists got to go home with a story about seeing mermaids. And at night, the odds of them spotting me... they would have to have lights, and I highly doubt they would risk that when they're moving drugs."

"What makes you think they'll move tonight?" Dale said. "With all the heat from Drexler and Jack getting arrested, I'd imagine he would just go dark."

"The arrest just happened this morning," Ari said. "Unless Corbett took the risk of calling to warn whoever is on the other side, they're going to show up to get their drugs for the weekend. They might show up even if he called and told them to stay away. They wouldn't want to get caught shorthanded."

Phoebe said, "Exactly. And Jack's arrest could force them to put a hold on other drops until the heat dies down. Tonight could be the biggest drop they've done in a while, just to build up their supply, and it could be our last chance to catch them in the act. I can follow the boat underwater, and the wolf can follow the truck on land."

Dale said, "And I shall remain here and be useless!"

It was obvious she was joking, but Ari reached out and took her hand. "Don't say that."

"I was..."

"I know. Still. I wouldn't even consider this if you weren't backing us up. Judging by when I witnessed their exchange, we should be fine if we head out around midnight. How long can you tread water, Phoebe?"

"All night, if I have to. I'll be tired in the morning, but I've done it before."

Dale said, "It's twenty miles from here to the Canadian shore, and that's if they go straight around the curve of the island. If they have other drop sites on other islands, who knows how far you'll have to travel before you find their Canadian endpoint. Add in the round trip to get back home, you might be swimming a hundred miles before dawn. If you get winded..."

Phoebe smiled. "I swam here from Vancouver. It was easier than dealing with customs. I just shipped my stuff ahead and dove into the water. Mermaids are built for long-distance. Trust me, I'll be fine. But Ari's right. It's going to be good knowing you're on the shore in case we need help."

Ari said, "We'll coordinate from here, and Phoebe will leave from her cabin's dock. I'll be at the clearing so I can follow the truck when it heads out. Hopefully they'll go back to Corbett's place to drop off the money. Even if they don't, we'll find out their base of operations. Dale, you'll keep the police department on speed-dial. If you have any reason to think something's gone wrong, do not hesitate to call. We won't have any way to contact you, but once we're in place, you should drive somewhere you can keep an eye on Corbett's place. Out of sight, but close enough you would see any fireworks."

"Sounds good to me," Phoebe said.

"If we're going to be running around all night, we should all get some rest. Phoebe, I know it'll be tough, but..."

She smiled. "If there's one thing I think I can handle right now, it's sleeping." She pushed her chair back and stood up. "I expect a bill, just so you know. We went through the whole pageantry of me giving you a dollar to hire you, but without you I'd... I'd never have been this close to getting justice for my sister. I probably never would have seen her killer arrested. You sacrificed your vacation, and that's not fair. So I want to make sure you get what's coming to you."

Ari nodded. "We, uh, should wake up around eleven so we can get something to eat before heading out. Do you need longer than an hour?"

Phoebe said, "Why would I... oh. Waiting an hour before you go swimming?" She chuckled. "No, there's no need for that. An eleven o'clock wakeup call should be fine. Even if we can't bring Corbett down, this will be a success. Penny would have really liked you both, and she would be glad to know you picked up our cause."

Ari said, "We'll do our best to honor her."

Phoebe wished them a goodnight and went into her bedroom. When they were alone Ari got out of her chair and knelt next to Dale's. With her head in Dale's lap, she put her arms around Dale's waist and held tightly to her.

"Never useless. You're the only reason I'm useful."

"I know, puppy." She stroked Ari's hair. "Just a joke. A bad joke. Sit up." Ari lifted her head and Dale kissed her lips. "Let's go to bed. We have a big night ahead of us."

Ari stood up and held out her hand. Dale closed her laptop, squeezed Ari's hand, and let herself be led into the bedroom.

Ari fell asleep almost as soon as the blankets were drawn up over her, a product of all her long nights and early mornings. Dale held her as she slept, smiling whenever Ari unconsciously snuggled closer or nuzzled her neck or cheek in the middle of a dream. There were times when Ari, even in human form, could be fairly canine. Those moments were more frequent when she was asleep. Dale gently ran her hands over her partner's curves, light enough so she wouldn't disturb her sleep but firmly enough that she could map out any knots or tight places that might require a rubdown before she went out for their mission. She found twisted cables across the spread of Ari's shoulders, a tense coil in the small of her back, and she didn't even want to think about what she would find if she explored her arms and legs.

She kissed Ari's temple, her expression twisted with concern.

Part of their vacation had been a way to forget their troubles if just for a little while. Now it was all she could think about. This unexpected investigation hadn't required very much from the wolf, and even that small amount of transformation had left her curled up and trembling in the woods. If they went back to Seattle and she started changing on a regular basis, how long would it be before every transformation required a half day of recovery?

Dale intended to keep the promise she made, the promise to end Ari's life if and when the time came, but she had hoped it was some years-away fantasy. But at the rate Ari was deteriorating she was afraid this would be their final vacation together. Dale would gladly stay with Ari at that point, through the pain and the trails of having a paralyzed girlfriend. It didn't matter to her if she had to feed and bathe and clothe her. As long as Ari was there, Dale would be there to love her.

She kissed Ari's cheek and Ari moved her lips against Dale's neck in dream speak.

There had to be a solution. The pot was helping, she knew, but it wasn't a cure. It would only help her manage the pain, not eliminate it. Ari's body was still suffering every time she put it through a transformation. Tonight would be a big test; doing covert surveillance would add to her stress, and that could exacerbate the pain she felt in the morning. How many massages would it take to get her back to normal? How much pot would she have to smoke? How long would she lay in bed on the verge of tears before she could stand up or walk?

Dale moved her lips to Ari's ear and whispered, "I'm going to save you, Ariadne Willow. I don't know how, but I know the answer is out there. Whatever it is and whatever I have to do, I'm going to save your life."

Ari murmured contentedly against Dale's shoulder, and Dale stroked her hair to calm her back to sleep. She needed to get to sleep as well, if both Ari and Phoebe were going to count on her later that night.

She knew she wasn't useless, and she knew she shouldn't have even said it at the table. She did like that Ari had been so quick to jump to her defense, however. She was Dale Frye, and she was far from useless. She would keep Ariadne safe, no matter how long it took or how far she had to go.

CHAPTER TWENTY-ONE

THE OFFICE was empty and cold, and Ariadne couldn't remember what she was doing there. The window was blank and lifeless as if the world ended just beyond the glass. She moved to the door and stepped out into the waiting room. Dale's desk was completely bare. Her computer and knickknacks were gone and Ari felt a twinge of apprehension at their absence. The entire room felt abandoned and the only illumination came from a soft blue shaft of moonlight shining through the window.

Ari stepped out into the corridor without being aware she had moved. Something growled behind her and she turned to see the wolf at the end of an impossibly long hallway. She knew it was her wolf, knew it the way a mother would know her child, but the sight of it struck fear in her heart. It shouldn't have been separate from her.

"Don't," she said.

The wolf took a slow step forward, dragging its forepaws along the floor. It swayed from one side to the other as it moved but its eyes remained locked on her. She knew its thoughts as it stalked forward, whether it was because she knew it was a dream or just because it was a part of her. Either way she knew it blamed her for the pain it felt with every change. It blamed her, and it knew that destroying her was the only way to not feel pain.

Body mine, the wolf said with its low and wall-drumming growl.

"No. It's ours. You're a part of me. You can't get rid of me and I can't get rid of you."

Can try.

She heard howling outside as she began to retreat. The wolf bared its fangs and lunged at her, and Ari turned to run. The door behind her was locked tight. She turned just as the wolf leapt at her and she had no choice but to lift her arms and cross them in front of her. She hit the wolf in the throat and shoved it back. It hit the ground and scrambled to get back onto its feet, and Ari knew she wouldn't survive a fair fight. She threw herself down onto the animal and tried to force its mouth shut, but it snapped at her hand. When it pulled back it had taken the last three fingers of her hand.

Blood poured down and matted the wolf's fur as it snapped at her again. Ari flailed wildly at the beast but it sank its fangs into her forearm again. It whipped its head and Ari's flesh was torn. She cried out and felt something clap down onto her mouth. She twisted and craned her neck to get free and closed her teeth around fingers, but someone slapped her hard enough to daze her.

"Stop! Stop, stop, stop," Dale chanted. "Ariadne! Stop it!"

Her panic faded enough for her to open her eyes. Dale was on top of her backlit by the actual moonlight. She had one hand clamped tight over Ari's mouth while the other was stroking her hair. Somehow she had managed to get Ari's arms pinned to her side by straddling her torso and squeezing her thighs. It only took a moment before Ari's flailing ceased and she began breathing more normally. Once she was sure Ari was awake she tentatively moved her hand to Ari's cheek.

"You were having a nightmare," Dale whispered. "You were crying out, kicking..."

"Did I hurt you?"

"You kicked me in the shin."

Ari's eyes welled up. "I'm sorry."

"Sh. Are you okay? What do you need?"

"You." She squirmed free and put her arms around Dale to pull her down. "Just hold me." She pressed her face to Dale's chest and kissed her through her shirt.

Dale slid down Ari's body so she was straddling her waist instead of her chest. Ari stroked Dale's back and looked toward the wall they shared with the other bedroom. "Did I yell?"

"No. But you were whimpering and making noises like you might start."

"Did I bite you? Oh, hell..."
"No. No, it's fine. You... you nipped me a little bit. You've done worse during sex."

Ari said, "Dale, if I bite you—"

Dale shushed her. They both knew that if an adult was bitten by a *canidae* they would become infected, and eventually the change would be forced on them. They would be able to fight it for a few weeks but eventually the need would become too strong and they would try transforming into a wolf. The resulting trauma always proved fatal, and from all accounts the death was extraordinarily painful. Ari lived in fear of accidentally biting Dale and sentencing her to that awful death.

"It's not." She put her hands on Dale's shoulders and pushed her up so they could look into each other's eyes. "I can't infect you, Dale. I won't live with that."

Dale bent down and kissed Ari's nose, then her eyebrows. "We don't know what's going to happen, okay? You could get hit by a bus tomorrow. I could get cancer and you'll have to take care of me long before the wolf cripples you. Or, maybe more believably, one day you might piss off the wrong person and we won't be able to wriggle our way out of it." Ari turned away but Dale forced her to hold eye contact. "The future depends on what we do on our way to reach it. That's the only thing we can control. So instead of worrying every second, let's focus on right now."

Ari kissed Dale's chin. "Thank you."

"Sure."

"How long do we have before we're supposed to get going?"

Dale reached for her phone. The light from the screen shone across her face and Ari couldn't resist reaching up to touch one green-tinted cheek.

"About forty-five minutes."

"Do you want to go back to sleep?"

Dale shook her head as the light snapped off and cast them back into darkness. "No, it would just make it harder to get up. We can just lie here."

"I have a better idea." Ari kissed Dale's neck, her hands under the blanket easing down Dale's panties. Dale smiled and held on to Ari as she was rolled onto her back. "If I'm worried about biting you, maybe I just need to replace that mental image with something pleasant. Now. What could I do to you with my mouth that could replace that image?" She pretended to think, then smiled as an idea occurred to her. "Oh! I think I know..."

Dale chuckled and slid her hands under the pillow as Ari sank under the blankets.

Ari dressed in a V-neck top and drawstring pants, both items she could easily slip on and off. She and Dale had just gone out into the main room when Phoebe came out to join them. She was dressed similar to Ari, in a flowing dress under a lightweight blouse. Dale was the only one dressed for real surveillance, in black pants and a black jacket. She also wore an olive-drab cap, a gift from another *canidae*, and Ari tweaked the brim after tucking a few stray hairs in place underneath it.

"Are we ready to go?" Ari asked.

Phoebe nodded. "I'm as ready as I'll ever be."

Ari said, "Okay. We'll go through the woods. I'll be with you to the cabin, then I'll continue on to the private dock and Dale will take your car to stakeout Corbett's place. She would take ours, but he's seen it before. He might be watching for it. We should set some kind of time limit on how long we're willing to wait. There's every chance nothing will happen tonight."

Dale said, "We give it until three in the morning. Approximately, since I doubt either of you will be wearing watches. If they haven't made their move by then, I doubt they would do anything closer to dawn. They wouldn't want their drug-running boat crossing paths with fishermen and ferries full of tourists."

"Are there fishermen out here?" Ari asked.

Phoebe said, "There are fishermen everywhere. Trust me."

"Okay," Ari said. "So by three or three-thirty, if nothing happens we come back here to regroup."

"Sounds good to me," Phoebe said.

They headed out with Dale leading the way and Ari bringing up the rear. Dale had a flashlight that she only used sporadically so they wouldn't be spotted from the road or the water. Phoebe looked at Dale, twisted to look at Ari, and chuckled under her breath.

"What?"

"I just realized that if we play this wrong, the sheriff might arrest us for running drugs."

Ari said, "Or if he shows up at the wrong time he could just ship us to the circus. A mermaid and a werewolf would probably bring in a lot of tourist dollars."

"At least in that case Dale would get away."

Ari said, "Obviously you've never seen her knife-throwing skills."

Dale chuckled and said, "You're lucky you didn't say the bearded lady."

"I'm the last person to make fun of a woman with facial hair," Ari said.

They arrived at the Alton cabin and paused so Ari and Dale

could say goodbye. They kissed, and Dale whispered in Ari's ear, "Be safe, Ariadne."

"You too. You've done enough stakeouts to know what to do. And the sheriff's office is on speed-dial on your phone. Don't hesitate if you think you need his help."

"I won't." She kissed Ari again. "I love you."

"I love you, too."

Dale moved her lips to Ari's ear. "I love you, too, wolf. Keep her safe."

Ari closed her eyes and nuzzled Dale's cheek. They stepped apart and Ari adjusted the strap of the bag on her shoulder. She waved to Phoebe and crossed the cabin's backyard, disappearing into the darkness before she reached the trees. Dale watched until she was completely out of sight before she turned to Phoebe.

"Sorry to be all sappy in front of you."

"It's fine." Phoebe smiled and held out the keys, then pulled them back. "I just realized something. You only have Ari's word that I'm a mermaid. You've never actually seen any proof."

"Ari's word is all I need."

Phoebe nodded. "I respect that, but... wanna see?"

Dale grinned. "Really? I was under the impression it involved nudity."

"I'll change underwater. It'll be fine."

Dale hesitated. They were in a rush, but she couldn't deny she was very damn intrigued. She'd loved mermaids since she was a little girl. When would she have another opportunity to see one? Phoebe could apparently read her decision on her face and chuckled. "Come on. It'll be quick."

They walked out onto the dock. It stretched out far enough that Dale could see the town on the inner curve of the island's shore, just a sprinkling of lights as opposed to Seattle's aggressive gleam. Without the light pollution they were able to see a whole sea of stars overhead, and the moon was reflected in the water just beyond the end of the dock. Phoebe stripped out of her jacket, placed her keys on top of it so Dale could take them afterward, and stepped out of her shoes.

"I have to be completely submerged for a few seconds. Kind of a pain when you're in a hurry, but it's a blessing when it comes to rainstorms and having water spilled on your lap in a restaurant." She sat on the edge of the dock with her feet dangling in the water. "Okay. Be right back."

Dale anticipated how it would look but she still gasped as Phoebe pushed off and sank into the water. The water rippled around the spot where she had gone in, a cluster of bubbles riding the miniature waves. Dale watched and tried to quiet her anxiety that she should be leaping to the rescue. *She's not drowning. She's safe, she's fine, I don't need to save her.*

The water broke and Phoebe emerged, gripping the edge of the dock with both hands. Dale took a step back as Phoebe hauled herself up onto the planks, swinging her hips up and dropping her tail down with a wet splat. She pulled her blouse over her head and tossing it aside. She unbuttoned her skirt and pushed it down as well. She looked up at Dale and smoothed her hair back against her skull.

"Well? What do you think?"

"You're beautiful," Dale said.

Her tail was silver-blue and shone in the moonlight, its scales stretching up past the smooth spot where her navel should have been. Dale was initially surprised that Phoebe would completely strip down in front of her, but Phoebe's breasts were smooth and without nipples. Even in the dim light Dale could tell that all of her skin had taken on a teal or light blue sheen. Her fingers were connected by thin webs. Dale took it all in before she looked at Phoebe's face and saw her eyes had turned milky-white.

"Oh!"

"Oh, yeah. Third eyelid."

"Right," Dale said. "Of course. For swimming. Wow." She

chuckled and ran her eyes over her again from head to fin. "This is spectacular."

Phoebe laughed. "Says the woman who sleeps with a werewolf."

"It's still amazing. Does... does it hurt?"

"No. I just get in the water, cross my ankles, and it just happens."

"Wow. Thank you for showing me."

Phoebe nodded. "I don't show it to many people. It feels like I'm making a spectacle of myself or they're gawking, but after everything you've done, I wanted you to see."

Dale said, "It was very much appreciated. Good luck tonight."

"To you as well," Phoebe said. "Hopefully I'll see you in a few hours."

She fell backward off the dock and Dale moved to the edge in time to see her fin disappearing into the black. The water rippled with her passage and Dale followed it to see Phoebe surface a few dozen yards out. She waved and then dove again.

Dale chuckled and shook her head. "Unbelievably cool. Wow." She picked up Phoebe's keys off the dock and carried her clothes up to the shore where she could find them when she came back. It was hard to be the "normal" part of their trio, but she was hanging out with mermaids, and she was an esteemed guest at one of Seattle's most popular *canidae* bars. She supposed that made her more special than the average Jane on the street.

She flipped the keys up into her palm and hurried around the cabin to get the car. They all had a long night ahead of them, and she didn't want to be late to her part of it.

Chapter Twenty-Two

ARI CHECKED to make sure the clearing was empty before she undressed, folding her clothes and placing them in her bag. She still wasn't used to carrying a bag with clothes in it when she ran as the wolf, but on the island she didn't have access to any of her usual stashes. The alternative was to wind up across town completely naked looking for a way home. She supposed Bowie wouldn't turn her away if she needed to use the phone, but she would also want a story. Ari didn't have a good excuse, so she would make do with the bag until they got home.

She rolled her shoulders and tried not to think of her nightmare as she slipped into the transformation. She'd always had a love-hate relationship with the wolf, but she would never chose to give it up. She had been born half-hunter and half-*canidae*, and the two natures cancelled each other out to prevent her from transforming. There was a possibility her wolfish nature would have eventually overwhelmed her father's influence, but her mother didn't take the chance. She allowed a doctor to perform a dangerous blood transfer to eliminate any trace of her father.

No matter how she had come about getting the wolf, it had been part of her since she was a child. She was twelve or thirteen the first time she transformed, the terror and amazement that came with becoming another creature tainted by the pain. Even with all the bad nights and lingering aches that even Dale didn't know about, she wouldn't give up the wolf even if it was an option. She didn't think even the shadiest doctor had a procedure that would cut the wolf out of a *canidae*.

She dropped to one knee with her palms flat on the grass like a relay runner at the starting line. She closed her eyes and focused on the *canidae* side of her.

I don't know if you sent that nightmare to me, or if it was just my own anxiety. Whatever it was, I don't want to fight you anymore. You're a part of me. The pain isn't your fault. It's your problem as much as it is mine. I know it's not your fault. Help me.

She opened her eyes and saw her hands had changed into paws. She felt the transformation pass through the rest of her body, the cramps and convulsions that came with it. Her fingers dug into the soft dirt and, when they relaxed, her palms had turned to pads. She stood up on her hind legs and shook out her fur, stretching her muscles again in their new form. She walked closer to shore and looked out over the water. Even her heightened senses couldn't pick up any indication of Phoebe out in the water. That gave her hope that their mission had at least a small chance of success.

Ari walked deeper into the woods where she hoped she wouldn't be seen. She found a spot where she could watch the clearing, sank down with her forepaws extended in front of her, and prepared for a long wait that might amount to nothing. Even if Corbett's people didn't show up she didn't want to take the chance and miss them. She put her head down on her paws and waited.

Phoebe cut through the strong currents, her arms at her side with webbed fingers splayed as she swam in circles through the harbor. She had time to explore before the boat arrived and she dove down to the kelp reefs, swimming alongside the myriad species of fishes and creatures that most people didn't get a chance to see. The greenlings and rockfish were well used to mermaids in their territory, although they were rare, and they didn't bother investigating her as she moved through the water. She and Penny had gone diving their first night on the island and being below without her felt wrong and isolated.

The few people who knew about her true nature didn't truly understand what it was like for a mermaid. It wasn't just swimming; it was moving into a different world. Once she transformed from one to the other, she was far more at home underwater than she was on shore. She could breathe freely, she could see further, and the water became a different kind of atmosphere. She was lighter underwater, and she could move far more efficiently with just a flick of her tail and the push of her arms. It was closer to flying than what most humans considered swimming, and she propelled herself down toward the seafloor like a bird dive-bombing a field.

When Phoebe finally went back toward the surface she saw the lower hull of a boat turning wide in the harbor. She watched as it turned toward the private dock and knew it was her target. She bent at the waist and pushed her fin out behind her, using her hands as rudders to guide her pursuit. She breached a few yards from the boat's starboard side, only her eyes and nose above the waves as she watched the boat settle against the dock. Its men stepped out and secured it as a pair of headlights swept through the darkness from the island. One of the men on the boat lifted his hand in greeting, and his partner handed him a heavy duffel bag.

"Everything kosher?" one of the boat men asked as he stepped from the wooden dock to the muddy grass.

Ari had moved to a better spot to watch as a driver she didn't recognize and the man she thought of as Passenger stood in front of their truck. Their headlights were still on, but they only illuminated them from the shoulders down. They wore muddy jeans, heavy work boots, and matching jackets that did nothing to identify them to her. The new driver took a drag off his cigarette before he responded.

"We have to full-disclosure something."

The boat man stopped. "Something went south?"

"It's under control now, but the boss wanted to be sure we had everything out in the open. Our usual pick-up guy is in jail."

"Jesus, Ken."

The new driver, Ken, held up his hands. "Hold on. Just listen to me. That incident we had earlier this week, with the girl we caught watching us? We thought that was all settled, but she had a sister and the sister hired a private eye."

Boat Man laughed snidely. "Oh, just a private eye sniffing around, then?" He turned and started walking back to the boat.

"Wait! There's no reason to let this get in the way, all right? Our guy Jack, he took the fall. He was a standup guy and did the right thing. He confessed to her murder and the sheriff arrested him this morning. We should hold off for the rest of the weekend but after that it'll be business as usual again. Sheriff is happy, the private eye will be gone by Monday, the sister will have a killer to blame. No one wants this to come crashing down, all right? Least of all the boss. So let's just calm down, finish tonight, and then take a few days off. The boss gave us a little extra to get you through the weekend, no extra charge. Just as a show of good faith."

Boat Man hesitated as he considered the offer. Ari could see that he had at least two partners on the boat watching him, unaware of the conversation taking place but aware he seemed to be dithering. They knew something was amiss but they didn't know what and it was making them tense.

Finally Boat Man walked back to the truck. "Our boss is going to call yours and have a little talk about springing this on us last minute."

"We wanted to be sure that everything was dealt with before we rocked the boat."

The exchange happened quickly and quietly. It was done mostly in the dark, with the Boat Man using a handheld light to check the bags in the back of the truck before he slung the straps across his shoulder. He took four bags that seemed full to bursting and held out his hand to Ken.

"Let our boss know when the next drop should happen. No more of these surprises."

"No more surprises."

Boat Man nodded and walked back to the dock. Out in the bay, Ari heard a very quiet splashing sound. A fish, or Phoebe diving in anticipation of following the boat back to where it had come from? Either way the men didn't pay any attention to the sound. The man returned to his boat and the locals got back into their truck. Ari stood up and stretched her legs. She hoped they were going back to Corbett's house and she would only have to run a few miles, but there was a chance they would make rounds all over the island. She dreaded the thought of going all the way out to the resort on the other side of the island but she would do whatever was necessary to officially connect these deals to Corbett.

The truck backed out of the clearing and out onto the road. Once they were underway, Ari left the clearing and began a pursuit. She was able to keep up fairly easily at a loping gate. The truck was traveling slow and cautiously so they wouldn't attract the attention of any police patrols. She caught up to them at stoplights and, even when they turned corners or dropped out of sight behind a building, she was easily able to spot them on side roads. She was definitely a fan of tracking people in a small town; less traffic and more places to hide, plus enough wide open spaces that she could still see the truck even if she was on a side street.

She waited for the truck to roll away from a stop sign and hoped Phoebe was having an equally fortunate hunt.

Dale parked at the edge of town and consulted her map. Corbett's property sprawled out over quite a bit of space outside of town, and there were no other properties nearby where she could unobtrusively park to watch for trouble. The main house was in a triangular clearing, and a secondary clearing held something that looked like a garage. The entire place was completely closed off from the street. She could see in, but only if she parked in front of the gate like Ari did on her first visit. She had been hoping to be a bit more inconspicuous than that, but she understood she might not have a choice.

She drove past the property into the darkness on the far side of Corbett's house, putting him between the car and the town. She pulled onto the first access road she spotted, pulled to the side of the road, and got out. She knew Ari would have preferred her to stay safe in the car but it just wasn't an option. Besides, if she stayed in the car she risked someone spotting her and coming along to see if she was all right. Small towns meant the kindness of strangers who would be all too willing to help someone who seemed to be stranded with a dead engine. An abandoned vehicle wasn't much better, but at least she wouldn't be forced to come up with an excuse on the fly.

The trees were spaced widely enough that she could pick out a path between them without getting lost. The glow of Corbett's property - brightly lit despite the fact it was now after midnight - was a beacon to keep her on track. She could also see the road from where she was, so she had little fear of ending up lost. She swept her boot over the ground to make sure she didn't have to worry about anything worse than dead leaves and sticky mud before she crouched next to a tree.

It was cold but not uncomfortably so, but she still found herself tucking her hands into the sleeves of her coat whenever she could. Corbett's house seemed completely still despite the lights she could see in the front windows. On the east side of the building was a colonnade with small area lights that shone up on the potted flowers that stood between each column. Every now and then she saw movement through the curtains but it was impossible to tell if it was Corbett or one of his men. She understood he was a celebrity and, as such, he might have security who patrolled the grounds to make sure stalkers didn't show up to do precisely what she was doing. Hopefully if one showed up she would have enough warning to get away.

"Werewolf running all over the island, mermaid swimming a hundred miles behind a boat of drug dealers... why do I feel like I got the raw deal here?" She sighed and watched her breath rise out in front of her, then reached back and flipped her hood up as she continued to stand guard. She had brought her cupped hands in front of her face to blow warm air into them when a truck pulled up to the open gate and drove onto the grounds.

Ari was thankful when she realized the men were going directly to Corbett's house, but she still followed them just in case they planned to drive by. When they pulled through the gate she turned and ran through the woods where leaping the gate had a smaller chance of being spotted from the house. She heard the truck give a quick blat of its horn to announce its arrival. Ari transformed with a grunt of pain, flexing her fingers and rolling her neck to work out the creeping pains that threatened to take hold. She was dripping sweat, and she used the towel she had put in her bag to give herself a quick rubdown. By the time she was dressed she assumed anyone in the house had moved to the front door to greet their drug runners, so she took that as the perfect window of opportunity to leap the fence.

Directly ahead of her across thirty or forty yards of lawn, was the eastern colonnade of the house. The grill was still set up, but for the first time in her experience it wasn't in service. To her left was the garage with all of its bays closed. Ari kept her head low and ran across the grass, ducking behind the garage before she looked at the house to see if anyone had spotted her. The smell she assumed Corbett had been covering with the grill was now glaringly obvious and it made her eyes burn. He was in the process of cooking meth, and the cast-off smoke was circulating around his property. She wished she wasn't wearing a V-neck so she could pull the material over her nose.

She took her phone out of the bag and turned on the camera. She took a few shots of the backyard to prove where she was, then crossed behind the garage to reach the back of Corbett's house. The reek got stronger and the burn spread from her eyes to her nose. She looked at the back of the house and saw the slanted double-doors of a cellar entrance. The aroma was so thick around that spot that she could almost see the fumes rising from below, and she checked the backyard to make sure she was still alone before she broke cover.

The door was unlocked and she hauled it open, still holding the phone in one hand as she looked down the stairs and saw Louis Fleming staring up at her.

"Miss Willow."

She dropped the door and ran, not bothering to look for a lock or something with which she could block the exit. If she could get to the wall, she was confident she could get up and over it while Fleming would have to go around. By the time he got to the woods she would already be the wolf. She made it halfway across the lawn before something sharp pinched her ass, and she cried out as her legs turned to rubber. She went down hard, her head bouncing off the turf as she reached back to pluck the feathered dart out of her jeans.

"Aw, thun uff ah bifth."

Fleming strolled up to her and grabbed the back of her collar to lift her up. She could barely move, but she got her hands up and fumbled with the clasp even as the leather cut off her air.

"Miss Willow. We were expecting you hours from now. But that's no matter. Mr. Corbett has had years to perfect his improvisation skills."

The collar came free and Ari fell again. Fleming tossed the collar aside, slipped his arm under hers, and pulled her up. She slumped against his side like a party girl who'd had one too many, her feet dragging behind her as he carried her back to the basement entrance. One of her eyes was closed; she couldn't even tell which one it was. Her tongue felt like a gag, and she knew her bottom lip was drooping enough that he had to worry about drool.

"Tran... kuh'd me..."

"Yes, Miss Willow. Why bother chasing a trespasser when we have all these lovely tranquilizers lying around? A bit brutal perhaps, but it gets the job done."

Going downstairs was terrifying; she spent the entire time afraid that he was going to drop her or that she was going to spontaneously swan dive to the concrete below. But she managed to reach the bottom without further injury. Fleming walked her to a long metal table, and she couldn't fight back as he swept her off her feet and placed her on the table.

"Whyooo do-un."

Fleming smiled as he prepared something she couldn't see. "I'm not doing anything, Miss Willow. I'm merely a facilitator." He placed a mask over her nose and mouth, blocking the stench of meth with a candy-sweet smell of gas. Ari's eyes rolled back almost immediately, but she heard Fleming's voice following her into the tunnel.

"You, Miss Willow, are going to tell us everything we ever wanted to know about *canidae*."

CHAPTER TWENTY-THREE

DALE WAS on her feet and had taken three running steps before her brain caught up with her body and forced it to stop. She spun and grabbed a tree, baring her teeth in a silent grimace of frustration as she slapped her palms against the trunk and felt shards of bark snapping off from the impact. For a moment it seemed as if everything was going perfectly. The truck arrived, honked, and Corbett came outside to greet the men. While they were talking was when all hell broke loose.

She had seen Ari run across the lawn away from the house, a hitch in her step from pain in her leg or hip, and then she went down. She went down hard, and for a moment Dale was positive she had been shot. But when the man appeared with a gun tucked against his side, Ari was moving and capable of standing upright as he walked her across the lawn. So shot with some kind of tranquilizer, most likely, and taken inside for god knew why.

Dale turned her back on the house, one of the hardest things she'd ever done, and forced herself to run back to the car. She told herself it was what Ari would tell her to do. If she stormed the house she would just get herself taken hostage and they'd both be up shit creek. She had to be smart, and she had to use the weapons at her disposal. Still, her eyes burned with tears as she got back in the car and started the engine.

She took a roundabout route back to town so she wouldn't have to pass in front of Corbett's house. They were probably so on edge that simply driving by would be considered suspicious. She waited until she was parked under a streetlight in town before she took out her phone and looked up the island's online directory. In Seattle she would have had no chance of success, but she figured small town plus an unusual name... and success. Sheriff Drexler's address was listed on the site, and she opened WorldMapp to find the street.

It was close, because everything on the island seemed close, and Dale managed to find the house in a matter of minutes. She planned to drive slowly and squint at house numbers in the dark to make sure she stopped at the right one, but she was spared the extra search when she saw his squad car parked in the driveway. There were no sidewalks, just drainage ditches running along the front of every lawn, and Dale parked with her tires in the soft mud.

She ran across the lawn as images of what Ari was going through running at the back of her mind. Torture, assault... worse. She didn't care about etiquette or politeness as she began pounding on the door, baring her teeth as she used the side of her hand to make the most noise. "Sheriff Drexler!"

A light came on in the main room and she backed away from the door, hands still balled into fists at her side as the door swung open. Drexler was wearing a white pajama shirt and gray sweatpants, eyeing her with a mixture of fury and confusion. His thick eyebrows knit together as he recognized her.

"Miss Frye?"

"He has her. Corbett, he... he has Ariadne. The drugs, they... made the drop-off and Ari followed them to his house, and he caught her. He has her."

Drexler processed the information in a flicker, his eyes darting down to the ground as he shifted from processing to planning. He nodded and motioned for her to come inside.

"I'll get my uniform on."

"Hurry."

He nodded and went down the hallway. Dale stood in the middle of his living room, hugging herself and trying not to cry, focusing instead on the framed photographs and awards hanging on either side of the sheriff's mantle. She was shaking with excess adrenaline, rocking her weight from one foot to the other. Down the hall she could hear Drexler speaking softly to someone, the opening and closing of a closet door, the sounds that he was moving as fast as he could to get ready, but she still wanted to tell him to hurry the hell up.

"Hey."

Dale startled at the voice and looked up to see a woman standing in the hallway to the bedroom. She was wearing a T-shirt several sizes too large for her, and Dale got the distinct impression she was naked underneath. Her dark hair was mussed and she looked extremely concerned.

"You're Ariadne's girlfriend?"

Dale nodded. "That's right."

"Tom's going to get her back. He's been growling and bitching about her all week, but I know he likes her. He respects people who challenge him, even if they get on his nerves. Especially then."

Dale couldn't help but smile. "He must love Ariadne, then."

The woman laughed gently. "I like Ariadne, too. I think she can take care of herself until you get to her."

"Thank you. When did you meet her?"

"I'm Lynne. I work at the police station."

Dale smiled. "Ari's mentioned you. She likes you, too."

Drexler came out of the bedroom in his uniform, instantly becoming a figure of authority rather than a middle-aged man pulled out of bed. Dale suddenly realized that she had caught him in bed with a much younger white employee, and she realized what a scandal that might be in a small town. She wanted to reassure them that she wouldn't say anything, but it seemed to carry more weight if she just didn't acknowledge it at all.

"I'll be back when I can," Drexler told Lynne. "Call Al. Let him know what's going on, get whoever is up to head out and back me up."

"I will."

They kissed quickly and whispered something to each other. Dale moved to the door and Drexler followed her out. She started for her car, but Drexler put a hand on her shoulder to guide her to the driveway.

"I think we might have more weight pulling up in this, wouldn't you say?"

"Oh... right. Yeah. Of course. Sorry."

"You have a lot on your mind. Get in. It's high time I did something about Mr. Corbett."

Ari kept her eyes closed when she came to, hoping she could gauge the situation before announcing she was awake. Unfortunately it was almost immediately clear that her position was distinctly horrible. She was still on the bed, but her wrists and ankles were held down by tight straps. She also felt them going across her waist and over her chest. She knew if she tried to move she would find herself completely pinned. She was still wearing the mask, and remnants of whatever gas Fleming used to knock her out were still evident around her mouth and nose. She breathed in enough traces to make her woozy when she finally opened her eyes.

Corbett was standing next to the table with an open book and a tray of tools. He glanced at her, smiled, and put a marker in his book before closing it.

"Hello, Ariadne. Don't bother trying to break the restraints. Even if you were at full strength it would be questionable. I want to apologize for how roughly you were brought here, but you did trespass on my property. If we could have done this in a more civilized manner perhaps you would have been spared the trauma." He shrugged and walked to the foot of the table. "I know you were only baiting me when you brought up *canidae*. You thought I was guilty and you would never have to make good on the promise, but it was a carrot I couldn't resist snatching up. You were right, and it worked, but you really shouldn't have planted the idea in my head."

Ari watched him with heavy-lidded eyes. It was all she could do to stay awake, but she wouldn't show weakness by passing out while he was watching her.

"Have you ever read Karl Magnusson's collection of essays regarding *canidae* in the modern world? I doubt you have. There's only the original copy, in Frankfurt, and it was hell just to get my hands on it. They wouldn't even let me take pictures of it. But it's the only article on so-called werewolves I've ever heard of that's devoid of myth and fear-mongering. It truly explores the plight of the *canidae* through history.

"It's devastating, really. Did you know your kind has been around for nearly as long as humans? You were the first shifters. A perfect marriage of man and nature. Of course, you were 'other,' and that made you frightening and dangerous. You were called monsters and eaters of children. You were forced to hide yourselves and wear human masks... that's not what you are, Ariadne Willow. You're not human. That isn't an insult, it's simply the truth. There have always been two species at the top of the food chain. You're just better at hiding. You aren't superior to us, but you're not below us either."

Ari blinked slowly, struggling to stay conscious. Her throat was raw and her eyes were tearing up. The scariest thing about Corbett's speech wasn't what he was saying but the fervor she could see in his face as he talked about her people.

"My goal is to help. That's all. I want to take away the stigma for your people. You hide and cower and you're hunted simply for being what you are. You can't even seek real medical help for fear of being discovered so you rely on back alley medicine and disgraced doctors. The fact you've survived into the twenty-first century is a testament to your tenacity."

Ari tried to speak behind the mask, but Corbett stopped her. He had stepped up to her right arm and pressed something cold against her shoulder. She made a wordless sound of distress and cringed away from him, but he pressed her back to the table.

"Don't speak. This will go much easier if you don't speak." He pulled and she realized he was measuring her arm. "I don't know if we can force you to change into the wolf for us. I hope you will agree to change for us without coercion. I want to get a comprehensive assessment of what happens when you become the wolf. Do your arms compress, are your legs the same length, and if not, where does the excess mass go? So many questions that need to be answered, so many mysteries about a *canidae*'s basic health. You could change the course of history for your people, Ariadne. You could be the Rosetta stone of wolf health. Can you imagine that? Millions of wolves finally able to seek medical help, or receive treatment, all because of you."

"You'll kill me," she slurred.

Corbett stopped and rested his hand on the edge of the table. "Science requires sacrifice. I am sorry. I have to be thorough, and that requires a dissection."

Ari's heart pounded as she scanned her eyes across the room looking for some last minute savior, some way out, but nothing presented itself.

"We'll discover how your muscles and bones interact during a transformation. We'll be able to study the way a human frame becomes lupine. Think of how this would change life for every *canidae* in the world."

"I'm broken," she whispered. "I'm sick. Wrong. You won't learn anything from me." Her words were slurred, but she struggled to make them clear. "Nothing you learn from me will be helpful."

"We'll put you under for the more painful things, but I'm afraid there are some procedures you must be conscious for. I apologize for that and I'll do my best to manage your pain, but at certain point pain medication skews the results."

"You're going to kill me," she repeated.

"An unfortunate consequence for the greater good."

He walked around the head of the table to measure her other arm, made a note, and then began on her legs. "I'll eventually have to remove your clothing. I want you to know my interest is analytical rather than prurient. I won't do you that indignity in your final hours."

Ari couldn't help but laugh. "What a prince."

He started to respond, but the phone he was using to keep track of her details chirped in his hand. He read something on the screen and scowled. "Oh, what is it now..." He put down his measuring tape and bent down to look at the machine feeding her with gas. He turned a dial and, with a hiss, the mask began to fill again. "I'll be right back. Pleasant dreams, Miss Willow."

She tried to fight the effects, but her eyes closed as her head lolled heavily to one side. She heard a door open and close, and Corbett's heavy footsteps on the stairs. She parted her lips to see if she could shout for help, but her tongue had become useless. Cotton closed around her senses and she slipped back into the comfort of unconsciousness.

The lights of Drexler's cruiser washed across the lawn, mixing with the yellow glow of his security lights to make the front of the house look unusually festive. Drexler was on the porch with Fleming while Dale remained halfway between the parked car and the front door. The sheriff had wanted her to stay in the car, and this was their compromise. Fleming had unequivocally denied the fact Ari was there, that they had partaken of any sort of drug deal, and basically anything else Dale had claimed. The truck was still parked in front of Drexler's car, but that in and of itself wasn't suspicious. Drexler finally demanded to speak with the owner of the house and refused to budge until he did.

Fleming sent a text, and a few minutes later Corbett arrived. "Sheriff Drexler. Sorry about that, I was just getting ready for bed." He looked at Dale without interest or curiosity. "To what do I owe this surprise visit?"

"I have reason to believe that you're holding someone against their will."

Corbett's face spread into a charming smile. "You're kidding. You think I abducted someone?" He looked at Dale again. "Did she tell you that? Who is that, anyway?"

"You're not talking to her, you're talking to me."

"Is she connected to that private investigator that's been harassing me all week? Murder, drugs, and now abduction... Sheriff, I'm sorry, but these women are obviously disturbed. Maybe they're fans, maybe they're stalking me, but I want them both arrested."

Drexler said, "If there's no merit to their claims, I'll reassess the situation. Right now I need to confirm that you're not holding anyone against their will in there."

"This is absurd. You're going to search my home to see if..." He put his hands on his hips. "I'm sorry, Sheriff Drexler, but no. I won't let you invade my privacy on the word of these disturbed women."

Dale looked toward the side lawn, frustrated, and her eyes settled on something small and black lying on the grass. "Sheriff..." She was already running toward it when Drexler yelled at her to stay where she was. Corbett shouted something as well but Dale wasn't listening. She stooped and picked up the collar from where Ari had dropped it, spinning to present it to Corbett.

"This is Ari's collar."

"I have seen her wearing that," Drexler said, turning to Corbett as his hand drifted to his holster. "Why is it on your property, Mr. Corbett?"

Corbett shook his head slowly. "I haven't the slightest~"

Dale didn't care to hear any more of his lies. She turned and dashed toward the house. Corbett shouted after her, and Drexler said, "Miss Frye, wait!" but she ignored them both. She clutched Ari's collar tightly in her hand as she ran in the direction Fleming had carried Ari's limp form and hoped she found an open door before they caught up with her.

The wolf was in charge. Ari was vaguely aware that the wolf part of her brain was fighting the drug, but she was still in human form. She couldn't change while she was strapped so tightly to the table. She opened her eyes and blinked slowly. She was a trapped animal who needed to escape, and everyone knew animals could chew off their own leg if it was caught in a trap. She looked down at her left hand. It would come with unbelievable pain and hopefully-temporary paralysis, but it was better than staying to be Corbett's guinea pig. She transformed her hand into a paw, her cry of anguish muffled by the mask. She pulled it free of the strap, the bones still throbbing from their change when she forced it back into a hand.

Tears flowed freely down her face as she fumbled with the mask. She pulled it away and gasped at the cold and untainted air before she moved her now-numb hand to undo the other straps. She released the one across her chest, then her other arm, and she sat up to free her legs. Her entire body was shaking, and she was drenched with sweat as she pulled her legs free. She rolled onto her side, fell off the edge of the table, and hit the ground hard.

"Ariadne!"

She tried to push herself up but her arms were too weak. Someone ran up to her and the wolf almost fought simply out of instinct before it recognized Dale's scent. She was gathered in Dale's arms, whimpering as she held tightly to her. She looked up as Corbett came downstairs, baring her teeth and stopping just short of barking when Drexler appeared behind him. The sheriff looked at Ari, then clapped his hand on Corbett's shoulder and slammed him hard against the wall.

"Wayne Corbett, you are under arrest..."

Ari nuzzled against Dale's shirt, trembling and whimpering under her breath, still too fog-minded to take control of her body. She wasn't too concerned, however. She would let the wolf drive for an hour or two. She knew as long as Dale was with her, she would be safe. Dale stroked her hair and whispered that she was safe, and Ari believed it. Her left hand was curled in her lap, the wrist bent inward so drastically that the thumb was almost touching her forearm. Her forefinger and ring finger were touching, the pinkie stood out to one side, and her middle finger arched over them all like a crane.

Dale closed her hand around the twisted fingers and kissed Ari's hair, repeating her mantra that they would be all right. Even now, after everything, Ari still could still believe it when it was coming from her.

CHAPTER TWENTY-FOUR

ARI CAME to her senses in the back of the sheriff's car, her left hand still cradled in her lap. Dale was holding her, and Ari turned and breathed deeply before she kissed the corner of Dale's eyebrow. "What happened? Where did you come from?"

Dale lifted her head. "Ari? Are you back, puppy?" She looked into Ari's eyes. "You were the wolf when we found you. Not... in form, but I could see that you weren't entirely there. The wolf took over. I think it saved your life."

The memory came back in bits and pieces. "The drugs knocked me out, but the wolf took over. She did save me. With a lot of help from you. Thank you."

Dale tried to smile, but it collapsed into a near sob before forming completely. "Oh, Ari." They kissed. "I'm so glad you're okay. When I saw you go down, I thought he'd shot you."

"You were watching?" Dale nodded. "I didn't see you. Sneaky girl."

"Don't change the subject."

"I'm not."

Dale stroked Ari's cheek and kissed her again. "I'm not going to be the person who says you can't do this job because it's too dangerous and I can't stand it. But I am going to say you can't do it without me. If you're going to be a private investigator, I'm going to be by your side. Every case, from now until you retire."

"Twist my arm," Ari said with a grin. "I mean, Bitches Investigation. It's always been plural."

"It has, hasn't it? I'm still your receptionist, I answer the phone and file the files, I make the coffee. But we're partners. All the way. Equals."

Ari chuckled. "When were we not? I'm the one who thought you should get licensed."

"I still don't think I want to go that far. I just want to be more than your assistant."

"You are. Always."

Dale smiled and stroked Ari's twisted hand. "This..."

"I had to slip it out of the restraints," Ari remembered. "The wolf turned my hand into a paw, then back. Two transformations in about ten seconds."

"Ari..."

"Don't yell at me. The wolf was driving."

"I wasn't going to yell." She tried to ease the fingers apart, but Ari hissed in pain. "Okay. Okay." She pushed her thumb under the fingers and rubbed the palm. "How is that?"

Ari nodded. "A little better."

Sheriff Drexler approached. "How are you feeling, Miss Willow?"

"A little better," she said again. "I'm not sure what he knocked me out with, but it was... it was strong. I'm still a little woozy."

"You're lucky that's all you were."

"Did he say anything about why he grabbed me?"

Drexler shook his head. "He's keeping his mouth shut for now, but we don't need him to talk. I saw that set-up." He looked at the house with a grimace of disgust. "Whatever he had planned for you down there, it was bad. We don't need to know his reasons. Probably wouldn't even make sense to us if we took the time to drag it out of him. We've got plenty to keep him in jail for a while even without that."

Ari said, "The meth lab?"

"Under his garage. Speaking of, I just got a call from the station. Seems Penelope Alton's sister showed up looking like a drowned rat. She says she knows where the drop-offs happen on the Canadian side, so I get to deal with the Canucks on this. That'll be a pain in my ass, thanks to you."

"Sorry, Sheriff."

"Yeah, I'll bet you are." He held out his hand. "There was a lot here I didn't want to see, Miss Willow. I made you go it alone, and that almost cost you a helluva lot. I hope you'll accept my apology."

Ari said, "None needed, sir."

He moved his hand to Dale. "Then to you, ma'am. I apologize for putting your girl in danger."

Dale accepted his hand. "All is forgiven, Sheriff. Besides, do you really think you could have stopped her? You tried your best to get her to just enjoy her vacation, and what good did it do?"

"Smart woman. Look, Donny is going to be here soon. I want her to check you out, just to make sure that gas didn't do any subtle harm. I don't want you fighting her, you hear me?"

"I'll try to behave," Ari said.

"Good." He thumped the top of the car and walked back to speak to Deputy Vaughn.

Ari put her head on Dale's shoulder and closed her eyes. "Joke's on you."

"Hm?"

"I don't think I could do this without you by my side. Ha ha, you got the raw end of the deal."

Dale laughed. "Sure. You go on thinking that, sucker."

Ari suddenly moved her hand up to her throat. "Oh, shit. My collar. I lost my collar somewhere." She sat up and looked out the window. "I think it was on the lawn..."

"Puppy... here. It's right here." Dale took it out of her pocket. "Dropping this was a good thing. It was how I convinced the sheriff you were inside."

Ari moved her hair out of the way. "Put it back on me, please."

Dale obliged, finding the right hole for the collar to be snug but not too tight. When it was back in place she bent down and kissed the leather, then Ari's skin.

"Better than some dumb diamond ring," Dale said.

"Light years better," Ari agreed, covering Dale's bracelet with her hand.

The rest of the night was a barrage of conversations, with deputies and Sheriff Drexler, recounting everything that had happened. Donny showed up looking like she had been yanked out of bed moments earlier, but she was still impeccably dressed. Her hair was mussed and her glasses were in her pocket rather than perched on her nose. She spoke to Drexler and then went to the cruiser where Ari and Dale were waiting.

"Miss Willow. Hello. Hi. Sorry to hear about, um..." She gestured at the house. "I've only heard bits and pieces, but I'm sure it was harrowing. I can't imagine." She shook her head. "I'll make this as brief and painless as I can. I'm sure you're eager to get home and get some sleep."

Ari said, "Listen... as a physician, there's... you may notice I'm not..."

"Be quiet, please." Donny placed her medical bag on the grass next to her. "I examined Miss Alton and I noticed some peculiarities. I hear her sister showed up soaking wet. Are you like them?"

"I'm... related. Different, but in the same arena."

Donny touched her face, patted her pockets, and put her glasses on once they had been located. "I've seen many variety of people on my table, Miss Willow. I've seen men who present as women, and I've seen vice versa." She touched the loose knot of her tie and cleared her throat. "I more than most know that it's the face you show the world that matters. Everything else? The things you keep hidden for one reason or another? Well, that's nobody's business."

Ari smiled. "Thank you, Donny."

"Of course." She looked at Dale, smiled a quick greeting, and then began her examination.

Drexler personally drove Ari and Dale back to the cabin. It was dawn by the time he parked in front of the porch, the new day's sunlight cutting through the canopy to make the clearing glow. The windows of the cabin reflected the wispy clouds overhead, and Ari didn't know if she'd ever seen a place look so inviting in her life. Dale got out of the car first and helped Ari stand, slipping under her arm to act as a crutch. Drexler rolled down his window.

"Try to stay out of trouble for the rest of your stay, Miss Willow. We have a lot of long days ahead of us, and I can't be running around cleaning up your messes."

Ari smiled. "I'll do my best, Sheriff."

He nodded to her, waved goodbye to Dale, and backed out of the driveway. When they reached the porch, the front door opened and Phoebe came out. She had showered and dressed, her hair bundled and draped over one shoulder as she looked at them.

"Is it really over?"

Ari said, "It is."

"I want... c-can you say..."

"Wayne Francis Corbett is under arrest for conspiracy to commit murder, abduction, attempted murder, and multiple drug charges. Penny came here to destroy his career. That's done. He's finished."

Phoebe stepped forward but then caught herself. "May I hug you? You look..."

"Hug me. Hugs don't hurt."

Phoebe hugged her and Dale both. "Thank you. I can't even begin to... thank you."

Ari said, "It was our pleasure."

Dale said, "Will you help me get her inside...?"

"Of course."

She took Ari's other side and together they helped her up the steps and into the cabin. They helped her into bed and Ari passed out almost immediately. She was exhausted, nauseated, and in agony. Too many transformations in too short a time, the drugs, the stress, everything combined to knock her out completely. She woke several times during the day, sometimes shaking so badly that the bed was knocking against the wall, and sometimes to dry-heave into a pot that was always quickly placed near her head when it was needed. Through all of her flickers of consciousness there was one constant: Dale never left her side.

When she finally woke for good, Dale was lying next to her and massaging the fingers of her left hand. The pinkie and ring finger were miraculously extended and without pain, and Dale was studiously working on the middle finger. Ari watched her for a moment before revealing she was awake.

"That's my favorite finger," she whispered.

Dale grinned. "I'm pretty fond of it, too."

Ari lifted her head and kissed Dale's neck. "I wish I could remember you swooping in to save me. Must have been pretty heroic."

"Please. I was fighting back tears the whole time. I was so sure we were too late."

"If you hadn't been there, no one could have gotten to me in time. You saved my life. I might be a werewolf, but you've been saving my life literally from the moment you came into it. I never knew what I would be without you, but now I know I would be dead if it wasn't for you."

Dale looked down at their joined hands. "Well, technically, you would never have been on the island this week if it wasn't for me, so-"

"Sh. You saved my life. You're not useless, you're the strongest and bravest person I've ever known. I'm lucky to have you in my life."

"Well," Dale said, "I have to be extra special to keep up with my wolf." She kissed Ari's lips, then looked down at their hands again. "How does that feel? Try moving your middle finger."

Ari carefully bent it, gasping quietly at the first twinge of pain. "It's okay. It's better."

Dale stroked the finger once more and then moved on to her forefinger. "It's getting worse."

"I know. If I had any other option, I wouldn't have done a partial transformation. I know those are stupid and dangerous and~"

"It's all getting worse, Ariadne. A year ago, I worried I might have to give you a rubdown after you changed. Now I'm worried you won't be able to stand up or move. I have nightmares about you lying next to a stash unable to call for help. I know that holding back the wolf would only make it worse in the long run, but honestly it's terrifying me. I don't want you to hurt."

"I know, baby," Ari whispered. She kissed Dale's forehead. She didn't want to promise they would find a solution, because honestly she had no idea what they were going to do. Time was running out. The day would come, and it would come soon, when she would be completely crippled in human form. "I'm scared, too."

They held each other while Dale continued to massage Ari's last finger. When she was finished Ari flexed her hand with only a twinge of pain in her wrist and the center of her palm. She knew that those final pangs would fade over the next few hours. She lifted her newly-capable hand to stroke Dale's cheek, brushing her thumb over Dale's bottom lip.

"Whatever happens, you and me, together."

Dale kissed the pad of Ari's thumb. "Always."

"You should sleep. Your night was as crazy as mine."

"Maybe not *as* crazy," Dale said as she nestled against Ari's chest. "I'm not overly tired, though. I think..."

Ari chuckled softly as Dale's voice trailed off into a sigh, and then her breathing deepened. Ari put her face in Dale's hair and breathed deeply. In the main room she could hear Phoebe moving around, trying to be quiet, and she was glad that the other woman had decided to stay with them even when the danger was past. "Phoebe might be a mermaid. I might be a werewolf. But you're Dale Elizabeth Frye, and that's a fucking amazing thing to be." She kissed the raised scar where Dale had survived a gunshot wound to the head and smiled. Dale was only human, and not special at all. That was what made her so unbelievably awe-inspiring. Ari closed her eyes and decided she would get some more sleep as well.

They finally returned to the world out of hunger, the smells of Phoebe's cooking too appealing for them to ignore any longer. Ari stopped short when she saw what Phoebe had created with the meager contents of the fridge and cupboards.

"Sorry," Phoebe said. "I told you cooking calms me down and I felt feeding you is the least I can do. So, uh, call it an early Thanksgiving."

"No apologies necessary," Ari said as she took a seat. She was ravenous now that she'd taken the time to heal. Her stomach made an embarrassingly loud noise as she began piling up her plate.

Dale said, "Sounds like you're still part wolf, puppy."

While they ate, Phoebe revealed she had been on the phone all day. "The sheriff charged Corbett with your kidnapping and the drug operation. Authorities on Vancouver Island have already started rounding up the people who were on the receiving end. And, um..."

She picked up her phone, brought the screen up, and passed it to Ari. "That's been all over social media today."

The Facebook post showed a promotional shot of Wayne Corbett standing on a boat, smiling into the camera, but the headline was nothing for him to smile about. "Conservationist and Animal Expert Wayne Corbett Arrested for Drugs, Kidnapping." The story continued on to reveal he was also under investigation for conspiracy to commit murder in the case of Penelope Alton, "the daughter of a scientist who once worked under Mr. Corbett."

Phoebe said, "As soon as Corbett was arrested, apparently Jack Granger started talking about a deal. He's going to reveal everything that happened to my sister."

"He might get leniency if he does that."

Phoebe nodded. "I know. But he'll still go to jail. And in return, the man who ruined our mother's life gets his grave dug a little deeper. I think Penny would make the same deal if the positions were reversed."

Ari passed the phone to Dale so she could read the article. "What are you going to do now?"

"The local funeral home offered to cremate her. So I'll let them do that, and then I'll take her home. I'll give her boyfriend a chance to say goodbye, and then I'll spread her ashes somewhere with lots of warm water." She smiled sadly. "It's where she would want to be. And you two. I don't know how I would have gotten through this week without you. I'm going to make sure you get properly compensated for... for everything you went through on Penny's behalf. Especially you, Ariadne."

Ari knew there was no sense in protesting, so she just nodded.

"I'll probably head out tomorrow. I know Evan is going to need the support. Besides, I think you two have more than earned to spend the rest of your vacation by yourselves."

Ari grinned. "Yeah, we wrapped everything up with almost a whole day to spare. Pretty efficient, now that I think about it."

Dale chuckled. "I hope you keep in touch with us after this. Let us know how you're doing."

"Of course," Phoebe said. "And if anyone I know ever needs a private eye, I'll definitely give them your card."

Ari said, "For now, let's just enjoy the fact that Wayne Fucking Corbett is finally going to pay for what he did, and enjoy our dinner." She lifted her cup. "To Penelope."

"To Penelope," Phoebe replied, tapping her cup against Ari's and Dale's.

CHAPTER TWENTY-FIVE

PHOEBE LEFT the island on Sunday morning. Ari and Dale drove her to the ferry lanes and said their goodbyes, lingering on the boardwalk until the ferry came and took her home. When she was gone they got in their car to go back to the cabin, but a police car pulled up behind them and flashed its lights. Ari groaned and rolled her eyes when she saw Drexler get out and stroll up to the driver's side window.

"You've gotta be kidding me."

Dale rolled down the window and Drexler leaned down to look in. "Sorry, Miss Willow. Couldn't resist. Call it old times' sake. You're not leaving, are you?"

"Tomorrow," Ari said.

"Good. You can refuse to come with me, but there's someone at the station who is insisting on having a word with you."

Ari frowned. "Corbett?"

Drexler nodded. "He says he's willing to confess to a load of the charges, but only if he can speak with you in private. It's almost as if he knew exactly what to say to give me a headache."

Ari looked at Dale and shrugged. "I guess I'm willing."

"This man put you through a lot the other night, Miss Willow. If you want to back out we can just tell him he's in no position to make demands."

"I want to hear what he has to say."

Drexler tapped the top of the car. "Okay then. You can follow me back. We can wrap this up right now."

Dale watched him go. "What do you think Corbett wants with you?"

"I don't know. But I know if I didn't go it would drive me crazy wondering."

"Me too."

They followed Drexler to the station, and found Lynne holding down the fort at her desk. "Good morning again, Ariadne," Lynne said. She looked past Ari at Dale and smiled bashfully as she averted her gaze. Ari looked between the two, aware that there was something going on but not quite sure of the details. They were both smiling, so she knew it wasn't bad, but she made a mental note to grill Dale about it when they were alone.

"Good morning, Lynne. Everything okay?"

Lynne nodded and fiddled with her pencil. "Everything's great. Hello, Miss Frye."

"Dale, please."

Lynne's smile widened and she nodded. "Dale, then."

They followed Drexler through the bullpen and Ari looked at Dale with a raised eyebrow. Dale chuckled and rubbed Ari's shoulder. "I'll tell you later."

Drexler led them to the holding cell where Ari had spent the night. Corbett was sitting on the cot, dressed in a drab brown jumpsuit. He was unshaven and looked as if he'd aged ten years in the day he'd been incarcerated, but he got to his feet as soon as he saw who was visiting him. Drexler stood between Ari and the bars.

"Mr. Corbett, Miss Willow has agreed to meet with you. This meeting will be completely private, as requested, but if you do anything..."

"I just want to talk to her. Nothing untoward, I assure you."

Drexler nodded and looked at Dale.

"Dale stays," Ari said.

Drexler said, "Whatever you want. I'll be right outside."

Once the door was closed, Corbett smiled at Ari and crossed his arms over his chest. "I'm sure you've been wondering what I'm going to say."

"Not particularly."

He looked at Dale. "And I assume she knows about you...? Your nature, I mean?"

Ari nodded. "She knows."

"I wanted to reassure you that I'm not going to say anything. I suppose I could try for an insanity defense by claiming I thought you were a werewolf, but I won't do that. Do you know why?"

"Because you think there's a chance you'll get out of there one day, and you want to be the one who makes the discovery. You want the credit for proving the existence of *canidae* and you're not going to risk that by shooting your mouth off."

Corbett chuckled. "You know me well. And if you know me that well, you know that I can afford some very good lawyers. I can make deals. I can get time off for good behavior. My career might be in shambles now, but in a few years when I get out? People will barely even remember why I was arrested. They'll be ready to forgive me. Martha Stewart, Michael Vick. People forget. Especially if I make my comeback with the world-shattering news that werewolves actually exist."

Ari didn't break her gaze. "Ambitious, Mr. Corbett."

He raised an eyebrow. "It won't take me long to prove. After all, now I know exactly where I can find a guinea pig. Bitches

Investigations, wasn't it?" He nodded and chuckled to himself. "Yeah... and Ariadne Willow is a pretty unusual name. Shouldn't be too difficult to find you."

Ari stepped closer to the bars. "Come after me, Mr. Corbett. See what happens."

They stared each other down, neither of them willing to lose the game of chicken.

"I'll kill you."

Ari and Corbett both turned to look at Dale. She didn't seem angry, or trembling with rage. She looked calm, which Ari found even more unsettling than red-faced fury.

"Dale...?"

"If he comes after you again, Ari, I'll kill him. What you were willing to do to her, just to further your own celebrity? If I ever see your face outside of a jail or a television screen, I'll kill you. I'm not threatening you, Wayne. I'm just telling you what is going to happen in no uncertain terms. I won't give you a chance to hurt her again. So what will happen if I see you again?"

He stared at her in shock.

"I asked you a question, Wayne."

"You'll try to kill me."

Dale smiled. "I won't try to do anything, Wayne." She pointed at Ari. "This woman has better things to do with her life than deal with your revenge bullshit. We're not going to walk out of here with you thinking you've scared her. So Wayne. You could get out of here tomorrow with your fancy lawyers, or you could get out of here in twenty years. It doesn't matter. If you show up in Ariadne Willow's life, what will I do?"

He met her gaze. "You'll kill me."

"I'm glad we had this talk, Mr. Corbett." She turned to Ari. "Did you want to say anything?"

"Not a damn thing." Ari didn't try to suppress her prideful grin as she linked her arm with Dale's. "Goodbye, Mr. Corbett."

He said, "I could still tell the world what I know about you!"

Ari laughed and faced him. "After you spent decades of your life researching *canidae*, digging up whatever you could find on us, you would let someone else take all the credit and get all the glory? You know what, Wayne? That might actually be worth it. Have a nice life, Wayne."

They walked out arm-in-arm. Drexler was standing guard outside the door and turned to look at them. "Everything went okay, then?"

"Absolutely," Ari said. "Although remind me to stay on Dale's good side."

Dale chuckled, and even Drexler cracked a smile. "Miss Willow, since you're leaving tomorrow, I hope you go the rest of your vacation without seeing me again."

"Don't take this the wrong way, Sheriff, but that would be amazing." She held out her hand, and he shook it. "Let us know when we need to be back for the trial."

"Will do. Enjoy the rest of your time here."

Ari nodded and led Dale out of the jail. "So, we should enjoy our last day on the island. Want to go whale-watching? Maybe take a scenic drive along the coast? Oh, I think there's a boating museum somewhere in town."

Dale tightened her grip on Ari's arm. "Take me home, and then just take me."

Ari laughed. "Sounds like a must-see attraction..."

After the bed, the shower, the couch, and then a bath, Ari suggested putting on the nicest clothes they had with them and going to have dinner at Bowie's restaurant. They couldn't have solved the case without her help, and Ari wanted to be sure she showed her appreciation before they went home. Ari picked out what she thought was her nicest shirt, but Dale kindly corrected her. When they arrived at the restaurant Ari was surprised to see the parking lot was full, and several cars had been parked on the street due to overflow.

"Wow. I didn't expect the place to be this busy."

"Looks like it's the place to eat here on the island."

Dale found a parking space at the end of the block, and they walked back to the restaurant holding hands. The town was beautifully silent and still, like the buzz of the daytime was just a show put on for the tourists and nighttime was a peek backstage. Out on the harbor boats were still bobbing and swaying on the waves like bejeweled buoys. Ari stopped Dale on the rise of a hill so the majority of the town was spread out in front of them. Dale furrowed her brow as Ari took both her hands and held them.

"Forever," Ari said. "As long or as short as it might be. With you."

Dale smiled. "Forever."

They kissed, embraced, and Ari took Dale's hand again to lead her the rest of the way to the restaurant. There was another couple ahead of them at the hostess station so Ari and Dale took a seat on the padded bench to wait. They had only been there for a few minutes before Bowie arrived, dressed in a dinner jacket, waistcoat, and thin black tie. Her hair had been wetted down and styled and, if Ari wasn't mistaken, she was even wearing makeup. Her eyes widened when she saw who was waiting.

"You finally decided to try my after-dark side, huh?" She looked at the couple who was ahead of them. "Jerry, Louise, these two are leaving the island in about twelve hours. Would you mind if they snuck ahead of you...?"

Louise was already waving them on before Bowie finished talking. "Absolutely not! Go, go." She touched Ari's elbow. "You have to try the Sea Spray Platter. It's absolutely divine."

Bowie said, "Okay, okay, Lou, save it for Yelp." She winked at the woman and took two menus from the slot on the hostess stand. "Come with me, ladies." She motioned with her chin for Ari and Dale to follow her. Ari remembered thinking the dining room would come to life at night but she was still impressed by the transformation.

The room was elegant and cozy, with soft music filtering through hidden speakers in the ceiling. Even though their table was in the midst of several other diners, Ari didn't feel crowded as she and Dale took their seats and accepted their menus from Bowie.

"I'll send your waitress right over. And don't worry about the cost. Everything is on the house."

"Oh, we couldn't..." Dale said, but Bowie cut her off with a wave of her hand.

"The rumor mill is going five hundred miles an hour today. I know what you did, and by tomorrow half the island will know. You did a great thing for this island." She stopped, choking up slightly, and she put a hand on Ari's shoulder. "You turned the page for this island, got justice for a girl, and you got Wayne Corbett arrested. And you did it all at the cost of your vacation. Dinner and a bottle of wine, my treat. Don't try to fight me on this, okay?"

"We won't," Ari promised.

"Good. Enjoy your meal, ladies."

Dale raised her eyebrows as Bowie left them. "Well, that was sweet of her."

"It was." Ari looked at her menu, sighed, and then put it down in front of her. "I'll be right back. I need to talk with her about something real quick."

"Is everything okay?"

"Yeah." She bent down and kissed the top of Dale's head as she passed, hurrying to catch up with Bowie before she disappeared into the kitchen.

Bowie saw her coming and stopped where she was, her shoulders sagging. "Ariadne, please. I've comped meals for a lot less than this in the past."

Ari shook her head. "It's not that. Is there somewhere we can talk privately?"

Bowie held Ari's gaze for a long moment, then she nodded and motioned her down a narrow hall. She opened the door at the end of the hall and led Ari into a small office.

"I wanted to talk to you about Corbett, and the whole drug pipeline he used to get drugs into Canada. It was a complicated system. A big system. He had to find people on Vancouver Island, he had to set up all the drops, and it ran like clockwork. It was really impressive." She leaned against the wall. "And if there's one thing I've learned about Corbett this week, it's that he doesn't do hard, intricate work when he can just steal someone else's."

Bowie was hugging herself, and she kept her head down as she paced toward the desk.

"I looked at this place, this magnificent restaurant, and I can't imagine what the overhead would be like. Buying the building, keeping it up and running... sure, you're probably making a profit now, but when you're just starting out...? A lot of places like this tend to die in the cradle. You managed to keep it afloat, which is impressive all by itself, but then at the same time you were diagnosed with breast cancer? You had a double mastectomy?" She shook her head. "The medical bills. Starting a new restaurant... well, technically starting two new restaurants. It's amazing you weren't destitute. So... what was it? I'm guessing pot?"

Bowie sighed heavily and sat on the edge of her desk. "Yeah. It helped, and I figured if I'm going to be buying pot anyway, I might as well buy in bulk. Turn it into a profit." She gave a cockeyed smile. "Even I was blown away by how big it got. And the money... good lord, the money." She loosened her tie and popped the top button of her shirt. "I got greedy. I justified everything I was doing, because suddenly I had enough money to blind myself."

"And when pot became legal..."

"Well, then the pipeline was worse than useless. I wanted to just toss it all, but then Corbett came in and bought it from me for an obscene amount of money. Again... leading cause of blindness is a full bank account. I knew what he was doing, but I had no idea... that girl...?" She blinked away her tears. "If I had just scuttled the damn pipeline, that would never have happened."

Ari said, "You had nothing to do with that. Corbett would have found a way even if you didn't sell, and she would have gone snooping without you. Don't put that on yourself."

Bowie wiped at her eyes. "Will you give me a few days? I need to find someone to take care of this place, and my house. I have a cat. I need to take care of the cat."

Ari frowned. "Where are you going?"

Bowie looked at her. "What? I'm... I-I'm going to jail. I accept that, but I just need a few days to put my affairs in order."

"How is the sheriff going to figure this out?"

"You're... going to tell him..."

Ari shook her head. "I'm a private investigator. I investigate the cases people hire me to solve. This? This is just something I figured out, and I wanted to confirm I was right. It's an ego thing."

"Why?" Bowie was crying now.

"You said Corbett was keeping this town afloat, that his cash was keeping it knit together. But that's not true. This place is what the town needs. A place where people can meet up, gossip, get advice. Losing the drugs and the money Corbett brought in might create some tough times for the island, but I think this place will help keep everyone above water. It'll give them hope. That's what they're going to need in the months ahead. So you broke the law a little bit a few years ago. Have you kept your nose clean since then?"

"Yeah. I mean, I still smoke..."

"Hey, so do I."

Bowie wiped her eyes, and Ari stepped forward to hug her. "Well, you're definitely getting your meal on the house now."

Ari laughed. "Excellent."

"Now get back out there. Free dinner or not, it's not wise to keep a lady as lovely as yours waiting."

"Right."

"I really do appreciate what you did for this town. Maybe now that we have to stand on our own two feet we can actually thrive rather than just... coasting."

Ari said, "With people like you and Drexler around, I'd put money on it."

Bowie smiled and then said, "Scout."

"Pardon?"

"I don't tell a lot of people my first name because I think it sounds silly. But it's Scout."

Ari smiled. "Scout Bowie. I like it. It... fits."

Bowie shrugged. "I wanted you to know."

"Thank you. So the Sea Spray Platter... is that as good as advertised?"

Bowie ushered her out of the office. "Better, but only the best for you and your lady. I'm thinking the surf-and-turf..."

EPILOGUE

IT WAS Sunday night, after they had packed most of their stuff to save time in the morning, during their one-last-time in the cabin's bed before they went home, when the seed of the idea was planted. Dale was pressing against Ari's back, their hips together and Ari's face in the pillow. In the heat of passion Dale decided to bend down and bite Ari's shoulder. Hard enough to hurt, but not enough to break the skin. Ari made a sound somewhere between surprise and pleasure, and Dale swept her tongue over the wounded flesh.

"Sorry..."

"No, it's okay," Ari panted. "*You* can bite *me* all you want."

Dale had grinned and focused on thrusting without even being aware that the idea had been born. It bounced around in her head until after the finished, and it blossomed while she was asleep. When she got up a little before three-thirty to use the bathroom it revealed itself to her as she stared bleary-eyed at the wall in front of the toilet. It was an idiotic idea, really. Stupid and... it was completely pointless to even bring it up. Still, she turned off the bathroom light and sat in the chair across from the bed instead of crawling back under the covers.

Ari reached out for her after about twenty minutes, gathering the blankets to her chest and then reaching out once more. She squeezed the pillow and murmured, "Dale? Are you okay in there?"

"I'm fine."

Ari opened her eyes. "Hey. I thought you were in the bathroom."

"I was. Now I'm watching you sleep."

"That's a boring show. Always puts me right out."

Dale smiled. "Ari, can I ask you a hypothetical question?"

She snuggled back to her pillow on the verge of passing out again. "Mm-hmm."

"What would happen if you bit me?"

Ari opened her eyes again. "I'm not going to talk about that."

"It's a hypoth~" She sighed. "Okay. Then tell me what happened to Detective Lorne when he was bitten during wolf manoth."

Ari sat up and the blanket fell away. She hadn't bothered getting dressed after their lovemaking, and the moonlight made her skin look iced-over. "Why are we talking about this?"

"Will you just humor me please?"

"Fine." Ari drew her legs up and crossed her arms over the knees. "When an adult is bitten by a *canidae*, they're infected. It's like a virus. It gets into them, i-it changes them. And they can fight the change for a little while. Three weeks, four at the outside, but eventually they can't hold back anymore. The wolf forces its way out, and their bodies can't deal with the strain. They die, Dale. Horribly, painfully. Sometimes they're just horrifically disfigured and they have to be mercy-killed. An adult's body can't deal with that kind of change. Bones break away at the joint and can't be rejoined. Spines snap. If they don't die, if they're not put out of their misery, they would be bone bags in constant pain."

Dale said, "But kids who are bitten..."

"*Canidae* change for the first time in puberty. A body that's still growing and evolving can handle the change and learn how to put itself back together."

Dale pushed her hair out of her face. "Okay. Here's the dumb hypothetical. What would happen if you got bitten?"

Ari frowned and shrugged. "Nothing."

"Why not?"

"I'm already a *canidae*. Haven't you noticed?"

"Yeah, but you're a bad *canidae*. No offense. The change hurts you, and it's hurt you ever since you were a little girl because it was done wrong. Your mother thought she was choosing the safer way, but it was just not enough. Close, but not enough." She got out of the chair and moved to the bed. "What if you're not technically a *canidae*? What if what your mother did was just enough to make you transform without making you one of them?" She brushed Ari's hair away from her face. "You've always had the wolf, and it's always felt like something separate from you. What if there's a reason for that? What if you don't have the same... connection... that your mother or Milo Duncan have? I mean, you hurt more than other *canidae*. You... you fell in love with a human, which is unusual enough it almost jumpstarted a war."

Ari was staring at the wall beyond Dale's shoulder. "I've been bitten before."

"Maybe it wasn't enough. Or, or maybe your blood confused the process... maybe you need to be bitten by whoever gave you the blood."

"Mom," Ari whispered.

Dale said, "If you were bitten, and if you were infected, you wouldn't die because your body already knows how to change. The bite would just give you the means to survive it. It would make you a true *canidae* once and for all."

Ari looked at her. "How did you come up with this?"

"I got the idea when I was humping you." Ari laughed and kissed her. "Do you think it will work?"

Ari sighed. "I have no idea. I really have no idea. But I think it makes sense. I think it makes enough sense that I'm willing to give it a shot."

Dale smiled. "Really?"

"We'll ask Dr. Frost about it, of course, and he'll be there when we do it. If we do it." She chuckled and shook her head. "But yeah. It sounds good to me." She touched Dale's cheek. "If it works, I may owe you my life all over again."

"I'll start running a tab."

Ari smiled and kissed her. "C'mere. Get a proper hero's reward..." She wrapped her arms around Dale's waist to pull her back down to the bed.

In the morning they reluctantly left the cabin and took the early ferry back to the mainland. Ari was still a bit uncomfortable about going onto the boat, especially after she had been thrown off the last boat she got aboard, so she stretched out on the bench with her head in Dale's lap. Dale covered Ari's face with her cap and held her hands, talking to her until they were underway.

"These things are so safe," Dale said. "They carry thousands of people back and forth every day. We have a fleet of cars and trucks underneath us. And on the rare occasion when a ferry does capsize or crash, it's international news."

"So we're going to be on the news, that's supposed to make me feel better?"

Dale chuckled. "Okay, maybe a bad example. Just relax, puppy. It'll be over before you know it."

Ari survived the trip - by the skin of her teeth, if her account was to be believed - and Dale drove them back to the city. The I-5 helped ease their transition back into the mainland reality of big cities; tall stone retaining walls crowned by evergreens blocked any views of the small towns they passed. It was as if it was giving them a buffer zone before overwhelming them with industrialization. Eventually, after driving beneath an overpass, the retaining walls fell away to reveal the fringes of northern Seattle.

"Home again, home again," Ari said.

Dale said, "Yep. We can go back."

"Yes. Do it. I think there's an off-ramp coming up..."

Dale laughed. "I was talking about next year. Anniversary, birthday..."

Ari said, "I meant now."

"I know." She looked over at her. "We can if you want. We have some savings, so if you want to turn it into a two-week vacation... not that the first week was much of a vacation..."

Ari looked over at Dale's left wrist, the bracelet loose enough to hang but not so loose that it was in danger of falling off or getting snagged on anything. "No. We set aside a week, we should hold to that. We need to get back to work. And we need to ask Dr. Frost and Mom about your idea."

"I hope it works, puppy."

"Me too. It's a good idea. A little unconventional, but... I think it has promise."

Dale picked up Ari's hand and kissed it. "We'll make sure we cover all the bases before we jump into anything. I don't want to risk some unforeseen consequence."

"In the meantime I'll just manage the wolf as best I can. Keep self-medicating."

"Yes."

Ari nodded and looked out the window. She didn't want to tell Dale her real fear about the bite. She had been bitten before with no effects whatsoever. But the only *canidae* to bite her badly enough to possibly infect her was Sadie Dillon, and she was a fox. Maybe the fox bite and wolf blood had cancelled each other out. Maybe if she was bitten by her mother it would trigger something. Maybe it would be the thing that finally took away her pain.

That wasn't here real fear, her main fear, the thing that kept her from being excited about the experiment. The logic behind it was that being bitten would make her a "proper" *canidae*, which would take away her pain. But no full-blood *canidae* had fallen in love with a human for over two centuries. She didn't see how being bitten could affect how she felt about Dale, but she had to admit the possibility. If they fell in love because she was "broken," how would fixing the problem affect her? Would she be the same person, or would she become more like her mother, or Milo?

Dale said, "You look deep in thought over there, puppy. Want to share?"

"Just wondering what it would be like to change without pain."

Dale smiled and patted Ari's leg. "It's going to be amazing. I can't wait."

Ari managed a convincing smile. "Neither can I."

If there was any chance the cure was worse than the disease, if giving up her pain came at the cost of her feelings for Dale, she would simply refuse to take it. Some things were worth suffering for.

"Dale..."

"Mm?"

"Sometimes I want to find those kids who were hitting me with PVC pipes so I can thank them. They gave you a reason to save me for the first time, and you haven't stopped since."

Dale smiled. "I might have to thank the little bastards, too."

Up ahead the highway cut an S through the greenery on either side. They were still a few minutes away from home and returning to their real life, so Ari put her fears aside. Their vacation might not have been exactly as relaxing as they'd anticipated but she got to spend the entire week with Dale. They made love, they spent time and effort for each other, and Dale had gotten a few full nights of sleep. So while they hadn't achieved all their goals, and even though her pain was as bad as it had ever been, Ari couldn't help but consider the week successful.

Now she was ready to get home and get back to their real lives. No matter how bad the pain got, she knew she could handle anything with Dale by her side.

Geonn Cannon is the author of over sixty novels, including the *Riley Parra* series which was adapted into an Emmy-nominated webseries by Tello Films. His novel *Can You Hear Me* was adapted into Static Space, an award-winning short film. He's also written two tie-in novels for the television series *Stargate SG-1*. He was the first male author to win a Golden Crown Literary Society Award for his novel *Gemini*, and he won a second for *Dogs of War*.

www.ingramcontent.com/pod-product-compliance
Lightning Source LLC
Chambersburg PA
CBHW071225210726

48293CB00002B/582